The Vengeance Squad Goes To England

SIDNEY W. FROST

Editors: Lisa Lickel (American), Julie Maria Peace (English)

Cover photo: © 2011 Sergej Borzov | Dreamstime.com

ISBN: 0-9830708-8-1
ISBN-13: 978-0-9830708-8-7

DEDICATION

This book is dedicated to my children and stepchildren. They get smarter and more understanding every year:

Eva Frost
David Frost
Julie Frost Golden
Lee Fegenbush Boyles
Erik Fegenbush
Dane Johnson
Tracy Johnson Schutte

AND IN MEMORY OF

Howard Donn "Tiny" Holden

September 1, 1936 – August 14, 2013

CHAPTER ONE

Tex removed his ten-gallon cowboy hat, swiped his brow and leaned back in his wheelchair to get his hug. I stood behind him knowing I'd be next. But nothing happened. Liz sat at the end of the conference table with her head in her hands.

My friend and former computer science student, Tex Thompson, locked his eyes on mine and I stared back at him in disbelief. Something was wrong. Liz Siedo, the happiest librarian in the world, the person who accepted God's will in every situation and hugged everyone who came within five feet of her, was either sick or depressed. She was the one who helped me most when my fiancé was murdered. Sarah died two years ago during a robbery weeks before we were to be married.

Tex put his hat back on and pulled out the chair on the side of the table nearest the door and rolled into its place. He reached behind his wheelchair, grabbed his laptop and set it on the table the way he always did at our meetings. I took the seat across from him, placed my steno pad and pen on the table and aligned them carefully.

We were in the Austin History Center's O'Henry room for what I thought would be a short, case close-out meeting. It was beginning to look like it might take much longer.

I had never seen a silent Liz. The fact that she didn't hug us was alarming. I didn't know what to say and I could tell Tex was at a loss for words, too. Since he'd known her longer than I had, I nodded my head toward Liz to encourage him to say something. He frowned and nodded right back, indicating he wanted me to talk to her.

I leaned over trying to get her to face me. "Liz, is there something wrong?" All I wanted to do was get the meeting over with so I could go see Angela. I had my flight reserved and was leaving next week on Christmas day. Angela had a rare holiday from work and wanted to show me where she lived and, she'd stressed, it was also where Sarah grew up.

Tex frowned.

I slapped my forehead to let him know I agreed it was a dumb question. As if he could do better. I cleared my throat and tried again.

"Liz. We know something is wrong," I said more firmly. I grabbed a quick glance at Tex and got an iffy thumbs-up. "Do you want to talk about what's bothering you?"

Liz let out a long sigh, a moan really, but continued to stare at the conference table.

"Ma'am," Tex said, "we don't mean to pry, but if there's anything we can do to help, you know we will. But we can't help unless you talk to us."

She inhaled for so long I thought she'd get dizzy, but she sat up slowly and gazed around the room as if she wasn't sure where she was. She stared at Tex, nodded slowly as if responding, before facing me.

"I know, boys. I know you'd help if you could. And I know you must be worried silly."

Tex raised both eyebrows at me. I shrugged.

Liz continued. "I don't usually let stuff like this bother me." She paused and looked at each of us before resuming. "But, for some reason I can't get past this thing with Virgil."

"What?" That surprised me. I glanced at Tex and it was his turn to shrug.

"Virgil?" I asked, wanting to make sure I'd heard her correctly. "I thought you were over him after you heard he was a con artist. Especially after we learned he was wanted in several states for absconding with all nature of property from women he was romancing."

Her one-time boyfriend had turned up out of nowhere and had worked as a volunteer at the library. He eventually got the attention of Liz and somehow got her believing he was interested in her. Not long after he and Liz began dating, Tex and I discovered Virgil was involved with another woman in town. We hadn't set out to check on him, but happened to see him while investigating a case unrelated to the library

"I am over him," she said, dabbing her eyes with a ball of tissue that was more gray than white. "It's not Virgil in particular."

"If it's not him, what is it, ma'am?" Tex asked.

She stared at the table as if searching for what to say. Seeing Liz less than fully in charge of any situation was new for me and probably Tex as well. We waited.

"I wasn't sure what was wrong for the longest time. As you boys know, I'm mostly happy. For several days I've been in a deep dark place, a place I've never been before. It bothered me, but I didn't let on about it. To be honest, it was a little scary. Now I'm beginning to understand what's happened."

She paused and looked at us as if deciding how to explain. "Virgil was the first man in my life since my alcoholic husband died. I don't know if I told you boys, but I loved my husband dearly and we had many good years together before the drink became his true love. That part was rough but it forced me to learn to live without him before he died. After his death, I went back to school and became a librarian. I was happy without a man in my life. But when Virgil came along sweet-talking me the way he did, and acting as if we were a couple and all, I began to think, why not. It felt right, and I deserved some happiness." She put her elbows on the table and dropped her head in her hands again. "At least it felt right until I learned his true intentions. Then it hurt. It hurt a lot. Now I know it's too late for me to have a loving relationship again." She sighed again and

4

appeared to melt. "Let's face it, boys. I'm officially an old maid."

It was a good thing Liz's eyes were covered after she said that. Otherwise she would have seen Tex suppress a guffaw. I don't know how he kept it in. I frowned at him, but that tickled him more so he rolled away bent over in silent laughter. His hat fell off his head.

Tex and I learned the truth about Virgil Golden while doing some detective work for Brian Donelson, the multimillionaire who brought his own bookmobile to work. Brian had asked us to find who was stalking him and his wife, Karen. What we learned was that Karen's stepson Heath was the stalker. But, much to our surprise, we'd spotted Virgil with Heath's mother, Cloris Parker. After a little digging, we learned he had a police record a mile long for deceiving women and embezzling money from non-profit organizations around the country. Evidently, he'd gotten close to Liz to get information about Brian and his wife Karen to help with Cloris's lawsuit.

"Liz," I said, standing between her and Tex in case she looked this way. "Don't let a criminal dictate your life. Especially one without morals like Virgil. You're a wonderful woman with many friends. If you want a man in your life, don't give up. I'm sure the right one will come along."

Liz focused on me. "Do you think so?"

"Yes. I do."

"I don't know." She spotted Tex. "Percy? What are you doing over there?"

Other than his parents, Liz was the only person who

called Tex by his real first name. Even his wife Jane called him Tex.

Tex coughed and sat up. "I…uh…I dropped my hat." He rolled back toward the table, stopping to pick it up on the way.

"Well," Liz said. "We need to forget all my tomfoolery anyway and get back to the meeting. I don't know about you two, but I'm looking forward to a little time off between cases. I want to do something fun for a change."

"Me too." I thought about Angela and my trip to England.

"I'm going to spend more time at home," said Tex. "My HONEY DO jar is so full I'll never get it all done. Actually, it's kinda embarrassing. I peeked in the jar last night just to get an idea of what to expect." He paused. "Know what I found?"

"What?" Liz asked.

Tex moved in close to us. "A note that said 'kiss wife,'" he said with a whisper.

"Oops," I said.

"Well, that doesn't sound difficult," Liz said. "How about you, Chris? Got any plans?"

"Sure do. I'm going to see Angela in England."

"Oh, how wonderful. Tell her hello for me."

"I will."

"Now," Liz said, opening a manila folder, "I guess there's nothing more to be done except declare this case closed."

We'd been searching for a woman in her late seventies who had gone missing about six weeks ago. The woman's daughter had asked Liz for help after the police had all but given up on the search. Unfortunately, all we found was her body. She was an Alzheimer's patient who had walked away from the home where she lived with her daughter and evidently got lost in the woods.

"Yes," I said. "It's a sad ending, but there's nothing more we can do."

Liz shuffled the papers from the file, and sighed. "I took the liberty of talking to our client. Even though we found her mother too late, she was relieved we were able to find the body. Said it gave her closure, but I know she's hurting."

"I just wish we'd found her mother alive," Tex said.

Liz scanned the papers again before putting them into the folder. "Not much else we can do. I'll file this away for the record. I talked to the police, and they may want a statement from each of you, too. I doubt it, though."

I stood and collected my notebook and pen. "Thank you, Liz. I guess that's all we can do."

Tex closed his laptop and stored it in the backpack hanging behind his wheelchair.

I walked toward the door, saying good-bye, and would have got away if Liz's phone hadn't rung.

"Hello," she said.

I waited. She listened only a short time before her face turned white and she slumped back into her chair as if she'd passed out. Her phone dropped from her limp body and hit the floor.

CHAPTER TWO

Tex rolled to her and fanned her with his hat. "Ma'am, ma'am, are you okay?"

"Oh, dear. Oh, dear," she said as she straightened.

I picked up her phone and placed it on the table in front of her.

"What happened?" I asked. My first thought was that the call was about her grandson. She'd raised Michael as her own after his parents were killed in a car accident. He'd lived a hard life and spent time in the Texas state prison system for multiple DUIs. But he'd turned his life around after that and was a student at Austin Community College where I worked. Liz had told me he hadn't had a drink since his release, as far as she knew.

"Did something happen to Michael?" Tex asked,

coming to the same conclusion I had.

Liz stared at him as if he was crazy. "Michael?" She shook her head. "No, not Michael. The bookmobile."

"The bookmobile?" Tex had been the one to find Karen, unconscious, hanging by her seatbelt when the bookmobile was sabotaged. They suspected it was the work of Virgil, but no one knew for sure and Virgil had disappeared after that. "Did something happen to the bookmobile again?" Tex asked.

"Another attack by Virgil?" I asked.

"No. Not Brian's bookmobile. *Our* bookmobile."

Tex looked at me with a frown.

"You don't have a bookmobile," I said, "other than Brian's."

Liz stood. "I'm talking about the money for the new bookmobile. The donations. The bookmobile fund." She swung her arms in the air like she was conducting an orchestra, emphasizing each word. "That was the bank on the phone. It's gone. The money is gone."

I could see my trip to England being postponed. I couldn't leave Liz now. "What happened?"

"The fund has been stolen." She sighed. "Stolen."

"How?" Tex asked.

"I don't know. It was such a shock to hear I didn't ask." She grabbed her phone and checked the display. "I guess they hung up."

"Tell us what you remember," Tex said.

"Here's what happened," she said. "I saw the latest monthly bank statement and noticed the balance was only $40,000. My records showed it should be more than $140,000. I'm the only one on the account and I keep my own running totals, updating it as donations come in. We haven't had any payouts yet, so recordkeeping has been simple."

"When was the last time you checked the bank's balance?" I asked.

"I don't know." Liz scratched her head. "I probably haven't opened those bank envelopes for several months. But, when I saw the discrepancy I figured there would be some simple explanation. I called the bank earlier this morning and they said they would investigate it. This call was to tell me the statement is correct. Turns out there are a number of payments made to companies I never heard of."

"Uh-oh," Tex said. "That sounds like something Virgil would do. Wasn't he accused of embezzling at several other non-profits around the country?"

I nodded.

"Virgil?" Liz asked. "He didn't have anything to do with the bank account."

"What about someone else in the library?" I asked.

"This isn't a city account. It's a personal one. It's in my name only. Since all the money was donated by friends and supporters, I set up a private account. The truth is, I didn't want to give the money to the city. I was afraid they might decide to spend it for something else."

"I know what you mean," Tex said. "Remember how the city council approved the concept of a bookmobile last year, but didn't budget a penny for it?"

"Right," Liz said. "That was what I was thinking about."

"Why do you want another bookmobile?" I asked.

"We can't rely on Brian and Karen to continue providing the service. When the council failed to fund the bookmobile last year, Brian promised to stay until September when the new budget is approved. The Donelsons are moving to Georgetown and taking their bookmobile with them." Liz put her hands on her ample hips. "What are we going to do? We had enough money to buy a nice bookmobile, and I was going to donate it to the city and get them to staff and maintain it. That was why I opened the latest bank statement, to check the balance to plan when I could purchase one. I figured we'd have enough money to order the vehicle."

"May we see your bank records?" I knew doing so could mess up my chance to be with Angela, but I had to ask. I couldn't leave Liz now. Not like this.

"Sure," she said. "But, why?"

"When we investigated Virgil we learned he'd stolen money before by setting up dummy companies and transferring money to them."

"He did?" Liz's eyes widened. "I knew he was a womanizer and liar, but I didn't know he was a thief as well."

We hadn't told her at the time. We knew she would be disappointed enough without giving her all the details.

She started pacing. Her body gradually transformed as she moved around the room. She went from slump-shouldered, poor-me, old maid forever to standing tall, assertive, sure of herself and angry. She straightened her flowered dress as she walked.

"Yes, ma'am he did," Tex said.

"Well," she said, "we'll see about that. Tex, go get my bank records. They're in the top drawer, left side of my desk. Chris, I want you to use your computer skills to find that rat and get my money back. Can you do that?"

Tex spun around and headed toward the door. "Yes, ma'am. He sure can," he hollered over his shoulder. "He sure can."

My vacation plans faded like a beautiful dream I tried desperately to remember after waking.

***

We called ourselves the Vengeance Squad. The name got started when Tex and I combined our talents to find Sarah's killers. We agreed not to tell Liz what we'd do when we caught the culprits. I bought a gun and learned how to use it. Tex had one, too, but as an ex-con he lost his the first time we were arrested. They let me keep mine after we were released so we eventually completed the job—and by that I don't mean we killed anyone. Still, we did help the police and feds round up some pretty unscrupulous guys.

Liz, the third member of our group, had not met Sarah and didn't know about my thoughts of personal revenge or Tex's plan to help. If she had, I'm sure she wouldn't have participated and probably would have turned us over to the cops herself. She helped mostly with research and through contacts with important people she knew, but she managed to get involved in the chase personally at the end.

I'm Chris McCowan, a computer science professor at

the local community college. Sarah, a nurse, had been gunned down during a robbery when she came to the aid of a wounded security guard. I'd taken her death hard and blamed myself for not doing a better job of protecting her. Survivor guilt, I guess. I'd taken a bullet in the leg, and after months of physical therapy, it only bothered me when I was stressed.

Tex attended several of my computer classes, including computer forensics. When Sarah was killed, he volunteered to help me find the ones responsible. He was in a wheelchair, so I didn't think he'd be much help. I was wrong about that. With his background as a marine, plus his time in prison and living on the streets, he helped in the ways I needed.

I hated the term, but some people call me a computer nerd, and I know Tex was concerned about my ability to do what needed to be done. He kept after me and eventually helped me get into shape physically and mentally. He took me to a pistol range where I learned I had a natural ability with handguns. The first person I fired at was lucky. All I did was shoot his trigger finger while he was aiming his pistol at Tex. In hindsight that was a risky thing to do. If I had been off slightly I could have caused the shooter to pull the trigger. It hadn't occurred to me that I might miss.

After Sarah's death I didn't shave or get dressed for weeks. I still haven't shaved, but now the stuff on my face is called a beard. The school talked me into working from home rather than not teach at all. I'm glad. I needed the money. By the time I got past the worst of the grieving, I'd grown accustomed to working from home and asked if I could continue. I think the college was afraid I was still suffering, so they agreed. Now, two years later, I was okay and the college still let me work from home.

I met Angela shortly after Sarah's death and we worked together to find the killers. A year after the case was closed she came back to Austin for a Christmas dinner at Liz's. That was when I knew I had a special feeling for her and she for me.

But, with her in England or off somewhere on an assignment for work, our communication was mostly by phone or webcam. During this semester break, I was going to England to be with her.

I heard Liz's voice and looked at her. How long had she been staring at me? "What?" I said.

"Can you use the computer to find Virgil?"

"I can't say for sure. Based on what we've learned about his activities in Austin, and after you report the theft of the bookmobile fund, I'm sure law enforcement agencies will be searching for him."

"But aren't there things you can do that they can't?"

Her question made me wonder if she knew more than we gave her credit for. "Maybe."

"I see things on TV crime shows all the time. Surely there's something we can do to find him. I've got to get that money back." Liz sighed. "The people entrusted me with their hard-earned dollars and I've let them down."

"Let's learn what happened first," I said. "Only then will I be able to tell you what we can do. You've got contacts with the city police and I'll ask Angela and my dad for help. We'll find that money. And, unless he's deposited it in a Swiss bank, we'll get it back."

We hadn't let Liz know all that was possible with computers. Some of it wasn't exactly legal. We would never do anything to hurt others, but we had poked around in some private computer files during our investigations. Although I never tried it I knew how simple it would be to transfer funds from one place to another.

I guess you could say computer hacking ran in the family. Dad was a computer science professor at the University of California in Long Beach. He also worked for the FBI doing some white-hat hacking. But he did it legally. Most of the time, he'd say. There was usually a court order or a national emergency to make his actions acceptable. I learned some techniques from him and we communicated about the craft from time to time. Dad didn't trust e-mail or the Internet in general. Sometimes we met in Denver, a good midway point between us, to discuss projects face-to-face.

Tex hurried into the room waving a piece of paper in the air and carrying a bunch of envelopes in his lap. "Wait till you see what I found," he said.

CHAPTER THREE

Tex tossed the envelopes onto the table as Liz and I peeped over his shoulder to examine the paper he placed on top of the pile of unopened bank statements. He glanced back, first at Liz and then toward me. "Here's how he did it."

"Are you talking about Virgil?" Liz asked.

"Yes," Tex said, holding the form so we could read it. "This authorization form says you added him to the bank account as joint owner."

"I certainly did not," she said.

"I understand," Tex said. "But somehow he got your signature on here and must have filed it at the bank."

"Where did you find it?" I asked.

"Under all those envelopes."

"Pretty brazen of him to put it there," I said.

"I don't understand," Liz said. "That's my signature, but I never would have signed such a thing."

"As your administrative assistant, he probably slipped it in with other documents for you to sign."

"I guess that's possible," she said, looking doubtful.

"Liz," I asked, "how long has it been since you checked the bank balance on this account?"

She flipped through the stack of sealed bank statements. "I guess it's been longer than I thought." She dropped the envelopes back on the table. "I'm not usually so sloppy with financial records. It's just that there was no need to open them since I'm the only one on the account." She paused as if thinking over what she'd said. "Well, I thought I was. I probably wouldn't have noticed it today, but this morning I received an interesting ad for a used bookmobile. That was why I decided it was time to verify what we could afford."

"If you never check the balance, how do you know what should be in the account?" Tex asked.

"Well, silly. Before I make a deposit, I record the amount of the donation along with the donor's name on a spreadsheet."

Tex raised both eyebrows. We knew how much she hated computers and it was hard to believe she'd created a spreadsheet.

"Spreadsheet?" Tex asked, giving her a look of incredulity. "You created a spreadsheet?"

"I certainly did. I carry it right here in my purse." She pulled out a worn, folded piece of mint green paper with lines on it. When she unfolded it I could see the handwritten entries on it, mostly in pencil with erasures in several places. I could also see entries for the date a donation was added, who it came from, and a running balance. The bottom line showed a total of $140,213.67.

"Oh," I said, "you mean a paper spreadsheet. I haven't seen one of those in years." I grabbed the paper and held it where Tex could see. "You should remember this. I showed one of these to the class when we talked about the history of computing."

Tex laughed. "Yes, sir. I remember that."

"What'd you think I was talking about?" Liz asked.

Tex stared at Liz's spreadsheet. "We were thinking about Microsoft Excel. That's an electronic spreadsheet you make on the computer."

"Oh, I think I learned that in college," she said. "But, remember, I told you none of that computer stuff made sense. I hired a special tutor to teach me enough to pass the tests. But, I only retained that knowledge long enough to graduate. Besides, all that computer stuff seems to keep changing." She grabbed her spreadsheet and straightened the creased folds before placing it on the table. "Here it is. My daddy used a spreadsheet like this for his bakery when I was a child. So what do we do now, boys?"

I picked up the envelopes and began to sort them by the postmark dates. "I suggest we study these statements to find when the money went missing. Perhaps we'll learn how it was done."

"Yeah," Tex said. "It shouldn't be hard to learn where the money went."

We all took a pile of envelopes, opened them, and placed the statements on the table in chronological order.

"Look at this," Liz said. "Here's a payment for $8,567.22 to Aurum Dealers of America."

"It was bad enough that Virgil left that authorization form," I said. "But this is certainly rubbing it in."

Tex picked up the statement and read it over. "Why do you say that?"

"Aurum Dealers of America?" I waited, but Tex stared blankly. "The symbol for gold is Au. It stands for aurum. Gold. Virgil Golden. He didn't try to hide his trail. It's like he wanted us to know who took the money. Just like the way he left that signed authorization form in the desk drawer."

"How'd you know the definition of aurum?" Liz asked.

"It's that photographic memory of his," Tex said. "He probably read it in high school and will never forget it."

It's actually eidetic memory, but Tex was right.

Liz held the bank statement in the air. "I could kick myself for not reading this when I got it."

"He's a con man," Tex said. "He probably noticed you never opened your bank statements. I bet he enjoyed knowing he could get away with stealing from you and still come to work every day."

"And take you on dates as well," I added, wondering too late if saying so might send Liz back into the doldrums.

"I guess," Liz said, apparently not upset by my comment. "I can't believe he could take nearly $9,000 in a single payment. That was pretty brazen of him, wasn't it?"

"Liz, you got a highlighter in that purse of yours?" I motioned to the black bag sitting on the floor next to her chair.

"Sure. Do we need one?"

"Let's highlight all the items on the statements that shouldn't be there."

Her eyes lit up. "Good idea." She raised her purse to her lap and started digging in it. Before long she found a yellow highlighter along with a half-eaten Tootsie Roll. She popped the candy into her mouth and marked a sloppy yellow line through the payment to Aurum Dealers of America.

I took the next envelope in chronological order.

"Wait," Tex said as he opened his laptop. "What was the amount paid to Aurum Dealers of America again?"

"What are you doing?" I asked.

"I'm making a computer spreadsheet of the payments so we can study them all in one place once we go through all the statements."

Liz smiled for the first time today. "Are you sure you don't want a sheet of my spreadsheet paper?"

"Oh, no," Tex said. "This'll be faster."

She picked up the first statement. "Okay, then. The amount was $8,567.22."

"Why don't you add the date and payee, too," I said.

Tex pondered that. "Good idea," he said.

After he made the last entry, he punched a few more keys and grinned. "Look at this," he said turning the screen to where Liz and I could see. "Most of the payments were made to a company with gold in its name."

"Actually, all are related to gold," I said.

Tex pulled the screen back where he could see it. "Are you sure? What about this one. Atomic Number 79?"

"Periodic table number for gold," I said.

"And the one called Precious Metals?" Liz asked. "I guess it could be a reference to gold also."

"Yeah," Tex said. "The rest are obvious. The Gilded Edge, Dental Gold Recyclers, Leaves of Gold, Go For the Gold Charity, Gold Plated Trophies, Golden Sweets, We Buy Used Gold, and The Gold Mine."

"Amazing," Liz said. "He wanted me to know what he did. He thinks he can get away with it."

"Boy, is he in for a big surprise," Tex said. "And did you see each monthly payment was an unusual amount while the total is exactly $100,000."

Liz had her hands on her hips and a look of determination on her face I'd not seen before. "Then that's exactly what we'll take from Virgil. No more, no less." The glare on her face relaxed some. "Boys, for the first time since we started working together I understand why we're called the Vengeance Squad."

Tex raised his eyebrows at me and I couldn't keep from laughing. Soon everyone was laughing.

"Liz, we haven't proved Virgil took the money," I said. "All we know is that a hundred grand is missing from the bookmobile fund and it was taken in smaller amounts over a period of time. Nearly a year."

"That's right, ma'am," Tex added. "We don't know for sure who did it."

"Virgil did it," she said. "We know he's the lowlife type who'd do such a thing. Find him and where he put

21

the money. Then all you have to do is take it from him the way he took it from me."

I glanced at Tex and wondered what we were getting ourselves into. Surely she knew we'd be breaking the law.

"We'll do our best," I said. "But we have to investigate this a little more before we do that. Like Tex said, we need to prove it was Virgil."

"I understand what you're saying. Just don't take too long about it. That weasel is getting away as we talk."

I could see my vacation plans evaporating.

***

I met Tex at Thundercloud Subs on West 12th Street thirty minutes later. It was a place I frequented when in Austin. Every time I came in for a meeting at the Austin History Center, I'd grab a meal there or across the street at House Park BBQ. This Thundercloud was one of several in town and it sat on the shores of Shoal Creek in an old building that had housed a variety of businesses over the years. The front of the outside was pale green and there was a giant replica of a sub sandwich on the roof. The inside was unlike most eating establishments. It wasn't dirty, but cluttered with mismatched furniture. Still the subs were wonderful and most people overlooked the ambience. There was a bookshelf where you could take books or drop off ones you'd read. I liked that and used it on occasion.

Tex and I ate in silence. I didn't know about him, but I was torn about what to do. Normally I would do anything for Liz. She was that type of person. And it wasn't just me. Everyone loved her. My inclination was to drop everything else in my life until we found Virgil and recovered the money he had taken.

But, was it the money? Liz had several friends who could afford to buy a bookmobile for the library, including Brian and several of his buddies. Tex had told me they had offered to purchase whatever she wanted. She'd declined and was proud of raising the funds through donations from the bookmobile patrons. Brian had admitted to Tex that he'd sneaked in some so-called anonymous contributions from time to time, but most of the money came from small donations made by the library regulars themselves. Tex learned Liz donated most of the raise she got when she'd been promoted to director of library services. She lived modestly.

As all this passed through my mind, I thought about the way Liz reacted when she learned about the stolen money. I had worked with her enough to know she was hurt deeply when she was faced with the truth about why Virgil had been so kind to her. Perhaps she had hoped he wasn't as bad as the police had said.

"I feel bad for Liz," I said.

"Me too." Tex wiped his mouth with his paper napkin. "I always thought Virgil was a slimeball. We should've investigated him when he first showed up at the library to volunteer."

"I know. Why didn't we?"

"Because he made Liz happy, I guess."

"Yeah," I said, "but we should've known he wasn't right for her. At least now they're checking everyone who wants to volunteer at the library."

Tex took a bite of his sub and chewed before he responded. "I love her to death, but she's not what you would call a beauty. What'd he see in her? That was what went through my mind when they started dating. I knew something was wrong. I just didn't want to admit it. I guess I didn't want Liz to miss out on the possibility of what could be. I wanted to believe Virgil saw her the way I do. Beautiful inside."

"I know what you mean." I retrieved a sliver of avocado that had slipped out of my sandwich and popped it into my mouth.

"We should have known. They were so different. Liz could care less about hair and clothes. He was always dressed like a banker with his coiffured black hair always in place. And, let's face it. Liz doesn't worry so much about her weight."

"I guess since we love her the way she is, it wasn't hard to think Virgil could, too."

Tex took another bite and the conversation stopped while we both chewed.

"Next time," he said, "I'm going to do a complete background check on anyone who asks her out."

"You think there will be a next time? She's pretty down on men right now."

"I know. Still, she deserves to be happy." Tex paused. "We'll find someone for her."

I shook my head. "No we won't. Especially not now. We've got enough to do to find Virgil."

"But she was so sad this morning."

"She was, wasn't she?" I said. "I've never seen that

side of her. But, after the bank called, she wasn't sad. She was angry."

"Yeah, but she's still not her old self. The Liz I want back is the one who's happy and confident, not just mad."

"Me too," I said. "So, what do we do now?"

Tex wiped the thunder sauce off his face again and shook his head. "I'm worried about this case. Anyone smart enough to steal a hundred grand from Liz is going to be hard to catch. Finding him doesn't mean we'll find the money. He probably hid it or spent it by now."

"That's what I was thinking. It may be too late to recover the bookmobile money."

"Yeah, the chance for success is low and, as I mentioned, I'm not sure I can work on it right now. With school out for the next four weeks, I'd planned to spend time with the family. I sort of promised Jane I'd be there for them this time. I don't know if I stressed how important it is for me to stay close to my wife and kids right now."

"I think you made it clear. And did you understand I would do anything for some time with Angela? And that I already purchased my plane tickets?"

We continued eating in silence.

"But, it's Liz," I said. "Why are we bothering to debate this? We can't tell her no."

"We can't hurt Liz," Tex said.

Silence.

"What can we do?" I asked.

Tex pondered that before he responded. "We have to talk to Jane and Angela. They know Liz. They'll understand and want us to help her no matter what. Let's make them decide."

"That's kinda chicken, isn't it?"

"Well, yeah."

"I think you've got the solution. We agree it's important to work fast to find this guy and so we have to start immediately. The only thing holding us back is your fear of hurting Jane and my desire to see Angela."

"Right. So, uh...will you come with me to talk to Jane?"

I laughed, but stifled it when I saw he was serious. I'd never seen Tex show fear, but I think he was definitely concerned about his marriage. "Sure," I said, wondering what I was going to say to Angela.

CHAPTER FOUR

Angela Hemsley was a spy. So secretive, I didn't know her last name until long after I'd met her and we'd completed our first case together. Angela was known to the President of the United States, and, although she couldn't talk about the circumstances, I'd learned from the president himself that she'd saved his life. Well, come to think about it, I guess he knows who I am as well. With the help of Angela, Liz, and Tex, I may have saved his life, too. Oh well, that was another story.

The next day I called Angela. There were times when I couldn't reach her for weeks, and, when we did talk, she couldn't say where she was or what she was doing.

I was lucky today. She answered on the fourth ring.

"Chris. Hi. I'm glad you called. I need to know your flight number so I can pick you up at the airport."

"Hello. How are you?" I ignored her question. Why was I nervous? We had kissed once and now she had invited me to visit her at her home. I noticed I had straightened all the objects on my desk while waiting for her to answer the phone. That was a bad sign. I do that mostly when I'm stressed. Or so I've been told.

"You do have your flight reservations, right?"

I loved her English accent, but she could sound like an American when she wanted to and had for the first year I'd known her. Once when I was with her while she was talking on the phone, I heard her speaking a language I couldn't identify. When I asked about it after her call ended, she'd said it wasn't important. I wondered how many other languages and accents she knew. I'd have to ask her someday. Right now I had to tell her about Liz and why I had to postpone my trip.

"About my arrival time. I'm afraid I have some bad news."

I waited for her to respond, but there was only dead air. "Are you there?" I asked.

"I'm waiting for the bad news."

"Oh. For a second I thought the connection was broken. You know how much I want to see you and spend time with you while neither one of us has to work. And, I was all set to leave. Even bought my ticket. But, this thing came up. It's about Liz."

Surely she'd understand. Angela loved Liz as much as we all did. We'd talked about it before. But I didn't want to miss this opportunity to see Angela. After all, I hadn't seen her in more than a year.

"Liz, huh. Tell me about it." She was abrupt and

clipped her words. She might be hurt, or disappointed. I wasn't sure. She was hard to read at times. Probably part of her job training.

"Liz has this bank account for funds collected from donors to buy a bookmobile for the city. She planned to donate the vehicle to the library as soon as she purchased it."

"And someone stole the money," Angela said.

"Right. Well, most of it. There's a hundred thousand dollars missing."

"Wow. I bet she's upset." I thought I heard some genuine concern coming from Angela. Surely she'd understand why I had to postpone my trip.

"She is. Or at least she was. Now she's just plain angry."

"If you're planning on helping instead of coming to see me, you must have a lead." Now she sounded angry. I was sure of it. Was she disappointed? Maybe both.

"Sort of," I said hesitantly. "There's a pretty strong indication Virgil took it."

"Ouch. Her old boyfriend?"

"Yes. Anyway, Tex and I are torn about what to do. He'd planned to give Jane his undivided attention during the semester break and I'd planned to visit you. But if we don't help Liz right away, Virgil, or whoever took the money, will have time to shift it around in ways that could make it impossible to find."

"I understand," she said, sounding as if she did.

"Good." Well, that was a relief. I had worried for nothing. Now I was a little disappointed. Had I subconsciously wanted her to give me an excuse to not help Liz? I went ahead and told her our plan. "Tex and I talked and decided that since you know Liz the way you do, you'd more than likely tell us to go ahead and help Liz. Am I right?"

There were several beats of silence and I was about ready to check again about the connection.

Angela's response surprised me. "I think you should take that plane to England." Her voice was firm, but I still couldn't read her reaction on the phone well enough to tell what she was feeling.

"Huh? I kind of thought you might tell me to postpone my trip."

"Well, you can if you want to, but I hope you'll come on as planned."

That was good to hear. "But, what about Liz?"

"No problem. I didn't know about the theft of the bookmobile fund, but I did know about Virgil and his cons around the world. Liz had said something to me about his English accent. But it wasn't until you mentioned him during a phone call that I became curious. That was when I put out some feelers at my agency. Turns out he's in London."

The hair on my arms popped out and stood at attention. "What? Virgil is there?"

"Yes." Now I could read her. That one little word conveyed the sense of humor I knew was Angela's.

I didn't say so, but I was glad I was still going to see her.

"Actually, I don't know exactly where he is at this moment, but I know he entered the UK via Heathrow airport November 3 on a flight from Atlanta. We didn't have a reason to follow him at the time, so I'm not sure if he is still in London or not."

"But there's a good chance he's somewhere in the United Kingdom?" I asked.

"Well, that's difficult to say. He could be anywhere in Europe by now since we didn't keep track of him. So, come on over. We can spend time together while we search for him."

"What a wonderful solution." I opened the trip itinerary e-mail and forwarded it to Angela. "I just sent you an e-mail detailing my trip, including my time of arrival. I'll see you soon."

"Good. And, Chris…"

"Yes?"

"Don't even think about bringing your Glock."

***

I laughed to myself as I ended the call to Angela. She admired my accuracy at the pistol range, but she worried about me carrying a gun. As a law enforcement agent, she didn't approve of amateurs like me being armed. It didn't matter. I hadn't planned to take the gun with me to England anyway.

As soon as I hung up from talking to her, I called Tex and then Liz to tell them about Virgil showing up in London. Tex got a little excited and expressed a desire to go with me until it hit him he'd promised Jane he'd stick close to home during the school break. Liz was the one who surprised me. It was like she didn't care where he was. She was back in the doldrums. The anger I'd

SIDNEY W. FROST

thought would make her strong again had been short-lived.

Three days later Jane called and invited me to the Thompson house for dinner. I accepted. Not only was she a creative and accomplished cook, I was getting tired of restaurant food. Not that I couldn't cook for myself. I was actually pretty good in the kitchen. Maybe I wasn't all that creative, but my ability to follow recipes to the letter resulted in some fine-tasting meals. My creativity came when I modified the recipes to match my tastes. Enchiladas, for example, were my favorite thing to cook. Not only that, I could make salsa, beans and rice to go with them the way they did in the Mexican food restaurants. Still, it wasn't much fun cooking for one.

Besides anticipating a home-cooked meal, I'd promised Tex I'd help smooth the way with Jane for him to help with the investigation for Liz and I knew he'd set up this invite. But, that was before we knew Virgil was in England. Now, Tex could spend more time with his wife while I saw Angela and looked for Virgil.

As soon as I entered the Thompson house carrying a canvas shopping bag, I was surrounded by love. Five-year-old Anna jumped into my arms and hugged me like a miniature Liz. Three-year-old Owen draped around my right leg causing me to drag him as I walked through the entry way toward the kitchen with him laughing louder with every step. Raymond, the chocolate Lab, bounced up and down on my left side as if he wanted to kiss me but knew he wasn't supposed to jump on people. Samantha, the Russian Blue cat, waited

32

in the kitchen doorway, twitching her tail seductively and glancing at me as if she didn't care who I was or why I was there while at the same time longing to be stroked.

"Unc'a Chris, when are you going to babysit us again?" Owen asked.

I'd grown attached to Anna and Owen more and more each time I visited the family and, on several occasions, served as a substitute sitter.

"I don't know, Owen. Soon, probably. I'll talk to your mom and dad about it tonight. Okay?"

He smiled at me, bobbing his head up and down. "Okay. Tell her tonight."

"You've got a load there," Jane said coming from the kitchen. "Get off Uncle Chris, kids. Sit, Raymond."

My mouth must have dropped more than I thought. Jane laughed.

"What happened to you?" I asked. The last time I saw her she'd been dumpy and overweight with puffed cheeks and dull, stringy hair. Now she was as slender as a model. It was December, but she wore a dark-blue tank top with "Fit Girl" on the front in shimmering silver. Shoulder muscles stood high above the straps of her top and her biceps were larger than mine.

"I got tired of being overweight and tired. I blamed it on having kids, but I knew it was from lack of exercise and eating the wrong foods."

"You are stunning. Have you considered entering one of those fitness contests? You look better than the competitors I've seen on TV."

She chuckled. "The judges agree with you, Chris."

She pointed to the mantel above the fireplace. There were various-sized trophies from one end to the other.

I read one and then another. "This is impressive. I can't believe you've changed so much since the last time I saw you."

"Then you need to visit more often. I think it's been about six months since you last babysat for us." She motioned toward the trophies. "It's more than winning contests. I feel so much better physically and mentally. The competitions keep me aimed in the right direction." She showed me her flexed biceps. "The only way to look this way is to exercise and eat properly."

"Amazing," I said.

"Thanks."

She gave the kids her sternest look. "I said to get off Uncle Chris. Now." Her voice demanded obedience and she got it.

I helped Anna to the floor and handed Jane the bag.

"What's this?" Jane asked.

"A bottle of red and a bottle of white. I wasn't sure what you were cooking for dinner."

"Well, thanks. Come on in." She turned to walk toward the counter and placed the wine bottles down gently. "I'll put the white in the refrigerator. Red will be fine for tonight. Tex is making spaghetti with Italian sausage. He's at the grill cooking the meat. Go say hi while I fix the salad."

I tried not to look disappointed as I went out the kitchen door, down the ramp and found Tex in his wheelchair turning sausages as flames popped in all directions. "Hey, buddy. Smells good."

"Hi," he said. "Nothing better than outdoor cooking. We get to do it pretty much year 'round here in Central Texas. Hope you're hungry. I made enough for an army."

I took a deep breath. "Mmm. I'm getting hungrier by the minute. I was hoping for one of Jane's meals, but I guess I'll have to put up with yours."

"You might be surprised. Well, actually, no one can mess up spaghetti and the sauce is from a bottle. Still, it's good."

"Speaking of Jane, what's it like being married to a sculptured goddess?" I asked.

He smiled. "Doesn't she look great? She's a member of the National Physique Committee, too."

"Why haven't you mentioned it before?"

"'Cause," Tex said, "I wanted to surprise you. I wish I could've seen your eyes pop out when you first saw her."

He used tongs to move the sausages from the fire to a warming pan. "This stuff's ready. Before we go in, I'd like your opinion on an idea I'm toying with."

"What's that?" I asked.

"Since Jane wants me to spend more time with the family. What if I tell her I'll skip a semester of school?"

I thought about the long painful route Tex had taken to get where he was now. "You've worked hard to get your degree and you're almost there. Don't postpone it."

"I don't want to, but I couldn't think of another way to help Liz and keep Jane happy, too." He shook his head.

"You'll find a way. Besides, with Virgil in England,

there's not much you can do right now to help Liz."

Tex crossed his arms, greasy tongs pointing in the air. "Virgil could be anywhere in Europe by now."

"Yes, but that's more than we knew before."

"I guess. But what do we do now? What do we tell Jane?"

"Be honest with her. Let's tell her everything we know."

CHAPTER FIVE

After dinner, Tex and I cleaned the kitchen while Jane bathed the kids and put them down for the night. When we were finished, we sat nervously in the family room, me in the easy chair, and he in his wheelchair next to the sofa. I could understand why he was worried, but I didn't know why I was so anxious. I'd worked out my problems with Angela and would get to see her and search for Virgil at the same time. Tex didn't have to do anything on the case while I was in England, but I knew he was concerned about letting Liz down. Although he didn't say a word while we waited for Jane to return, I guessed he was worried about disappointing her, too. And that was the way it should have been.

Jane stormed into the room and took a seat on the sofa. "Okay. Anna and Owen are in bed. Which one of you sissies is going to tell me what's going on?"

I stared at Tex, knowing my face showed surprise as much as his did.

"Don't worry, I can't read minds." She nodded toward Tex. "I've been married to this guy long enough to know something's going on and that he probably invited you over tonight to soften the blow. Since the day I met him in the hospital, recovering from his accident, till now, I could read him like a children's book." She turned her gaze to me. "Not that you're not invited to come over anytime. The kids love you, you know. When I tucked them in they begged to have you babysit again."

"I love them, too," was all I managed to say.

Jane continued to stare at me with intent, ignoring her husband. "The accident did more than put him in a wheelchair. It ended his hopes of going to Iraq. To fight for his country."

"He said you saved his life."

She put aside her anger and looked at Tex lovingly. "Well, not his life. As hospital chaplain, if anything, I may have helped save his soul. He probably told you he was pretty upset with God about what had happened. All I did was listen and before I knew it I'd fallen in love with him."

Tex smiled, but I could tell he was still nervous about where the conversation was going.

"The man I fell in love with was sober and he's not had a drink since."

"Hasn't needed one, either," Tex said.

"Right. But we know that addicts sometimes beat one

addiction by replacing it with another." She looked at me as if daring me to disagree with her. "Lately he's been working too much. That's why I arranged a month-long vacation for us so we can be together more, part of that time will be with the children and part of the time will be for the two of us." She smiled at Tex so sweetly I felt like an intruder in the room.

Her smile quickly disappeared. She pierced me with her eyes making me wonder why she was angry with me, if that was what it was, unless she thought I enabled Tex's work addiction.

She focused on Tex. "You've known about our plans for how long?"

"Uh…uh…a long time."

"Right. Plus, I've reminded you about it every week for the past two months so you don't have an excuse for not knowing."

"What are you going to do on your vacation?" I asked.

Tex shrugged and turned to Jane.

"Nothing, she said. "Absolutely nothing. There's no classes for Tex, no homework, and no library work. We're both taking off and staying home. If we feel like going somewhere, we will. A vacation doesn't mean you have to go somewhere. It doesn't have to be costly. The main thing I want to do is be together."

"Of course, we'd have the kids to care for," Tex said.

Jane frowned. "You never listen. Your parents are keeping the kids part of the time. It's just you and me while they're gone. There will be no excuses for not honoring each other with our full attention."

Tex had been estranged from his parents for years. Liz and I tried to find them for months, but it wasn't until they read about us saving the president's life in Houston that they contacted Liz and she got them together with Tex. That was when they learned they were grandparents.

"Oh," Tex said. "I forgot." He frowned. "They're not going to smoke around the kids, are they?"

"No. I'm sure they won't if we ask them not to. Besides, they're both trying to quit."

"*Trying* won't cut it," Tex said. "I don't want my kids exposed to cigarette smoke the way I was."

"Now, back to business," Jane said. "What are you two up to? And don't act so scared. I know something's going on. What haven't you told me? You two have been sneaking around like a couple of teens, talking behind my back."

Tex nodded cautiously and then gulped.

"Well," Jane continued, "let me tell you right now, it'd better be a matter of somebody's life or death if you hope to get out of this vacation I've planned."

Tex, my usually loud-mouthed friend, was mute. The room was silent longer than I could stand. "You're right, Jane. We have been trying to choose how best to tell you about something that came up that could affect us all during the next month. We decided to present you with all the facts and let you decide what to do."

"I already know what I'm going to do," she said. "But go ahead. I'll listen."

I cleared my voice and began. "First of all, it's not life or death. Not exactly. But the situation is timely. If we don't act immediately, there could be emotional pain for someone we all love."

"Must have something to do with Liz," Jane said.

Tex caught my eye and smiled.

"Right. This is about Liz," I said.

"I should've known. She's been like a mother to Tex ever since he met her. So what's she into now?"

"A hundred thousand dollars has been stolen from a personal bank account she set up to buy a bookmobile for the library. We suspect the money was taken by Virgil."

"Virgil?" Jane asked. "The guy she was dating?"

"Yes."

"Yikes. Now I understand what you mean by emotional pain. Poor woman. I thought she'd fallen for him too quickly."

Tex appeared hopeful by Jane's remark. "Yes, and if we hurry we may be able to catch him."

Jane turned to me, ignoring Tex. "Tell me what you know so far."

"We've just begun to study this case. To be honest, we're not absolutely positive it was Virgil who took the money. We may find it's someone trying to make it look like he did it."

"Why do you say that?" she asked.

"The money was paid in small amounts, all less than ten thousand dollars to companies with 'gold' in their name."

"Gold?"

"Yes. Virgil's last name is Golden."

"Oh, I see. So either he was stupid enough to leave a

trail or someone set him up."

"Or," Tex said, "he left the trail on purpose, wanting to brag about what he did."

"What else do you know?" Jane asked.

"We know he entered England on a flight from Atlanta on November 3. We don't know where he went next."

Jane counted on her fingers. "That was, what, seven weeks ago. He could be anywhere by now."

"That's right," I said. "But that gives us a place to begin.

She crossed her arms. "Still, him being somewhere in the United Kingdom, or Europe for that matter, is not enough to make an immediate search necessary."

She was right, but I knew I was going to England anyway. I looked at Tex and could tell he didn't have a good response either.

I grabbed a huge breath. "We know. I had a trip to England planned before we learned Virgil went there."

"To see Angela?"

"Yes. While I'm there I'll see what we can learn about Virgil. Tex and Liz could help from here."

"Okay," Jane said, smiling for the first time since she came into the room. She stood and sauntered to Tex. "I think this will work. If you need his help while you're in England, I'll help too." She wrapped an arm around her husband. "We're going to be together and enjoy our vacation even if that means a few hours now and then doing some research for Liz."

Tex smiled.

***

On Monday, Tex, Liz, and I met in the bookmobile which was parked at the loading ramp behind the Austin History Center. It was Tex's idea. He thought Virgil might have bugged the O'Henry room where we usually met.

I didn't think Virgil would have gone to the trouble but I guessed he could do it if he wanted to. Stealing a hundred grand from Liz was more difficult than planting a hearing device. But why would he want to listen in to what Liz said now? He'd finished his business here. Still, I'd learned to trust Tex's instincts when it came to understanding the minds of criminals.

Liz sat in the librarian's chair in the front. It was actually the passenger seat that turned around to face the rear of the bookmobile. Tex had rolled in on the metal ramp the librarians use to load the mobile library and was parked near the door, close to Liz. I was in the back sitting at the checkout desk. The vehicle wasn't so large that I felt separated from the others.

I gazed at the ceiling and around the room. If there was a bug in here, it could be easily hidden behind all the books. "Are you sure there are no bugs in here?" I asked Tex.

"Yep. Jimbo did a sweep as soon as Brian and Karen brought the bookmobile in this morning. It's clean. Since they keep the vehicle at their house overnight, Virgil would have less chance of placing a listening device in it."

"That's not true," Liz said. "Virgil got his hands on the

bookmobile at their house once." She paused. "Actually, the police don't know for sure, but they suspect it was Virgil who took a wheel off and caused it to roll off the side of the hill with poor Karen inside."

"That's right," Tex said, "But don't worry, this baby is bug free now."

I didn't know all the details, but I think Tex met Jimbo in prison and he was now a private detective. "Why didn't you get Jimbo to check the O'Henry room?" I asked.

"I did. He's checking it now. It'll take longer, though. The bookmobile is smaller and easier to check."

"What about Brian and Karen?" I asked. "Aren't they going out today?"

"No, silly," Liz said. "It's Christmas Eve. They brought it in and left it so we can get it serviced at the city garage. The Donelsons are taking a few days off for the holidays."

With us separated the way we were it wasn't an ideal meeting place, but it was worth it knowing we could talk without being heard. I don't know about the others, but I liked the smell of used books. Sounds weird, I guess, but being on the bookmobile reminded me of the many pleasant hours I'd spent in a multitude of libraries, some mobile and some not, from elementary school through graduate school

"Okay," Liz said, "from what I understand, Chris is going to England to see Angela. While he's there, he'll try to track down Virgil. Percy will be on vacation, but is staying home with his family and will join the search only if necessary."

"Yes, ma'am," Tex said. "And, if I'm needed, Jane is coming with me. I'm sorry, but I must dedicate this semester break to my wife. She's done so much for me over the years. It's my turn to do for her."

"I understand," Liz said. "You don't need to apologize to me. You make that lovely wife of yours happy. Okay?"

Tex beamed.

"Now," Liz continued her summary report. "I'm staying right here. I wish there was something I could do to help you, Chris."

"Thanks," I said. "I'll call you if I learn anything. By the way, have you closed that account yet?"

Her eyes bulged. "No. Do you think he'll hit it again? I assumed that would be the end of it with him gone and all."

"No, ma'am," Tex said. "Once he got access to the bank account, he could get to it from anywhere in the world."

"Donations are still coming in," I said. "He may have been waiting for the balance to get larger."

"That doesn't explain why he took exactly $100,000," Tex said.

"I hadn't thought of that," I said. "That hundred grand may have been a goal. Still, if he sees some easy money, he might grab it anyway."

"Well," Liz said, "I wish you'd told me all this last week. The rest of the money's probably gone now."

"I've got an idea," I said. "Let's leave the account open with a balance of ten thousand."

"Why?" Liz asked.

"Oh, I see," Tex said. "You want to trap him, right?"

"Yes. That, plus we don't want him to know we're on to him."

"But, ten thousand?" she said. "That's a lot of money for a 'maybe' result. Couldn't we leave a hundred or even a thousand?"

"I know it's a lot, but not compared to the hundred thousand he already took. If you don't leave at least ten grand, I'm afraid he'll spot the trap and not do anything that will help us find him."

"He's right," Tex said.

"Okay," she said, "I'll go to the bank to do that in person after we finish here. Anything else we need to talk about?"

"Not that I can think of," I said. "I'll stay in contact with both of you from England."

CHAPTER SIX

I left the meeting thinking about Angela. Although we talked frequently, our relationship had been nearly all long-distance. The kiss from a year ago stayed in my memory and I knew from our conversations she cared for me. Still, I didn't know what to expect when I saw her. Her job took her around the globe. Mine took me from Georgetown to Cedar Park, Texas, at least on the few days I didn't work from home. How could we ever be together?

There was also the guilt. Was it too soon after Sarah's death to think about another woman? Was it fair to Angela to pursue a romantic friendship with her knowing how much I had loved Sarah? Did Angela want more of a relationship? I had more questions than answers, but one thing I knew, I needed to talk to Sarah.

I drove my pickup to the Grace Garden Columbarium where her cremains were interred. The bench wasn't inviting in cold weather, but I sat there anyway with my head bowed, waiting to feel Sarah's presence as I had so many times before. Soon, it happened. She was there. Perhaps it was only the cold weather, but I felt the hairs on my arms rise.

"Sarah?" I straightened myself on the bench, half expecting to see her. "I feel you're with me now." I knew she was there in spirit only, but I couldn't help looking around. "But I understand you are with the Lord."

I waited, knowing there would be no response. There never was. But it didn't matter. I still felt I was somehow closer to her here.

"I miss you more than mere words can express. When you departed, you left a hole in my heart and an emptiness in my world. I remember you saying you wanted me to find someone to be happy with, but it is so hard to do."

"I guess you know all that. I came to tell you about my plan to go to London to see Angela. If only you could tell me what to do. I feel as if I'm betraying you by going."

I bowed my head again. "Please, help me. Do I let myself love someone else? Is it possible to love two people as much as I think I do?

"This trip tomorrow frightens me. I've always told you I didn't think I'd ever love another woman, but somehow it's happened. Still, she may not have the same feelings for me. To make things more difficult, we live far apart and I don't know what to do about that. If only you could talk to me and help me decide what to do."

A sudden wind arose in the garden, stirring dead leaves that were sheltered in the corners. It was an unusually strong wind with a circular motion that picked up the leaves and surrounded me. The sudden burst of air caused me to stand and gasp.

Then, just as suddenly, calmness covered me and I felt a peace I hadn't known since Sarah's death. I remembered her last words to me, and knew it was okay to go to Angela.

***

I spotted her through the glass wall beyond the customs area at Gatwick Airport before she knew I was there. It gave me time to savor the moment without her knowing she was being admired.

The first time I saw her was after she'd broken into my Georgetown apartment. I didn't know her name for days afterwards so I called her the dark-haired beauty. That name came back to me instantly. Brown hair, brown eyes, with a smile that could light up a room. She came across as the gentle girl-next-door-type in her jeans and white blouse, holding her coat in her arms, but she could subdue a man twice her size.

I stood there, knowing there was a grin on my face. She spotted me and I saw what I was waiting for. Her smile. I waved and walked toward her, dragging my overnight bag. I had no idea what would happen next, but I knew I wanted to hold her in my arms and prayed she wanted to be held.

When I got to her, I dropped the handle of my suitcase and put my arms around her. She fit perfectly against me and my arms wrapped around her so naturally I felt at home there. I hugged her romantically, not the way Liz hugs, and I pushed back slightly and kissed her full on the lips. She kissed me back and came close for another embrace. It happened quickly and without warning, and I knew it was irrational, but that feeling of unfaithfulness to Sarah engulfed me. I backed away from Angela, catching my breath.

"Thank you for meeting me at the airport," I said, shaking off the guilt and telling myself it was illogical.

She looked into my eyes as if studying my face. Had she caught my momentary relapse?

"No problem," she said. "The express to London is simple to use unless you've never done it before. I came to show you the first time. Besides, I wanted to see you sooner." She smiled.

Her comment warmed me, but also made me feel as if a spotlight was beating down on me. I didn't respond, but I'm sure my expression conveyed how pleased I was to hear her say that.

"I'm glad you kept the beard. It looks good on you. I couldn't tell on Skype."

So, that was why she had been studying my face. "Thanks. I'm beginning to like it, too."

The "express" Angela referred to was a fast train that ran about every fifteen minutes between Gatwick Airport and Victoria Station in central London. The trip would take about thirty minutes and land us close to her flat.

"It's good to see you," I said.

She grabbed my hand and turned to walk away. "Let's talk on the train."

She checked her watch and walked faster, as if knowing a train would be departing soon. And, sure enough, it was. We jumped on just in time and were leaving the airport in a matter of seconds. Angela found two seats next to each other and a place to stow my bag. I took off my coat and held it in my lap the way she did hers. As soon as the train left the airport I could see the open fields were dotted with thin pockets of snow. There wasn't much of the white stuff, but enough to make the view compelling. Further along I saw sheep that appeared yellow against the purer white of the snow.

"How cold does it get here?" I asked.

"The low was minus seven or so last winter, but it's not been that cold this year. Minus four, maybe."

I quickly converted that to Fahrenheit. "You mean nineteen or twenty-five degrees in American?"

She laughed. "Yes, approximately."

My special memory helped at the oddest times.

"Jet-lagged?" she asked.

"I slept some on the plane, but right now I feel like it's time to go to bed."

"It's not. Our day is just beginning. It's easier to adjust if you stay awake as long as you can."

"I'll try." I grabbed my phone. "I need to check for messages."

She nodded.

"Uh-oh, " I said. "Here's one from Liz…"

"She says the thief has struck again," Angela said before I had a chance to read more. "Remaining balance went to a company in Bulgaria called Twenty-Four Carats."

"Oh, she cc'd you?"

"No. She called me." Angela sounded angry.

I didn't know why a call from Liz would upset her. I was feeling light-headed from the time change, but I had to know what was wrong.

"Is there something wrong?" I asked.

Angela stared out the window. I watched, too, as we went through a forest. Glistening ice encased the smaller leafless branches of the trees making them look like monster fingers.

I waited, but when she didn't respond I tried to find an answer to why she might be angry at Liz. Nothing came to me.

She turned away from the window, still not looking at me. "I'm sorry. Nothing's wrong. I guess it's my job. I have this holiday, but we both know they could call me in at any time and our visit would be over."

I nodded, still not understanding.

She continued. "I want to be with you. I wish we didn't have to think about Liz and Virgil or your friend Tex for a short time."

Now I understood. She had a knack for being direct and saying what she felt. And, in this case, it was what I wanted to hear. Still, I was at a loss for words.

She peered into my eyes and I saw a vulnerability in her that she'd never shown me. "I know that sounds selfish of me, but you asked."

"No. That's not selfish. That's why I'm here. To see you. That's what I want, too."

The train decelerated slightly. I could tell more by the sound than feel. Out the window I saw the backyards of homes zipping by.

"I know," she said, "but you also have an obligation to Liz. Her problem is time-sensitive. I understand. And, I said we could look for Virgil while you were here. We still can, but I just want us to have time to do things together, to talk, to do nothing. I want to take a real vacation with you no matter how short it might be. And, since I can't promise they won't call me back to work, I have no right to ask you to take off entirely."

What she said pained me and thrilled me at the same time. She wanted to be with me as much as I wanted to be with her. She had feelings for me. Right at this moment I wanted to pretend I hadn't received the e-mail from Liz.

But I couldn't.

The train was barely moving as it entered the station.

"I want to be with you, too," I said. "And I'll give you my full attention just as soon as I can. But I have to see what I can do to follow this new lead to Virgil. This trap was my idea and Liz will lose an additional ten grand if I can't fix this. I didn't think Virgil would take the bait so fast. I'm sorry."

As the train came to a stop Angela stood without acknowledging my apology. We put on our coats and I grabbed my luggage. I followed her out the door, anticipating a new adventure.

CHAPTER SEVEN

We exited the station onto Victoria Street, just across from the Victoria Palace Theatre. The marquee announced *Billy Elliot* was showing. The snow we'd seen from the train outside of the city wasn't as prevalent in central London. It was cold and everyone was bundled up, but the only snow I saw was in places protected from the sun.

Angela put on a rain hat and hooked her arm in mine as if we'd been a couple for years. I pulled my suitcase with my other hand, pleased with the way she nestled close to me. I checked the sky to get my bearings, but the cloud covering offered little help. I thought we were headed east on Victoria Street. It didn't matter since I had a competent guide.

"The sidewalk is so crowded here," I said.

"Not bad, today. By the way, we call it pavement."

"Oh? What do you call the pavement?"

"Are you talking about the street?"

People were going in both directions. Some followed by wheeled luggage the way I was, some talked on phones as they walked, but mostly everyone was in a hurry to get somewhere. I'd gotten used to the slower pace in Georgetown, Texas, where I lived and Cedar Park, Texas where I worked, both close to Austin. One thing about London I liked was that everyone was courteous.

"How do you get used to all the people?" I asked.

Angela laughed. "Are you kidding? This is nothing compared to a working day."

"What do you mean? Is this a holiday?"

"Today's Boxing Day."

"What's that?"

Angela stopped, withdrew the arm she'd had around mine, and looked mystified.

"Boxing Day is celebrated on the 26th of December. It is a national holiday in the UK, Ireland, and Canada."

She was so beautiful standing there teaching me about her world. Her brown hair poked out of her canvas rain hat, and her brown eyes glistened. The winter coat she wore came to mid-thigh and was zipped to her chin.

"So you have two holidays in a row at Christmas time."

"Right."

"Why is Boxing Day so close to Christmas? Do the boxers wear Santa costumes?"

She laughed. "Don't be silly. Boxing Day doesn't have anything to do with the sport." She grabbed my arm again and continued to lead us in the same direction on Victoria Street, weaving in and out of people walking toward us.

"So, why is it called Boxing Day?"

"It has to do with Christmas boxes. There are some disagreements about how the name came about. I was taught it has to do with those more fortunate sharing with the poor. The day after Christmas they would box up the leftover food along with some gifts and take it to those who had little."

She stopped in front of a pub called The Albert. "This is it," she said.

"You live in a pub?" I checked the street signs. Victoria Street on the front of the building and Buckingham Gate on the side.

She laughed. "Well, sort of." She pointed to the floors above The Albert. "I live up there. The office is nearby and this flat comes with the job. It's a way of making sure I can get to work in a hurry, if need be. It's also convenient to the train and Underground in case I need to go somewhere else."

"It's convenient to the pub, too."

"Right. I have to admit I eat here more than I should. When I'm at home in Somerset, I'm more likely to cook." She pulled me close and offered my favorite smile. "We'll go there tomorrow," she said.

"I'd like that." I was pleased she planned to take me to see her home. Still, I had a lump in my throat knowing we'd be close to where Sarah grew up.

We entered the pub and a burly guy in a tight black tee shirt smiled and waved from behind the bar. Angela waved back and led me to a hallway near the front of the pub. "My place is on the top floor. We call it the fourth floor, but you would call it the fifth. Here, we start numbering with zero for the ground floor."

"I see. Where's the elevator?"

She laughed. "The *lift* is down that hall there, but we don't need it. Think of it as exercise. Do you need me to carry your bag?" she asked with a twinkle in her eye.

"Oh, no," I said. "I can manage."

I followed her as she climbed a narrow wooden staircase with wooden steps, concave from wear, that creaked as we stepped on them.

"How old is this place?" I asked, thinking specifically about the stairwell. The outside of the building was sturdy and didn't seem so old. In contrast, the wood in the stairwell had probably been hand planed long ago, perhaps before modern machinery was invented.

"The pub dates back to the mid-1800s, but I think the building itself was built in 1615."

We reached the top floor and went down a hallway made from the same old wood as the stairwell. She stopped in front of a nondescript wooden door with no number on it. She pulled a key chain from her purse, opened the door, and led me in. I was surprised by what I saw. Barren was the word that best described the room. In one corner stood a single bed covered with what looked like a threadbare olive-colored army blanket. A kitchen of sorts was in another corner. It consisted of a narrow counter barely wide enough for the small sink in the middle. A hotel-sized refrigerator huddled to the right of the counter with a micro microwave oven sitting on top of it. No cabinets or drawers that I could see. A few pans along with plates, bowls and utensils were stacked on the countertop on either side of the sink.

I turned in a circle, pulling my suitcase with me. I didn't see another bed. There was a small bathroom with the door open, but apparently no other rooms.

I turned to Angela. "Uhh...I know this is not your own place, but I'm surprised how sparse it is. Do you stay here often?"

She laughed and handed me a key. "You're kidding, right? You don't think I live in this place, do you? This is where you're staying. My flat is across the hall."

"Oh," I said, feeling relieved and a little embarrassed. "Yeah. I was just kidding." We hadn't talked about sleeping arrangements, but I hadn't considered a separate flat would be available for me. I'd assumed I'd be on a couch somewhere or perhaps a nearby hotel.

"The agency owns the building. This room is used mainly for agents and guests who are passing through the city. They let me use it when I have guests. Don't worry, you can come over to my place for meals."

She frowned as if seeing the room for the first time. "You okay with it?"

"Oh, sure. It's great."

"Good. If not, we can get you a room in a hotel."

"No. This is fine. I'd rather be near you than in some hotel."

She smiled. "Okay. I'll give you chance to unpack and freshen up. But, whatever you do, don't lie down. If you do you'll fall asleep. Come on over when you're ready and you can use my computer to take care of that business for Liz."

"Okay. I promise not to fall asleep. I'll be there in a few minutes. The door across from mine?"

"Yes," she said as she walked into the hall and opened a door. "This one."

I was relieved to learn Angela didn't live in a place like this. It was fine for me, though. I supposed she had to live in worse places at times while on assignments.

I found one of those folding racks for luggage and plopped my suitcase on it. I put my toiletries bag in the tiny bathroom. It was too small for a tub, but there was a shower and that was all I needed. I didn't see a closet, but I found a peg behind the bathroom door with several wire clothes hangers. I hung my two shirts and two pairs of pants on that peg. Everything else I left in the opened suitcase. The room was small and there wasn't much furniture, but it was clean and close to Angela.

***

"It's open," Angela said a few minutes later in response to my knock.

I turned the knob and went in.

Nice.

Her main room was at least twice the size of mine and she had a separate bedroom and a larger bathroom. The kitchen area was in the main room still, but it was huge compared to mine. In another corner of the room was a desk with a computer on it, a comfortable-looking chair and a bookshelf on the wall behind the desk. Liz would like the bookshelf. It was well stocked and the books were aligned, mostly. I straightened a few of them.

There were curtains on the windows and a variety of framed pictures hung on the walls. The wall paint and carpets were nicer than in my room. Everything in Angela's flat was coordinated and fresh. Just looking, you'd never dream the building was from the 1600s.

"Now, this is lovely. Especially compared to the flat I'm in across the hall."

"Thank you." She laughed. "That's why I showed you your room first. Actually, I straightened your place before you arrived. You should have seen it before."

"Hard to believe it could be worse, but thanks. I'm pleased to have it."

She smiled. "Did you see my curtains?" she asked, pointing at the windows in her place.

"Yes. I love them."

I also loved looking at her.

"I'm glad. I made them myself. I was aiming for a more feminine touch. I think it worked, don't you?"

"Yes. Very nice."

"If you're hungry," she said, "we can grab a quick meal downstairs at the pub. I'd cook something, but I've been in Bath for a while and there's not much in the pantry. We'd have to shop first. I have a feeling you're going to want to use my computer before we eat." She nodded toward her desk.

"I guess I should, but let me say first how wonderful

you look and how much I appreciate your invitation to visit."

She moved into my arms and hugged me.

"Thank you." She kissed my cheek. "Now do your work for Liz."

"Okay," I said, wishing she would stay in my arms and we could forget about Liz and Virgil and the rest of the world. "I could meet you downstairs at the pub if you're hungry."

"I'm okay," she said. "In fact, I'd like to watch you work. I'm trying to learn as much about computers as possible."

"I don't mind you watching, but this part is nothing you don't already know. I'm going to log into Liz's account with the password she gave me and dig into her bank account."

I sat at the desk and Angela took a side chair and moved close. I found her browser and pointed it to Liz's bank. I logged in as Liz without referring to notes.

"I see you're using that exceptional memory of yours."

"Well, you know Liz and computers. Actually her password isn't too hard to remember."

"You mean like '1234'?"

"Well not that simple. Liz didn't know how to access the account electronically until we helped her. The bank required a combination of letters, upper and lower case, and numbers. So, we came up with capital-L-number-1-lowercase-b-r-a-r-y. It is easy for her to remember, but follows the password rules."

"How did Virgil get access to her account if she didn't

have it set up for online?"

"He smiled at her while getting her to sign a form making him a co-owner on the account."

"Oh, that old ruse."

"Yes. He was a volunteer at the library and worked himself up to serving as her personal assistant. He often had legitimate forms for her to sign. After he took her to dinner a few times and gained her trust, it was probably not that difficult for him to get her signature. She doesn't remember it happening, but agrees it could have. Remember, he was feigning interest in her and she was falling for him."

"Wow. I'm sorry she got hurt like that."

"Yeah, he's an old-school con artist, but he knows enough about computers to take money from her bank account. That worries me some. We don't know the full extent of his computer capabilities, which means we don't know what to expect from him next. So far, he's covered his electronic trail before we could get to him." I wondered if he knew how to steal from his victims without conning them into signing a form the way he did Liz.

"Mind if I change your mouse for my left-handedness? I'll switch it back when I finish."

She smiled. "No problem."

I punched a few keys and waited for the display to refresh. "Okay. I'm in."

Angela moved in and stared at the screen. She was close enough for me to smell the pleasant scent I had noticed when she'd hugged me.

I stared at the display on the screen. "The balance is

ten dollars. That's different. In the past, he's always taken an amount less than ten thousand dollars. He took everything this time. Well, everything but the minimum the bank requires to keep the account open. The balance was a little over ten grand. That means he had to get into the account first and determine the balance. I wasn't sure what he'd done in the past." I scanned the transactions. "Ah, here is the ACH payment he made to Twenty-Four Karats."

"ACH is a bank-to-bank transfer, right?"

"Yes. Automated Clearing House. Now, I need to try to find the bank where the money was sent. For all the previous transactions the receiving account was closed before we could get there. We're hoping it'll be different this time, since he just took the money yesterday."

"I hope you can catch him."

I did a few magic steps, explaining them to Angela as I went. What I did wasn't entirely legal, but she knew my dad and had used his talents on cases of her own. I don't think she was comfortable with what we did. Still, I think she trusted us not to use our hacking talents the wrong way.

"Here it is," I said as a Bulgarian bank website screen appeared. "And the money is gone."

"What? What happened?"

"It's an online bank so we don't know where it is physically. The money was withdrawn just as soon as it cleared. It's all gone. There is a balance of ten US dollars left in Twenty-Four Karats' Bulgarian account."

"Sorry. Can you see where the money went?"

"No. The notation says a cashier's check was mailed,

but it doesn't show where."

"So, what's next?"

I shook my head, thinking, but nothing came to mind. I straightened the keyboard and aligned the papers and pens on Angela's desk, making them parallel and equidistant. She kept a neat house, so perhaps I'd inadvertently moved some things around. I scanned the desk. All better now.

Angela giggled.

"What?"

"You. When you're stressed you try to correct it by getting everything around you in order."

Normally, I'd be embarrassed for someone to know that about me. But I didn't mind Angela knowing. "I guess I do. I'm sorry."

"No. It's okay. I understand."

I think she really did. Maybe better than I did.

"You asked what I was going to do next. There's nothing more I can do with Virgil's bank account and we know from the previous withdrawals he'll close the account soon. I guess I'll call Liz and give her the bad news. I caused her to lose another ten thousand. What time is it in Austin?"

Angela glanced at her wristwatch. "It's a quarter to five in the morning there."

"Oops. Too early for Liz. She gets to work by seven, though. I'll call her later. There's nothing she can do about it now anyway."

CHAPTER EIGHT

"Is it time to go to bed yet?"

Angela looked at me incredulously with one eyebrow arched.

"To sleep. I've been awake all night."

"It's eleven thirty in the morning. I thought you said you slept on the plane."

"A little. Maybe during the third movie. Still, I feel so tired. How about a short nap?"

"No napping. You've got jet lag. The best way to get past it is to adjust to the schedule here. You can imagine how much I travel so I know what works."

"Okay, but if you want me to stay awake, I'm going to have to walk. That sofa of yours is calling my name." To prove it, I plopped on it. I did it as a joke, but, it felt so good I couldn't keep my eyes from closing.

She grabbed my hands and pulled me to my feet. It was eerie how strong she was.

"How about a quick tour of the city?" she asked. "This is your first time in London, right?"

I was on my feet, but rocked slightly from left to right when she let go of my hands. "Yes, but I'm in no condition for a tour. How about tomorrow?"

"I'm not talking about a long tour. Just a ride on a city bus to keep you from falling asleep. We'll have a late lunch, grab some coffee, and see a few sights."

"And go to bed?"

She laughed. "Yes. You can go to sleep early if you like. But not before eight."

"Eight? Okay, I can do that."

"Good. Tomorrow, I'll show you more of London. Plus, we're meeting Andrew in the pub downstairs for an authentic English meal."

"Andrew is coming here?" Andrew was Sarah's brother who had initially blamed me for her death. He'd thought I should have somehow prevented her from getting into the fray when she went to save the security guard's life. He apologized later after he learned the whole story, but I wasn't sure he meant it. I hadn't talked to him again after that. To be honest, there were times when I wondered if he was right. I was stronger than Sarah and could have prevented her from running to that wounded man. But, she was a nurse, and she felt she had to help. If I had stopped her she would be alive today, but it may have ended our relationship. Of course I would give that up for her life.

"He lives and works in London."

"What does he want?" It felt strange to learn he had talked to Angela.

"Want? I don't know. After I told him you would be visiting, he said he'd love to see you."

"It'll be good to see him, too. Thanks for setting it up." I wasn't sure why I said that. He and I hadn't taken time to talk to each other and had nothing in common. Not anymore.

"I didn't arrange anything. He called to have lunch with me and I told him you'd be here. That's all."

"Oh." I wondered if they had lunch regularly. All this talk about Andrew made me to think more about Sarah. I never wanted to forget her, but I didn't know what Angela would think if she knew Sarah was on my mind as much as she was after all this time.

We grabbed our coats and left Angela's flat for a venture designed to force me to stay awake until eight tonight.

***

It was cold outside, but not unbearable. I saw a sign that showed the temperature was three degrees Celsius, or thirty-eight Fahrenheit. Luckily, we didn't have far to walk. We climbed aboard the first red double-decker bus that came by. She paid the fare for both of us and led the way to the upper deck. It was one with an enclosed upper floor. I took a window seat and she sat next to me.

I trusted she knew best, but I longed for sleep. The heated bus made it more difficult to keep my eyes open.

I took off my coat and held it in my lap.

"I know you're drowsy," she said, "so I'll tell you about the sights as we go. Perhaps my brilliant commentary will cause you to want to stay awake."

I leaned my head against the glass, hoping the cold would spark my attention. "Okay. But, first tell me why everyone is driving on the wrong side of the road."

"What do you mean? You Americans are the ones who drive on the wrong side."

"Hey. There's Scotland Yard." I pointed to a building we were passing with a big sign near the street. "Is that where you work?"

She scrunched her nose. "I don't work for Scotland Yard. You know that. They're like your city police. I'm more like your CIA."

"So where's your office?"

"Well, it's not marked like Scotland Yard."

"Is it near here?"

"We have many different locations."

"You're not going to tell me, are you?"

I counted black cabs while Angela described where we were. I saw a maroon-colored cab and wondered why it was different. I didn't ask. That's when I saw a building I recognized.

"There's Big Ben!" I said.

"Right. And there you've got the Houses of Parliament as well."

"Oh, and there's that Ferris wheel. I saw it on the news. I didn't realize how big it is."

"It's called the London Eye," she said. "It was built as part of London's millennium celebrations."

The bus turned left before the bridge that would have crossed the River Thames and taken us over to the side with the London Eye. We followed the water line on a narrow road across from it. I saw boats, mostly large ones that appeared to be small restaurants, some docked and some moving slowly on the river. People walked along the tree-covered area between the street where we were and the water. I imagined the area would be full of tourists in warmer times of the year.

"You were right," I said. "This is keeping me awake. I don't want to miss anything."

She pressed her shoulder into mine in a sort of a hug gesture. I liked it.

We passed a tall, slender monument of some type that came to a point on top. "What's that?" I asked, pointing to where it stood between us and the river.

"That's called Cleopatra's Needle. It's an Egyptian obelisk. There's one like it in New York City and a similar one in Paris."

We continued along the river, and I turned from side to side, taking it all in.

Angela pointed ahead. "We're coming to Waterloo Bridge."

The road we were on was taking us under the bridge. As we neared it, I saw three red double-decker buses approaching.

After a while we turned left, away from the river. Angela pointed. "That's Blackfriars Station."

"That's another thing I want to do while I'm in London."

"What's that?"

"I want to learn how to use the Underground. I hear it's the best way to get around."

"It is. I considered taking it today, but sitting on this bus will keep you awake longer."

Angela leaned across me toward the window, close enough for me to smell her perfume or shampoo or whatever it was. It was subtle, but it made me want to stay close to her.

"We're going to get off in a couple of blocks," she said. "There's this place that makes the best pizza in London. It's like Naples pizza, if you know what I mean."

I didn't, but assumed it was good. "Didn't you tell me you're part Italian?"

"Yes. My grandparents on my mother's side came from Naples."

At the next stop, Angela climbed off the bus with me behind her. She led the way to the pizza place. It wasn't one of the chains I frequented back home.

"Let me order," Angela said. "You can get us a table and napkins. Oh, and grab a bottle of those dried red peppers over there."

After getting the condiments and finding a place near the window I hung my coat over the back of my chair. Angela returned with two large glasses of a cloudy liquid.

"What's that?" I asked.

"Lemonade. Not exactly a winter drink, but I thought it might help you stay awake. They make this fresh from lemons shipped in from Naples."

I took a sip that turned into a gulp. "Excellent choice," I said.

She took off her coat and put it in one of the extra chairs at our table. "The owners moved to London about ten years ago and their pizzas are made the same way the first pizzas were made in Naples. I ordered one with tomato slices and Italian sausage. I think you'll like it."

As she talked, I enjoyed watching her. She had a charming smile, especially when she was happy, and her whole body took on a sense of contentment when she talked about something she loved. Even pizza.

A young woman with long dark hair the same shade as Angela's brought a large pizza and two plates. The first thing I noticed was how thin the crust was. I had grown accustomed to a thicker one. I wondered if I'd like it. But after taking a bite, I knew why Angela liked this place. Delicious was the only word that came to me, but it was more than that. It lit up my taste buds like nothing before.

We ate silently for a while and I savored every bite.

"Okay," she said. "Next stop is the coffee shop. That pizza woke you, I'm sure, but I'm not taking any chances. Besides, I have a favorite place to go for coffee."

The coffee shop was across the street from the pizzeria. When we got there, Angela pulled a silver-colored Thermos from her handbag.

"Fill this, please," she said to the barista. "No need to rinse it. It's clean." He looked as if he didn't care and hadn't planned to wash it anyway.

After returning the filled Thermos to her handbag, she headed toward the door.

"I thought we were going to have coffee at your favorite place," I said.

"We are. Just wait." She motioned with her head for me to follow her.

She walked briskly away from the coffee shop as I pushed to keep up. In front of us was a tall building with a dome on top.

"What's that?" I asked.

"That's where we're going. St. Paul's Cathedral."

We continued along the sidewalk until we were in front of the enormous church.

"I recognize this place. Those steps especially. Wasn't there a movie filmed here?"

"You're probably thinking of *Mary Poppins*."

"That's it. Dick Van Dyke and Julie Andrews. Right?"

"That's the one. There have been other movies made in and around the church. One of the Harry Potter movies and the latest *Sherlock Holmes* movie."

After we entered the church, and after she'd showed me around, she led the way to a wide staircase in a corner. She grabbed my arm and we started up.

"Where does this go?" I asked.

"You'll see. Not only will this keep you awake, you'll be truly amazed when you get there."

There were few people on the stairway. We kept going up until we eventually reached an area where we could walk all around the dome.

I peeked over the rail at the interior of the church below. "You're right. This is beautiful."

She laughed. "We're in the Whispering Gallery—only about a third of the way to where we're going."

I looked up, but didn't see any way to go further.

"Where are the stairs?" I asked.

"Follow me," she said.

She led me to a stairway behind a wall. One where we had to stop and twist when we met people coming toward us. After what felt like forever, we reached a point where we went outside into the cold air.

"Ah, this must be it. Lovely," I said.

"No. We're not there yet. This is the Stone Gallery. We're about two-thirds the way."

Soon, she walked up again, and I followed. When she stopped, I knew we'd reached the top.

"Here we are," she said. "The Golden Gallery."

"Five hundred and twenty-eight steps," I said.

"That's correct. How'd you know? Did you read that somewhere?"

"No. I counted."

"Why?"

"I don't know. Just one of those weird things I do."

She laughed. "We are eighty-five meters from the cathedral floor."

My mind converted meters to feet automatically. Two hundred eighty-seven, almost two hundred eighty-eight feet. But I didn't tell her. I didn't want to scare her off with what Mom called my uniqueness.

The view was unbelievable. Cool wind whipped around us, but it wasn't all that uncomfortable. Invigorating. Just what I needed to stay awake. I pulled the collar of my jacket around my neck and walked all around the top of the dome, stopping only to gaze at the city below from the various vantage points. The rooftops reminded me of the chimney sweep dance scene in *Mary Poppins*. The view of the river from this vantage point was spectacular. Making full circle, I found Angela sitting on the edge of a wall about as tall as a chair drinking coffee from the lid of the Thermos. Steam rose from the cup. I took her picture with my phone.

She smiled and passed the cup to me. The smell of fresh coffee was awakening in itself. I took a sip, still holding my phone in my other hand, then returned the cup to her.

"What time is it back home now?" I asked.

She checked her watch. "Half past eight in the morning."

"Austin time?"

"Yes."

"Okay, six thirty in California. Mom will be awake. I'm going to call her." That was the second time I'd asked Angela to convert time for me. It was also the last. My unusual memory would take over, and from now on I would know the time here, in Georgetown, and in Redondo Beach.

I tapped in Mom's number and waited. Angela shook her head, but smiled and handed me the coffee cup when my other hand was free. Another couple popped through the opening to our level and stared at me, my phone and my coffee. I toasted them with the cup.

"Hello." Mom sounded surprised.

"Mom. Guess where I am?"

"London, I hope. That's where you said you were going."

"Yeah, but where in London?"

"I have no idea."

Angela took the cup from me and refilled it. She took a sip and motioned it toward me. I shook my head.

"I'm on the top of St. Paul's Cathedral with Angela. We're having coffee."

"Is that allowed, dear? A cathedral? That's not a good place for a picnic."

"We climbed five hundred and twenty-eight steps. We're taking a break for the walk down."

"Okay, dear. Just don't spill any coffee on the church and be careful."

"Okay, Mom. Love you." She didn't understand. She'd have to see the place to know what I was talking about. It is near impossible to describe beauty to someone. They had to see it themselves.

That was the highlight of the day. Of my trip, for that matter. The day would be perfect, however, if I could quit thinking about why Andrew called Angela about lunch.

CHAPTER NINE

"Okay to Skype Liz?" I asked as soon as we got back to Angela's flat.

"Sure. Does she Skype?"

I laughed. "I guess we'll see. Tex set it up for her, but I doubt if she's ever used it."

I clicked on Angela's Skype icon and called Liz. Angela reached over and uncovered the webcam button.

"I don't leave that open. Not since some nerd videotaped me."

"Probably because you broke into his apartment."

"Not that nerd," she said, laughing.

I was referring to a time before we'd met. Someone had burglarized my place so I installed surveillance cameras and caught the next person who tried it. That person happened to be Angela. That's when I realized my emotions hadn't died with Sarah, that it might be possible to do what she said to me with her dying breath—to move on. So I was working on it now, with Angela. Not because of what she'd done but because of what I saw in the video. Her beauty, which was considerable, but also her confidence. She'd been searching my apartment and didn't care what anyone thought about it. At least that was the way she came across in the video. Looking at another woman in that way so soon after Sarah's death made me feel angry with myself.

Liz's computer answered and I could see her sitting behind her desk.

"Hi, Liz," I said.

She stood and all I could see was one huge pink flower on her dress.

"Tex! Come quick. My computer is talking to me. I don't know what to do."

Her face filled the screen. She got blurry and then all I could see was her mouth and chin.

"Hello, computer," she said.

Angela moved in next to me. "Liz, this is Chris and Angela. You're too close to the camera lens. Back up a little."

"Tex! Hurry. It's Chris and Angela."

I turned toward Angela. "I wonder what Tex is doing at work. He's supposed to be off having quality time with Jane."

"Calm down, ma'am. You can do this. Sit in your chair and relax. Good. Now, lean in toward the screen just a little. Whoa. That's enough. Now what do you see?"

"Oh. I see Chris."

"Hi, Liz," I said.

Angela moved in again. "Hello, Liz."

"Well, I'll be. Hi to you both. Are you all the way over in England?"

"Yes we are," I said. "What's Tex doing there? He should be home with Jane."

Jane's face popped onto the screen. "Everything's okay. He's not working. He's teaching me to be an investigator. I love it. Wait until we tell you what we learned from Cloris. Liz has a question first."

Liz moved in too close again and we got a great view of her nose and the hair on her upper lip. "Chris, were you able to find where Virgil sent that money?"

"Yes, but by the time I got into his bank account the ten grand was gone. His Bulgarian account has a balance of ten dollars and if he does what he's done before, it'll be closed soon like the others. By the time I got to a computer, it was all over. He moves fast and we've hit another dead-end. I'm sorry it cost you so much."

Liz backed away from the webcam enough to where I could see the disappointment on her face. What hurt me the most was the contrast with her usual perky attitude.

"That's okay," she said. "I know you did your best."

Tex popped into view, pushing his ten-gallon hat back on his head. "Sorry, Doc. I know you were counting on getting to his account in time. But don't give up on finding that slimeball. Pardon my French, ma'am." He turned toward Liz.

"That's okay, Percy. I've called him worse, but not around other people."

Tex appeared on the screen again. "Jane and I have cultivated a friendship with Cloris Parker, Virgil's former girlfriend. Well, Jane, mostly. Jane figured that if he had conned Liz he probably conned Cloris as well. We knew about the pickup truck he leased in her name and dumped into the lake when he took off. Turns out he not only left her to pay for the pickup, he also took her life savings. Upwards of thirty thousand dollars are missing from her bank account. She told us she'd love to get her hands on him."

"What are you going to do now?" I asked.

Jane moved into view. "Cloris told me that when he left he promised he'd contact her and fly her to where he was."

"His promises aren't worth much," Angela said.

"That's for sure," Liz said.

"I know," Jane said. "But, from what Cloris told us, they had gotten pretty close. Cloris said they'd talked about marriage. Sorry, Liz."

"Don't matter to me," Liz said. "I could care less what he did or didn't do."

Jane continued. "I don't think he'd seriously marry Cloris, but he might get lonely and contact her."

"Well, if he does, will she tell you?" I asked.

"Yes, I believe she will," Jane said. "Especially since we promised to help her get her money back. I showed her the newspaper clipping from Houston when y'all saved the president's life last year."

"Good," I said. "Maybe that will help her trust us. Keep me posted. I haven't slept yet, so I better sign off." I wanted to say it would be hard for me to ever trust Cloris. Especially after what happened in Austin while Virgil was living with her. When Brian hired us to investigate her son, we saw a mean, angry mother. Not someone Liz and Jane could befriend.

Liz's face popped in again, again a little too close, but with a huge smile this time. "I wish I could hug you two." She made a hug sound and got closer to the camera. "Y'all enjoy your time together."

"We will," we said in unison.

Angela remained close to me after the Skype session ended. I wished I wasn't so sleepy. I wanted to enjoy every second with her.

***

I had that strange feeling of waking and not remembering where I was and wondering if I was actually dreaming and not waking at all. Light sneaked in around the edges of the window curtains. Not bright sunlight, but daylight blurred by low-lying clouds from a sun not yet high enough to peek over the buildings. I scanned the room. Uh-oh. I was on Angela's sofa. I must have fallen asleep where I was sitting last night. It was all a blur. I sat up and looked under the blanket. My shoes and socks were gone, but I was wearing the clothes I had on for the flight over.

"Good morning," she said with her lovely English

accent. "Are you feeling better?"

"Good morning," I said, my voice barely working. "Yes. I feel rested. Sorry I didn't make it to my room."

"That's okay. Once you fell asleep, I didn't have the heart to wake you. Actually, I tried, but you were sleeping so deeply, I decided it would be best to let you stay here."

"Did I make it to eight p.m. the way we planned?"

"Almost. You fell asleep about seven thirty."

"Sorry. Thanks for taking off my shoes."

"That's okay. I think you'll feel better today. You're probably hungry though. If you want to go to your room for a shower and change, I'll make us breakfast."

I got up, grabbed my shoes and socks, and noticed my belt was gone. "Did you take my belt off, too?"

"Oh, yeah," she said. "It's there on the table along with your wallet. I didn't think they'd be comfortable for sleeping."

I scooped up my things. "Thanks. I'm headed for the shower now. I'll see you in a few minutes."

"Just come on over when you're ready. No need to knock. I'll leave the door unlocked."

After a quick shower, I put on fresh clothes and brushed my teeth. Music was playing when I opened Angela's door. She was standing at the kitchen counter and apparently didn't hear me come in. I decided to kiss her on the back of her neck. Before I had a chance to reach my goal I found myself sprawled on the floor six feet from where her foot hit me in the stomach. I gasped for air.

"Chris! Are you okay?"

I inhaled again, taking in enough air to make my lungs happy. "I'm sorry."

"Don't sneak up on me like that," she said as she checked on me.

"All I wanted to do was kiss that beautiful neck of yours. I sometimes forget you were trained in the James Bond school of self-defense."

She cringed. "I'm sorry. I should have warned you not to do that without letting me know first."

"That would take away the surprise."

"You want surprise? This is what you get." She helped me to my feet. "Are you sure you're okay? I've been known to crack a sternum from time to time."

I rubbed my abdomen. "Yes. I think so. At least I'm breathing again."

"To tell the truth, when I turned and saw it was you, it was too late to stop my reaction, but I did manage to hold back on the power."

"That was holding back?"

"Yes. Otherwise you'd be unconscious, or worse."

"Well, don't worry. No more spontaneous displays of affection for you."

"I think you should try again. It should be okay if I know you're in the room." She turned around with her back to me. "Now, kiss me."

"Kiss you? From the back?"

"Yes. The way you'd planned."

I moved to her and put my arms around her waist and nuzzled her neck. I didn't want to stop and I didn't until she turned around and kissed me full on the mouth.

When we parted, she pulled away gently and gazed into my eyes with the warmest look I had ever seen. Her cheeks were flushed. "One of these days we're going to have to talk about this."

"What?" I asked.

"This thing that's happening between us."

I didn't let go of her. "I know."

She kissed me again, her lips both soft and firm. I felt emotions I hadn't allowed to surface for a long time.

She backed away while she kept her right hand on my arm and looked into my eyes. "I knew this would happen. I waited a year after Sarah's death to show you how I felt about you and now it's been another year. Still, I don't know if you're ready for someone new in your life."

I couldn't believe my ears. I hadn't known. All I knew for sure was that I was attracted to her and it felt right. Knowing Angela had feelings for me was an answer to prayer.

"But you know it can never be."

What did she say? "Huh? What do you mean?" Was it because of Sarah?

"It won't work. We live in different worlds. You're a college professor in a small town and I'm… Well, we both know what I am. I travel the world. Sometimes I'm away for months. You already know there are times when I can't be reached for days, sometimes weeks. That's not what you need."

"It's too late," I said. "I'm already in love with you."

I was serious about loving her, but said it the way I did for humor. It wasn't funny to her. She looked as if she'd been slapped, pausing only momentarily before she turned and walked away.

She went into her bedroom and shut the door. I was stunned. "Angela," I said through the door. "I'm sorry. I didn't mean to anger you."

"I know you didn't. I'm okay," she said, sounding anything but okay. "I need a minute."

When she came out I could see her eyes were red.

"I'm sorry," I said again.

"For saying you love me?"

"No. Not that. I'm sorry for the way I said it. What I wanted to say was that I want to find a way we can be together. I do love you."

"I know. What upset me was the realization that if I couldn't have a relationship with you, someone who loves me and whom I love, I will never have a meaningful relationship."

"You love me?"

"Is that what you took from what I said?"

I couldn't help from smiling and soon she was mirroring me.

"Yes, I love you, too," she said.

"We can make it work. We must."

"Okay. But not today. Today we have fun. Now sit at the table. Breakfast is ready and we can't eat too late because we're having lunch with Andrew."

CHAPTER TEN

We met Andrew at the pub a little after one. Given a choice, I would have opted to spend more time with Angela. Alone. We'd talked about loving each other, but that was about as far as she would go.

Not me. I had already begun to think about marriage, and that was what was on my mind when I walked into the pub and saw Andrew waving at us from across the room.

Those thoughts evaporated when I saw him and was reminded of Sarah. I'd forgotten how much they looked alike. He was a year older and had the same shade of red hair that Sarah had. His height and his smile were similar to hers. How could I have thought of Angela the way I had with Sarah still so much a part of my life? Was I ready to marry someone else? I hoped I hadn't missed my chance for happiness.

He moved toward me with an outstretched hand. Our right hands gripped and he held my arm with his left hand. I was aware of the black suit. It looked like the same one he'd worn to Sarah's memorial service. His thin black tie, old-fashioned in the States, fit snugly against the buttoned collar of his white shirt. I noticed several men similarly dressed.

"Chris. Good to see you, mate. I'm sorry I haven't kept in touch. I meant to. For Sarah's sake, you know. Besides, I like you."

"Hey," Angela said. "No greeting for me?"

"Sorry, love. I only saw you last week." He glanced at me. "I haven't seen this bloke since Sarah's memorial service. What was that? Two years ago?"

"About," I said. Did he call her love? What did he mean about seeing Angela last week? Were they dating? She hadn't mentioned that, but I knew they were friends. Probably only friends. No reason to obsess about him. She said she loved me. Besides, what right do I have to be jealous of him while I'm standing here thinking about Sarah?

"I got us a table," Andrew said, nodding to his left. He led the way to a booth near the rear of the restaurant with a window facing Buckingham Gate Street. He moved his coat over and offered us a seat.

"I think I'll order," Angela said. "Do you want to come with me, Chris? I'll show you how it works."

"Sure," I said.

She recommended the lunch special, so we paid the cashier at the bar and walked to the left where there was a serving line like you might find in a cafeteria back home, except there were fewer selections. Angela described the choices, along with her recommendations, and we both filled our plates. When we got back to the table, a waitress was serving Andrew a sandwich on a large platter with an enormous mound of fries, or chips, as they were called here.

"I'm tired of pub food," he said. "I'm sure I'll go back to it soon, but right now all I want is a sandwich."

Angela sat on the bench across from Andrew and moved in to give me room to sit next to her. Had I jumped the gun telling her I loved her? She said it, too. Did she mean it the way I did? She was trying to tell me a relationship between us would never work. Was it because of Andrew? Was I going crazy?

Her hand was on my thigh. I looked at her eyes. I glanced at Andrew. He was polishing off half his ham on rye. I turned back to her. "It's okay," she said, almost a whisper.

"What?" Had she read my thoughts?

"Your setting. It's straight."

I realized I had been realigning my plate and utensils the way I did when I was stressed. She probably thought I did it all the time. I didn't. At least I didn't think so.

I nodded at her.

Andrew ignored my compulsion. "Angela tells me you're here to catch a thief," he said. "How's it going?"

Did she tell him that instead of telling him I came to visit her? Maybe she didn't want him to know about us. "Nothing yet. I tracked him to a bank account, but he'd emptied it before I could get the money back."

"You can do that?" Andrew asked.

Angela merely smiled and indicated I had to get myself out of that one. "Well, no. Not legally. Perhaps I shouldn't have mentioned that to you, with you being in the banking business."

He laughed. "Don't worry. We're almost family. I know we got off on the wrong foot, but Mum and Dad told me what you did for Sarah and how you got shot trying to protect her. And mainly how much you loved Sis. So, if you need any help whilst in London, just let me know. Legal stuff, you understand." His narrowed eyes locked on to mine when he added that last bit.

A stinging ache shot through my right leg at the spot the bullet entered. That was odd. I hadn't felt pain like that in a long time.

"Thanks, Andrew," I said. "I might take you up on that offer."

***

The next day Angela and I exited the train in Bath a little before noon. Thanks to her, my body had adjusted to local time. My arm vibrated as my bag bounced along the narrow cobblestone streets and alleys for a couple of blocks until we reached a wooden garage door next to a building that would be in the national historical registry back home, but was probably considered contemporary in the United Kingdom. The doors didn't appear to be strong enough to keep anyone out for long, but Angela unlocked the layered steel Yale padlock anyway and I helped pull the doors open, one to the left and one to the right. Inside was a dark-blue Mini Cooper as shiny and clean as the ones you'd see sitting in the dealer's showroom.

"I'm away from home so often I rent this garage for convenience. There's not much in the way of public transport to the village where I live." She walked around to the front of the vehicle. "Let me take the battery charger off, then I'll back out while you close for me." She removed the battery cables and hung them on the wall.

"Nice," I said, admiring her car. "Looks brand new."

She smiled. "I've had it a couple of years, but I don't drive much."

"I love that dark shade of blue."

"Me too. The dealer calls it Tahiti blue."

Angela backed out and waited while I closed and locked the garage. I climbed in on the left side.

She drove up the cobblestone road and circled what I thought could be the center of the town. The buildings were old, but I couldn't keep from noticing how majestic they were. I took in the view. So much to enjoy.

"Don't worry. We'll tour Bath later," she said as if reading my mind. "First, I want to show you where Sarah lived and grew up." She checked her watch. "I told Roger and Ruth we'd be at the farm by one."

I grabbed for a handle as Angela sped through an intersection without slowing. It was exhilarating and I wished we had more roundabouts back home. They were much more effective than traffic lights. The Mini Cooper hung close to the road and I didn't feel pulled from side to side the way I did in some vehicles as she followed the curved road into the woods at a gradually increasing speed. I got a little nervous when she drove on the wrong side of the road several times to go around double-parked cars.

"How do you know Roger and Ruth?" I asked.

"We're neighbors. But before that, I had met them while visiting Sarah and Andrew."

I got together with Sarah's parents who lived on a farm near Georgetown, Texas at least once a month, but I hadn't seen Ruth and Roger, Sarah's aunt and uncle, since the memorial service. I had mixed feelings about meeting with them today. Ruth and I hit it off pretty good back then, but Roger took Andrew's side in initially blaming me for Sarah's death. Unlike Andrew, Roger had yet to apologize. I didn't know what to expect now after two years had passed and wondered if he was still angry?

We zoomed through a small town called Radstock and then followed a curved road with only enough room for one car into an area of farms. We eventually got to the village of Hemington.

Sarah's aunt and uncle were standing in front of the third house on the left. Roger leaned against a gray Land Rover that blocked half the road. Angela stopped in front of the Land Rover. Roger scowled while Ruth smiled and waved.

I climbed out and gave Ruth a hug. She hugged me back with enthusiasm and kissed my cheeks. A tear fell from one of her eyes. I probably reminded her of Sarah.

"Hello, Roger," I said as I reached for his hand. He was slumped against his vehicle and made no effort to the hand I held out toward him.

"Roger, say hello to Chris," Ruth said. "I'm so glad you could come, Chris. I want you to know I pray for you every day." She jerked her eyes toward Roger but didn't make another attempt to get him to talk.

I suspected he knew she wouldn't give up pestering him by the sigh he let out. He slowly pushed away from his car and shook my hand. "Hello, boy. You okay?"

"I'm doing fine," I said, knowing now he was still angry with me. Sarah's dad, Roger's brother, had never been angry with me. Not once did he or Ann blame me for Sarah's death, nor did they let me blame myself.

Roger smiled when Angela came up to where he was and gave her a big hug. "Angela, dear. So nice to see you again. It's been a long time."

"Hi, Roger. I've been busy. They let me off for Christmas so I thought I'd show Chris where Sarah grew up."

Roger's smile disappeared. "Good. He needs to see it." His piercing eyes were on me as he spoke to Angela.

"I think it's delightful to see you again," Ruth said, wrapping an arm around mine.

Roger led the way to a door on the side of the house. "This is where Sarah lived from the time she was born until she moved to Texas to become a nurse." He shook his head. "Worst idea ever. She'd still be alive if she'd stayed here."

"Now shush that talk," Ruth said. She still had her arm locked with mine as we walked. "Sarah was so happy about living in the States, and she was especially pleased when she met you, Chris."

Roger stopped at the door. "This house is more than two hundred years old and there have been generations of Eason families living here," he said. "The farm out back wasn't always owned by the family, though. There was a time when the lands were leased to the farmers, don't you know."

"Why did Ann and Paul leave this place?" I asked.

"Mostly to be close to Sarah," Ruth said. "They worshiped that girl."

Roger made a negative sound. "That and the fact they couldn't make enough money farming what's left of the land. The government, don't you see, built a motorway down the middle of the farm and took away their income. Of course the government paid them for the land, but it was nothing compared to what the land could've made over the years. Paul had thought Andrew or Sarah might take it over some day. Weren't fair, I say."

"So no one's working the farm, now?" I asked.

"We are," Roger said, puffing out his chest. "Plus our own. Although we've got some hired help, you see."

"Are you living here?" I asked.

"No," Ruth said. "No one lives here now. Except when Paul and Ann come home from time to time. Our home is close by."

"Do Paul and Ann visit often?" I asked.

"Not so much, anymore," Roger said, glowering at me. "Too many unpleasant memories, I suspect."

I couldn't let that stand. "I find that hard to believe. I see them often and when I do, they talk about how believers must trust God when they lose someone dear to them. They're always telling me how Sarah would want me to get on with my life."

Roger nodded toward Angela. "I see you're doing that, son."

"Roger!" Ruth said without explaining.

"Sorry," he said sheepishly, to Angela, not me.

"What about Andrew?" I asked.

"He couldn't make a living at it now that the place has been reduced in size so much," Roger said. "Probably best. That boy never did like farming. Kids are different now. They watch TV and read and they all want to leave the farm and do something else. Like Sarah wanting to be a nurse. Children don't stay home the way they used to. Andrew's a banker in London, don't you know. Paul says Andrew is quite successful in his job."

"Yes," I said. "We saw him yesterday. He likes his work."

"Work? He should like it. Sitting around all day in some fancy office wearing his Sunday clothes. He never was much help around the farm. Even as a kid. He's too skinny."

"Shush," Ruth said. "He's a sweet boy."

Roger unlocked the door and we walked into a small room. I felt as if I was entering a basement. The stone walls were undecorated and the ceiling was low. It was more than an entryway, but not much larger. There was a sink on the driveway side of the room and a large top-opening freezer in the corner. The room was cold and smelled moldy.

Roger led the way to the adjoining room which was

a small dining room, just large enough for a table in the middle with chairs all around.

The kitchen next to the dining room included a small table with two chairs they probably used for breakfast, plus a recliner and TV, making half the room look more like a family room.

There was a larger room in the back of the house that spanned the width of the building. "What is this room?" I asked.

Roger waved across the room. "It's the living room now, but it used to be where they kept the chickens. They could collect the eggs without going outside. It was smelly, but it was what was done then. At some time in our history, the chickens were moved out and the space converted for human use."

As we went from room to room, I had a sense of Sarah being there. But the feeling of her presence was stronger when we went up the narrow staircase to the bedrooms.

Ruth took my arm again, holding tighter than before, as if preparing to support me if need be. "This is…was Sarah's room," she said in a whisper. I turned toward Ruth in time to see another tear rolling down her cheek. Angela was behind us.

Ruth led me in and stood close by while I took it in. The room was small in comparison to bedrooms back home. The furnishings were simple as well. A single bed on one side of the room covered with a quilt made from squares of various shades of blue. I wondered when Sarah slept there last. I peeked at Angela, but she had picked up a doll off the bed and was examining it.

A large wooden cabinet stood in one corner with a matching chest of drawers next to it. I took a deep breath and smelled her. As I inhaled, guilt poured in with the memories. I found Angela's eyes locked on me. I looked away and moved toward the door. I don't know why, but I didn't want her to see me cry.

She knew. I don't know whether she was upset or wanted to protect me, but she decided it was time to leave.

"Thank you, Roger and Ruth," she said with a strong voice, one that didn't encourage discussion. "But I think we'd better go and let Chris rest. Jet lag, you understand."

Ruth hugged me. "Yes, of course, we should let you get some relaxation. You two are coming for dinner, right?"

"Yes," Angela said. "We'll be at your house at six."

That was the first I'd heard about it, but it didn't matter. All I knew was I had to leave Sarah's room and get out of her house.

CHAPTER ELEVEN

"You want to drive?" Angela asked.

That was when I realized I was outside the car on the driver's side. "Oh, no. I forgot the steering wheel is over here."

I started to walk away, but she tossed me the keys. I climbed in and waited while she got in on the passenger side. I started the engine and pulled out onto the road. It was weird driving from the right side, but not as bad as I thought it would be. Fortunately, we were on a small farm road with no other cars. If one came toward me, I would have had to remember to move to the left.

I drove slowly, taking time to look at the neighborhood. We hadn't gone far when I saw the oldest church I had ever seen. I pulled over and stopped in front. "Is this where you go?"

"Sometimes," she said. "I haven't been to many services since I'm gone so much."

"Can we go in?"

"Sure." She pointed. "Park over there."

I pulled into a parking spot and turned off the engine. As we walked through a graveyard to get to the entrance on the side opposite from the road, a thin layer of ice over the ground cover crunched with each step we took. Snowdrifts remained in shaded areas, as if placed there by an artist. Halfway to the door, Angela took my hand in hers just as naturally as breathing. I considered stopping to talk about Sarah, and how it felt to see her house. And about us, Angela and me. But, I couldn't. We needed to do that soon. Maybe tonight. The church appeared as old as Sarah's house and the other homes in the village. Still, there was something about the shape that made me think it could be older.

"Do you know the history of this place?"

Angela stopped and looked at the tower on the right. "We can Google it from the house, but I read once it is a Norman church built sometime in the twelfth century. I think it's been renovated several times over the years though."

We entered and I could tell it was well cared for and regularly used. There were wooden pews enough for fifty or sixty people. The chancel area was small, but there was room for the organ console to the right of the pulpit.

I sat on one of the pews to take it all in. Angela moved in next to me, close enough for our thighs to touch. There were books in a holder on the back of the seat in front of us. I took one and thumbed through it.

"This is similar to the Book of Common Prayer we use at home," I said, motioning the book toward her.

Its age and the dampness of the area could be why, but this church smelled different from mine. It wasn't unpleasant. Comforting would be a better description. I thought about Sarah being here. Perhaps she sat in this pew. But I didn't feel her the way I sometimes did. I wondered if it was because of Angela's stronger presence.

Eventually, without discussing it, we departed and made our way to Angela's house.

We could have walked from Sarah's house to Angela's house. Her place wasn't much different from the one where Sarah had lived. Angela's was old, stone, and built close to the road, the same as Sarah's. We unloaded my suitcase and went in. She showed me around and then pointed out the guest bedroom which was downstairs. Her bedroom was upstairs.

Although her home was much like Sarah's on the outside, the inside was much different. Perhaps it was because the place where Sarah grew up was her parents' home. Angela bought her house and lived there alone. The entire house was furnished and decorated for her taste, not just her bedroom. Outside, the house reminded me of a museum. Inside was bright with modern furniture and filled with photos and souvenirs from around the world. I smiled when I saw an antique Dr Pepper sign on one wall. She said she'd bought in Dublin, Texas on a rare holiday.

Dinner at Roger and Ruth's house was uneventful

except that the food was wonderful. Roger had charcoal-broiled lamb shanks and I had never tasted anything like it. I had the feeling it was a meal reserved for special guests. For dessert, Ruth served a delicious blackberry crumble covered with unsweetened whipped cream she called clotted cream.

***

The next morning, I woke to the sound of a rooster crowing. That was something I hadn't heard before. At least, not that I could remember. Once I was awake, I could hear kitchen noises, too, followed by the smell of fresh coffee. I slipped on my jeans and a corduroy shirt and walked toward the kitchen. Before I got there I became aware of my bare feet on the cold rock floor and I went back for shoes.

"Good morning," I said as I entered the kitchen.

Angela was wearing running shorts and a tee shirt. I could see she had on running shoes.

"Good morning," she said with a smile. "Did you sleep okay?"

"Sure did. Rooster woke me. Have you been out already?"

"Yes. I left you a note, but threw it away when I got back and you were still sleeping. I run in the mornings when I'm here. In London, I go to the gym for exercise."

I found the coffee and poured a cup. "Mmm. This is what I need."

"Good. Hope you're hungry. I decided to make you a big breakfast since I didn't offer you much to eat in

London. I called at the grocery store in Radstock while I was out to get supplies."

I remembered the little town we'd driven through on our way from Bath. "You ran all the way to Radstock?"

She laughed. "It's only three miles."

"And three miles back. Besides, it is cold."

"It's not cold if you run. Sit down. This is ready."

I took a seat at the small kitchen table she'd indicated and she placed a large plate in front of me and another across from me. On each was two eggs, sunny side up, potatoes and a piece of thinly-sliced meat.

"What is this?" I asked, poking my fork at the meat.

"That's bacon."

"No it's not." I laughed.

"It's English bacon. You're used to that little crispy bacon we get in the States, but try this. You might like it."

I did. It wasn't bad. Not bacon. Everything was delicious and I quickly cleaned my plate.

Angela pushed away from the table and watched me while she sipped her coffee. "This might be a good time to talk," she said.

That sounded scary. My mind jumped to all the bad news that could follow. The possibility that hurt the most she'd already said. We couldn't have a real relationship because of her job.

"Do we have to? I was enjoying being with you."

She smiled and shook her head slowly. "Still, we need to agree on what we are doing. And we can't do that without discussing it."

"You're right. I..." I didn't know where to start.

"I saw the pain on your face in Sarah's room." Angela paused and our eyes locked. "Are you sure you're ready for this visit, to be with me, as you said?"

I felt slapped and exposed. I was positive she saw my pain and felt my heartbeat as it rapidly increased. "Yes, it hurt to be there. More than I thought it would. And, at first, I didn't want you to know how I felt. But if we are to have a meaningful relationship, we'll need to be honest with each other about our feelings."

She turned away. "I can't compete with your memories of Sarah."

"It's not a competition. I have memories, yes, but I'd never compare you with her."

"Sure you would. It's okay. I understand. I shouldn't have said that."

"Right now I don't think I can honestly say I won't think about her and what could have been, but I'll try—
"

"No. That's not what I'm saying. I don't want you to forget her. I'm just not sure you're ready for another relationship."

"I feel I am when I talk to you and when I'm with you. I didn't know visiting her home would affect me the way it did, but I'm glad you took me there. It was sad, but it doesn't change how I feel about you."

"I don't know why we're talking about this anyway. With my job we could never be together for long. I shouldn't have let things get this far. I was crazy to want you to visit. Nothing can come of it. We both know that."

Maybe she was right. Could I live this close to where Sarah lived? Could I put up with Roger and his constant reminder that I was to blame for his niece's death?

Her cell phone rang. Her nostrils flared as her eyes shot toward the phone. She didn't answer it right away. Instead, she sighed louder than usual, and took a deep breath. "It's work. I must take this."

She took her phone and left the kitchen without saying more. I heard her climb the narrow staircase. I didn't like the look on her face when she saw who called. Was our time together over so soon?

In a few minutes she was standing in front of me with a knapsack on her shoulder and a pistol strapped to her right calf, bunching up her trousers.

I took in the sight without a word, knowing what it meant. She had warned me it could happen. My pulse rate rose and I felt slightly faint and out of control.

I heard a helicopter getting closer and closer. When I looked out the kitchen window, I saw it landing in the field just beyond a rock wall. Every whop of the blades as the engine idled reminded me of when Sarah was shot. I shook my head to block the painful thoughts that only confused me. I wanted to think about Angela, not Sarah.

Clearly there wasn't time to do what Angela said we needed to do. We hadn't talked enough about our situation, much less made decisions about it. I hadn't given her all the options and choices. She didn't know how much I would sacrifice to be with her. We only had time to hold each other and say good-bye. She gave me her keys and asked me to lock up when I left and to take her car back to the garage in town. She knew I'd remember where it was. She reminded me about the battery charger and gave me the key to her flat in London. She said to stay there for as long as I wanted. She wanted to show me more of her part of the world if she got back in time.

She held me in her arms, but instead of appreciating Angela's closeness, all I could do was think about Sarah and the day she died. On that day when the helicopter went whop, whop, whop.

When Angela let go and looked into my eyes one last time before turning away, I saw tears.

As she walked toward the sound of the engines, I wanted to ask her where she was going and when I would see her again, but I knew she couldn't tell me. I went outside and saw military markings on the helicopter. My selfishness made me wonder if I could survive the loss of another love.

After she was aboard, the helicopter lifted and gained altitude rapidly as it flew over the church, leaving trees quaking along the route. I didn't see Angela, but I imagined she was at the side window watching as I waved.

Then she was gone and the silence was deafening.

***

I washed the dishes and stayed at the Hemington house for a couple of days, hoping she'd return and say it'd been a false alarm. When Ruth heard Angela had been called back to work, she invited me to eat with them, and insisted I join them to bring in the new year. From what they said, I don't think they understood the nature of Angela's job. I didn't feel festive, but I couldn't find a way to say no without hurting Ruth's feelings. So I went, but I didn't celebrate much. On New Year's Day, I closed the house, drove to Bath and locked the Mini Cooper in Angela's garage.

The train trip back to London was lonely. I felt destined to feel that way the rest of my life. The London room she'd reserved for me was stark, but I had the key to her flat and she'd said to make myself at home. When the time was right, I'd call Tex and see how things were going with Cloris. With Angela gone, I didn't have a local contact to help me trace Virgil. I wondered if Andrew might know someone in law enforcement who might talk to me.

I was on her sofa with my feet propped on the coffee table getting ready to punch in Andrew's number when she called.

"I can only talk a few minutes." It was more of a whisper than regular speech, but I loved hearing her voice.

"I'm just glad you called."

"I'm sorry I had to leave, and I'm sorry we didn't finish our talk."

"Me too."

She paused. "I thought I'd have more time off than that."

"I know." I was confused about our future, but I couldn't ask her now.

"It's just another reason you'd be better off…"

I cut her off. "Hush. I don't want to hear that. We'll work it out. I've been thinking about giving up teaching and becoming an international private investigator."

She laughed softly. "No you haven't. You love teaching."

I did. It was nice that she knew that. But how could we ever be together? If nothing changes, nothing changes. "You're right. I do like it. But, I'd give it up at the drop of a hat to be with you."

"Well, don't do anything rash until we finish our talk."

All sounds on the phone disappeared and I thought I'd lost her. "Angela?" I asked.

She whispered rapidly. "Got to go. Love you." She disconnected before I could respond.

I was still alone, but now loved.

My life was such a jumble and I didn't know what to do. The search for Virgil had fizzled and my vacation time with Angela had ended abruptly, or was at least postponed indefinitely. School resumed in two weeks, but, I was thinking of ways to stay in London until Angela returned. I grabbed my phone to try Andrew's number, but before I had a chance, it rang again. I looked at it quickly, thinking it was Angela calling back, but Tex's name popped on the screen instead.

"Hello," I said.

"We got a lead," he said.

"Happy New Year," I said.

"Huh? Oh, yeah, happy New Year."

His voice was strong and his accent emphasized when he got excited. "So, what's the lead?"

"Remember how Jane thought Virgil would call Cloris?"

I could see him push his ten-gallon hat off his forehead the way he always did. "Yes, Jane said it was possible he had fallen for Cloris for real and actually missed her."

"Right. That's what happened."

"So, did Cloris tell you where he is?"

"Naw. She doesn't know. But he wants to see her."

"Tell me what he said."

"He said he'd fly her to England to join him."

"Using her money," I said.

"Yeah," Tex laughed. "She picked up on that. She told us she cussed him out for taking her life savings. Said it was like stealing from her little boy."

"Little boy?" I asked. "He's twenty-two or twenty-three, I think."

"Right. Anyway, he said he took the money for them to have in England. She asked him where he was and he hung up. I don't know if her question scared him off or what."

"So, we don't know where he is?" I said.

"Chris, this is Jane."

"Hello, Jane."

"What Tex didn't tell you is that we've built a rapport with Cloris and I think she'll help us find him as soon as she knows his whereabouts."

"So, you think he'll call again?" I asked.

"Yes. I'm sure of that. It's probably best she didn't act too anxious to see him. Might make him suspicious. We suggested she go meet him, and I think she will after we promised we'd help get her money back from him. Then, when she goes to see him…"

"I follow her and we've got him—or his money."

"Right. You and Angela, right?"

"Well…" I stalled. "She got called back to work, but I'm at her flat in London and I plan to wait until she returns."

There was a long silence. "Isn't she sometimes gone for months at a time?" Tex asked.

"Well, yes. But, I can do my work from here if I'm still waiting when the Spring semester begins."

"Dear, dear, Chris," Jane said. "I don't know if you two are meant for each other or not."

"I think it's too late to think about that. I'm already in love with her."

"Then I'll keep my mouth shut."

"Chris?" It was Tex again. "Sounds like you're all alone there. I'm sorry to hear that. What's the address? We'll ask Cloris to find you when she gets there."

I gave Tex the address, wondering only briefly if it was supposed to be a secret. Angela hadn't said not to tell anyone.

CHAPTER TWELVE

Three days later someone knocked on the door to Angela's flat while I was on her computer Googling places in London to see. I'd been spending more and more time at her place. I only went across the hall to my room when it was time to turn in for the night. I'd just returned from a trip to Greenwich to see the sights there. It was cold, but many of the more interesting exhibits were indoors. Outside, I stood in two time zones and asked a stranger to snap my photo with my phone.

My heart beat a little faster when I realized the knock could mean Angela was back. Since she'd given me her keychain when she left, she might not have another key with her. The possibility of seeing her again so soon thrilled me. I smiled as I threw the door open wide.

It wasn't Angela.

"Surprise," Tex said, peeking from under his ten-gallon cowboy hat.

"Bet you didn't expect to see us," Jane said, standing behind his wheelchair with her hands on the handles.

Cloris pushed her way around the two of them slowly, shaking her head and making a tsking sound. I had not met her, but I'd seen her from a distance when we were investigating her son Heath.

"I'm Cloris," she said. Her eyes were streaked with red.

"Hello. Nice to meet you. I didn't expect you so soon, but…"

Cloris pushed past me and entered the room. "They'll explain," she said, nodding toward Tex and Jane. "I need to use the john."

"Okay," I said, pointing. "It's just down that way."

When she was gone, Jane grabbed my arm and pulled me close and spoke softly. "Hope you don't mind our little surprise. We had to come. Cloris said she wouldn't talk to you. We've got her trust, but it took forever to open her up. She doesn't know you and said she wouldn't come here alone. Then, when Liz offered to pay for our trip over, we couldn't say no."

"Cloris trusts Jane," Tex said. "Not me."

"Yes." Jane was still whispering. "She talks to me because I listen and respond. I think she likes Tex, too. Mainly after I told her how he got past his alcohol dependency. The way she reacted, I think she may have the same problem, or suspects she does."

"Come on in." I stepped into the hallway. "Where's your luggage?"

"Down at the pub," Jane said. "I mentioned Angela's name and the bartender said it would be okay to leave our bags there while I took Tex up on the elevator. That thing was just barely large enough for the three of us. I'll go back and get the luggage in a minute."

"Yeah," Tex said. "I'm just glad Jane's been working on strength conditioning for as long as she has. She's had to handle me as well as the luggage. I have a new appreciation for how great it is in America for those of us in chairs."

Cloris returned. She stared out the window. "Sure cold in this God-forsaken place. I hadn't planned on that. I might have to buy a winter coat as well as some gloves. This is gonna be one expensive trip." She eased herself onto the sofa, sitting primly with her black purse perched on her knees.

"Chris," Jane said, "there was another reason Tex and I came."

"What's that?" I asked.

"When you told us Angela got called back to work, we worried about you being alone. We decided to join you." She laughed.

"Thanks," I said. "Where are you staying?"

Jane swung a muscled arm around the room. "Here, I hope. Tex thought you'd let us. We can't afford much and we don't need anything fancy."

Uh-oh. I hoped Angela wouldn't mind. Tex and Jane could stay here since I had a room across the hall. But, what about Cloris?

"All of you?" I asked. Cloris was on the sofa, about to nod off. Her head was on the arm of the sofa, but her feet were still on the floor.

"Just me and Jane," Tex said. "Cloris has a place near here. Virgil picked it out. She's going there as soon as we talk and make some plans."

"I think we have room. I'm sure Angela wouldn't mind. I have a room across the hall. I sleep there, but spend most of my time here."

"Good," Jane said. "Now, let's plan this sting operation before Cloris falls asleep."

"What?" Cloris asked, sitting up straight with her eyes wide open. "What did I miss?"

"Nothing," Jane said. "Don't fall asleep. We need to talk before you go to the hotel."

"Is Virgil staying at the hotel, too?" I asked.

"We don't think so," Tex said. "He told her to check in and he'd contact her there. He said he had to be careful in case anyone was following her."

"Did he pay for the room?" I asked.

"No," Jane said. "She had to put it on her credit card."

"The thieving snake," Cloris said. "Why can't I just see him and beat the money out of him like I planned?"

"Because," Jane said, "he'd beat you worse, or he'd run away and we'd never find him again. If that happened you'd never see your money."

"Well, just how are you going to get my money from him?" Cloris asked.

Tex pointed at me. "This guy has a special talent for breaking into the Internet. He's going to find Virgil's bank account and transfer your money back to you."

"How much are we talking about?" I asked her.

"He took everything I had. Twenty-five thousand. I'd

saved it for my son's college. Heath never wanted to go to the university, but I'd still like to give him the opportunity to go if he changes his mind someday. I worked hard for that money." She looked me in the eyes. "Real hard, you understand."

"We'll do our best to get it back for you, ma'am," Tex said. "But we'll need you to help us find Virgil."

"Since he suspects Cloris could be followed," I said, "we're going have to be extra careful. He knows me and Tex, so Jane will be the only one who can get close enough to be seen."

"I agree," Tex said. "Okay with you, honey?"

"That's fine," Jane said. "I kind of like detective work." She turned to me. "Tex brought his makeup and disguises for both of us. We can use that to change our appearance."

"Okay," I said. "That might help, but it's hard to hide that wheelchair."

Tex had learned to play a variety of roles when he lived on the streets and depended on handouts. He could change his look as well as his voice. I'd seen him in action several times when we were on an assignment. Once he made himself into an old man with me as his disinterested assistant who pushed him around just so he could get a young store clerk to talk more. Another time, he looked so much like an illegal coming across the border from Mexico he fooled the real ones, and got them to help with his wheelchair. Of course it didn't hurt that he spoke fluent Spanish with a Mexican accent.

"Tex, I know how good you are with makeup and costumes, and we may call on your talents while we're here. But let me remind you of the time you put Virgil on top of the bookmobile. From what I heard, he was pretty upset after that. He'll probably freak out every time he sees a wheelchair."

"What was that?" Jane asked. "He put Virgil on top of a bookmobile? He never told me about that."

"Tell us what happened," Cloris said.

I turned to Tex. "You didn't tell Jane? For once you didn't brag about something. That's hard to believe."

"I never brag."

"Yes you do," Jane said. "Unless it's about something you think I might not like. So, what happened?"

"It was right after we'd learned Virgil was a con man," I said. "We wanted to let Liz know he wasn't who she thought he was. I wanted to tell her, but Tex suggested we get her friend the police chief to do it. I agreed and left to go to school. What happened after that, Tex?"

He smiled. "I saw Virgil at the library doing his volunteer work, so I got this idea and called some of my friends from the old days to help me."

"I bet I know who that was," Jane said. "Jimbo, for one."

"Yeah," Tex said. "So, while the chief was talking to Liz, me and my buddies stripped Virgil of all his clothes, hogtied and gagged him and put him on top of the bookmobile that was parked at the library loading dock."

"What happened next?" Cloris asked. She was wide awake and showing interest for the first time since she got here.

Tex continued the story. "Brian arrived about that time to load the bookmobile and didn't appreciate the joke we'd pulled on Virgil. He offered to help him down, but Virgil wouldn't get off that vehicle naked. Some street bum had taken his clothes by that time, so Brian gave him the dirty clothes the streetwalker had left in the garbage bin. Virgil put them on and hightailed it out of there like greased lighting."

Cloris laughed. "I remember the day he came home smelling so bad. He wouldn't talk about it, but he never went back to the library after that. Served him right. Thanks, Tex."

"Jane," I said, "if you're going to be the one exposed to Virgil, you must be careful at all times. This guy is trouble. The police believe he tried to kill Brian's wife Karen on several occasions."

"Pshaw," Cloris said. "I don't think he'd kill anyone." "He's always been gentle with me. Other than being a liar and a thief, he's a nice guy."

"Still," I said, "we should all be careful around him. There's no telling what he might do if he felt threatened. So, how will we know when he contacts Cloris?"

"Good question," Jane said. "There are several scenarios to consider."

I winked at Tex. Jane was getting in to this detective work. Tex grinned. He'd somehow managed to find a way to work on the case and his marriage at the same time.

"First," she continued, "Virgil could be waiting for her in her hotel room when she gets there. Second, he could come later. Third, he could contact her and tell her to meet him somewhere else."

"Fourth," I added, "he may get spooked and not show at all."

"Right," Jane said. "In that case, he'll probably contact her and tell her to meet him elsewhere."

Cloris shook her head. "Why does it have to be so complicated? I'll call you when I get to the room unless he's there. If he calls, I'll have time to call you and tell you what he says."

"What if he shows up later without calling?" Jane asked.

"If he does, we could miss him," I said. "We can't watch the building around the clock."

"How's this? I'll call every hour during daytime and in the evening until bedtime." Cloris said. "When I don't call, you know he's there. I'll stall before I leave so you'll have time to get there."

"That's it," Jane said. "Can you make that every thirty minutes?"

"Where is this place?" I asked.

"It's close," Tex said. "Less than a mile away."

"Okay," Cloris said. "Every thirty minutes."

Shortly after that decision, she left. I went with her as far as the pub and moved Tex's and Jane's luggage to Angela's room.

About a half hour after I returned to Angela's room, Jane's phone rang.

She answered it and mouthed, "Cloris," to let us know it was her.

"Okay. Be careful." Jane hung up the phone. "She's in her room alone."

***

Tex, Jane, and I discussed whether we should try to see some of the sights while waiting for Cloris to call or not call every thirty minutes, but we decided against it. We needed to stay close to where Cloris was staying. I worked on the textbook I was writing while Tex and Jane napped. I encouraged them to stay awake the way Angela did me, but I couldn't convince them it was worth it. Jane jumped every time the phone rang, but Tex slept through the calls. If Cloris's call was late, and it often was, I was the only one awake. I'd wonder if Virgil was with her. But before I panicked enough to wake Jane and Tex, Cloris would call and apologize, giving some inane reason for not calling sooner. Several times, it sounded as if the woman was drunk. Either that or she was suffering from severe jet lag. I still had doubts about counting on her to help us find Virgil. I kept remembering how she'd sued Karen.

One good thing came out of sitting around waiting on Virgil to contact Cloris. That was when I got the idea to build a drone.

We'd still have to find Virgil, but a drone would let us get in close enough to find information about his bank account without having to break in to his room.

The next time Jane was awake I told her I had to run an errand. Before I left, I made a pot of coffee and talked to her until I was sure she was awake enough to take action if Cloris didn't call. I could hear Tex snoring in the bedroom.

After talking to the manager at the pub downstairs, I found a remote-controlled helicopter at a hobby store a few blocks away. The rest of the equipment, webcam, monitor, and connectors, I found at an electronics store he told me about. I was in my room putting it together when someone knocked.

"Who is it?" I called through the door.

"It's me," Tex said.

"Come on in."

He opened the door and rolled in. "What's that?" He indicated my new toy.

"Guess. You arrived just in time for a demonstration." I turned on the helicopter and grabbed the control unit. The aircraft buzzed around the room until the props got tangled in a curtain and I turned off the engine.

"Oops. I still need some practice flying this thing. Let me try again."

Tex laughed.

I moved the helicopter to a spot away from the window and pressed the lever on the control unit, gently this time. The helicopter rose slowly into the air where I let it hover before turning it to face Tex.

"Now check the monitor. Quick."

"What? Where?" he asked.

"On the table there."

He looked. "Hey. That's me. You got a webcam on that helicopter."

"Yeah. Except it's not just a helicopter anymore. It's a drone. We're going to break into Virgil's room with this and see what's there. That is, if we ever find him."

"Well, that's why I came over. Cloris just called.

Virgil wants her to meet him at the Garrick Inn in Stratford-upon-Avon in Warwickshire."

"When?"

"Tomorrow at noon."

"Good. That'll give me more time to practice controlling this drone. Also, we'll need to find out where it is and how to get there."

"Hey, guys," Jane said as she entered the room talking on her cell phone. "It's Liz. She called to check on our progress. I'm just glad I had something to report."

"Tell her hello for me," I said.

Jane nodded. "Chris and Tex said to tell you hello and they miss you."

I looked at Tex and shook my head, but it was a nice thing for Jane to do.

"Yes, they both said they missed you," Jane lied. "Tomorrow Cloris is going to meet Virgil at the Garrick Inn in a place called Stratford-upon-Avon."

I shook my head and waved my arms to get Jane's attention, but it was too late. She'd spilled the beans. Liz was one of those people who couldn't keep secrets, and who talked to everyone she met.

Jane frowned at me, but continued talking to Liz. "Okay, sweetie, take care. We'll call you after the sting."

Jane put away her phone and turned to me. "What were you trying to say?"

"I was trying to tell you not to give Liz details about what we're doing. She's not great at keeping her mouth shut."

"I thought it would be encouraging for her to know we have a solid lead on Virgil. Besides, what could she possibly do from Austin to interfere with what we're doing?"

"I guess you're right. I worry too much, sometimes."

"Come on, you two," Tex said. "Let's use Angela's computer and check on where we're going tomorrow."

"I just hope we get back by Thursday," Jane said.

"Why's that?" I asked.

"I entered a bodybuilding contest for women. It's here in London."

Tex smiled.

"Why'd you do that?" I asked.

"Because that's what I do. I saw it on the Internet before we left home and applied since we were going to be here."

"She's good," Tex said. "Be nice to get another trophy. Especially one from another country. I bet you'll be the only one from your gym who can say she's an international winner."

I found Stratford on the map. "There's no reason why you can't come back for the competition. Stratford's not that far away. We don't know what might happen with Virgil, but if we do get delayed, I can follow him while you and Tex return to London." I preferred to work alone anyway.

We found a website about the Garrick Inn that included a menu, history, and a photo of the exterior. I wanted to see what it looked like inside to know if we could hide from Virgil.

Later, back in my room, I practiced flying the remote-controlled helicopter more before I packed it in my suitcase for the trip to Stratford.

***

The combination bus and train ride from London to Stratford took us three hours. Determining the route beforehand took about the same amount of time. There was some frustration from not knowing what we were doing. Cloris had asked Virgil where the inn was and how to get there. All he told her was it was where Shakespeare was born and raised. I called Andrew and asked him about going to Stratford. He didn't ask why I wanted to go to Shakespeare's hometown. He must have assumed it was part of my tour of England. However, he did ask about Angela, forcing me to say she'd been called back to work. He said he knew what that was like, and made me wonder more about what was going on between them.

In planning our trip to Stratford, we had to assume Virgil could be furtively watching Cloris. Especially since he knew where she was and where she was going. So we decided to keep our distance from her just in case. Besides, I didn't trust her much. She probably wouldn't deliberately rat us out, but she wasn't the most reliable person I'd met. My concern now was whether she could get to the Inn alone.

Jane talked to her by phone to finalize our plans. I worried some that Virgil might have had her room bugged and could be listening as she talked to us. I don't think he'd go to that much trouble. He didn't know we were over here.

We talked about what to do when we got to the

Garrick Inn, and everyone agreed we had to be flexible. Primarily because we didn't have time to check on the place ahead of time. We decided Tex would be in disguise and he and Jane would try to get a table near the entrance. I would ask for a table near the rear of the restaurant. Cloris would sit somewhere in the middle where Virgil could easily see her when he came in. I emphasized our goal was for Jane to follow him when he left the restaurant so we could learn where he was staying. I don't know what we'd do if he drove off in a car, though.

We got there early to get a sense of the place and pick where we would sit. We'd read about the Inn on the web before we left London, but I learned more by reading a sign on the outside that said it was built in the 1400s and was the oldest pub in Stratford. The exterior was made of wood that could be that old. White stucco was plastered in between the timbers.

When we got inside, the oak beams and stone floors caught my attention. The tables were arranged in cozy nooks and crannies, providing the tables along the walls with some privacy. Perfect for our goal of seeing Virgil without being seen by him. The bar opened on two sides, and I found a table where I could watch the back door while still being able to see the front door.

Tex and Jane sat in a cubbyhole near the front entrance. He was disguised as an old man, complete with makeup and a gray wig, but we didn't want to take a chance on him being recognized by Virgil so Jane faced the room while Tex faced the wall behind her.

I was wearing an English flat cap Tex had pulled

from his costume cache in hopes it would change my looks. I think it worked. It not only modified my appearance, it helped me fit in with the locals. I also planned to keep my head down after Virgil arrived and try not to make eye contact with him. I had my suitcase next to the table. All it contained was the remote-controlled helicopter and the rest of the equipment I had put together to call it a drone. I was ready to fly at a moment's notice. Sort of. There were still many unknowns about how well the drone would work in a live situation.

Tex and Jane were getting into the acting. They looked like the other customers, but with a little too much emoting for my taste. I'd have to tell them my observations later—a critique for future performances. Cloris was the one I was worried about. She was nervous, her head jerked toward the front door every time it opened. She also stared at Tex and Jane, or me. She wasn't good at this game. If Virgil had been watching her, all he had to do was follow her sightline and he'd see each of us, one by one. I wondered if she could pull this off. I saw a tall bar drink on her table and remembered Jane's concern about Cloris's drinking. She could ruin this opportunity to follow Virgil if she drank too much.

The front door opened once more. A man stood in the shadows longer than other people who had come in. When he stepped into the light I could see it was Virgil. He scanned the room. I turned away before his eyes reached mine, but couldn't resist watching him after that. He wore a bulky brown coat and a dark hat with a narrow brim. He paused in the entryway, looked left and right, before walking to Cloris's table and sitting across from her.

I wished we'd put a wire on her so we could hear what he said. We didn't have one and it would have taken more time than we had to build one. Besides, our goal was to follow Virgil to learn where he was staying. We wanted to search his room, get his bank information, and retrieve the money he'd stolen. That was all.

So, the scene was perfectly set. Virgil had picked the time and place, but Cloris had gotten him to her table. Jane was ready to follow him out the front door, and I was prepared to follow him if he tried to leave by the rear door. All we had to do now was wait for him to leave so we could follow. I couldn't help feeling a little smug for what we'd done.

"Well, there you are!" The voice wasn't English. It was a combination of Texan and North Carolinian. It could only be one person, but I couldn't believe she could possibly be here at this time.

CHAPTER THIRTEEN

What was Liz Siedo doing in Stratford? I could see our carefully prepared plan falling apart.

Virgil stood, looking as shocked as I felt. Liz lumbered toward him, dragging a suitcase that had twisted so its wheels were up and the bag slid noisily along the stone floor. Suddenly, the suitcase took flight. Holding the extended handle, Liz swung it in a wide arc ending near Virgil's head. He blocked the blow with his hands. Still, the impact knocked him to the floor, his chair upended. He stared in fear. Liz had the suitcase poised for another strike. Virgil twisted away, but she stepped toward him and let him have it again with her luggage. For a large woman, she handled the weapon with ease, striking him on the right shoulder this time.

"Where's my money, you cad?" she yelled, raising her

suitcase in the air once more.

The patrons who had been seated near Virgil and Cloris were standing now, moving away from the swinging suitcase. I grabbed the drone, still neatly packed in my suitcase, and moved in closer to see what was happening and to help Liz if need be. So far she was getting the best of him while Cloris stood back and enjoyed it. Some of the customers and waiting staff looked as frightened as Virgil. A few laughed. Those who don't know Liz the way I did were often fooled by her size and lack of muscle tone. She could move quickly when she wanted to. Today was one of those times.

Just as the suitcase came down a third time, Virgil rolled. But it didn't faze Liz who had the suitcase airborne again and aimed straight for him. He turned the wrong way this time and the bag caught him in the chest. I heard him gasp, but it wasn't enough to keep him down. He was on his haunches and scooting away before she could strike again. When he was far enough away, he stood and ran toward the door, only to find his path blocked by Tex and his wheelchair.

"You!" he said. Virgil turned toward Cloris. "Thanks a lot, woman."

Virgil grabbed the wheelchair and started to move it out of the way. Jane jumped on his back and stopped his effort to move Tex. She was stronger than Virgil, but he twisted and turned and got her off by bumping her against the wall. She let go, and fell onto a table knocking partially filled plates to the floor. The clatter of dishes and glasses sounded throughout the inn. Two men wearing white aprons appeared from the back and moved through the crowd toward Virgil.

I walked slowly toward the action, pulling the suitcase housing the drone with me. Jane appeared to be okay. My concern was that Virgil had seen the one person he didn't know. The one person who could have followed him without spooking him.

Just as the two employees reached Virgil, he climbed on Tex's wheelchair and jumped over it. In seconds he was through the door.

I made my way to the front and followed him. I got there in time to see him turn left and race down the center of High Street.

It took only a few seconds to get the drone into the air, making me hopeful I could follow him.

But it wasn't to be.

All I could see on the monitor was the sky and an occasional rooftop. I hadn't included controls to allow the drone to show what was below the helicopter. The camera pointed straight ahead and I couldn't point the helicopter down. It was out of eyesight and I didn't want to risk crashing it into a building. To avoid losing the helicopter, I flew it over the houses and brought it back. When it landed I heard applause behind me. I turned around and saw a crowd of customers and servers standing there clapping. I wasn't sure why. Perhaps they thought I was trying to catch Virgil.

We went back inside and found a table for five to talk about what to do next. We thought we might have to pay for the damage to the restaurant, but the manager brought us all a free lunch and apologized for the stranger's actions.

"Liz," I said, "I guess you know you blew our sting operation."

"I'm sorry. I couldn't help it. When I saw that thief, I had to go after him. I didn't know what y'all had planned. I didn't know you were in this place."

"You should have told us you were coming," Jane said.

"Yeah," Tex said. "When you called we thought you were in Texas."

Liz smiled. "I wanted to surprise you. I was on a private jet with Matt and Marie and we were about to land somewhere in Birmingham. That's in England, you know. Not the Alabama town. They told me how to get to Stratford, and here I am."

"You did, indeed, surprise us," I said. "That's for sure."

Matt and Marie Thomas owned restaurants in Austin and Denver. Probably other places I didn't know about. Matt was one of the Combine group who supports the Vengeance Squad from time to time.

"How'd you get them to fly you to England?" I asked.

"They were on their way to France to study some new ways of cooking. They dropped me off and told me to call if I need a ride home."

"Speaking of surprises," Cloris said, snickering. "Did you see the look on Virgil's face when you walked? Priceless. And the look of fear when you had him on the floor?" She laughed. It was the first time I'd seen her happy. Probably because she'd had a couple of drinks since we got to the Inn and she had another one in her hand now.

"I like you," Cloris said to Liz. The two had not officially met, but it wasn't long before that acted as if they were old friends.

"That was funny," Liz said, more relaxed now. "I guess I got carried away. I never hit anyone before. I owe him an apology."

"I wouldn't worry about him complaining," I said. "Not after what he did to you."

"I don't think you hurt him much," Tex said. "Besides, he deserved what he got. Still, I guess we're back to step one."

"Yeah," I said. "Only difference is that now Virgil knows we're tracking him and he knows he can't trust Cloris. And, he's seen Jane."

"So," Jane said, "you're saying it's worse than before."

"I might as well go home," Cloris said.

"We all might as well go home," I said.

"I'm sorry," Liz said. Her bottom lip quivered as she looked around the room.

CHAPTER FOURTEEN

I hoped Angela wouldn't mind, but I invited everyone to her place in London. Liz had reserved a hotel room, but she was so upset about causing us to lose our chance to follow Virgil, she canceled it and asked if she could stay with us. Honestly, I worried about her more now than any time since Tex introduced her to me two years ago. I had never seen her depressed before, and Tex, who had known her longer, said the same.

When we got back to London, we agreed that Tex and Jane would stay in Angela's bedroom and Liz would sleep on the sofa. I had my little flat across the hall. Cloris still had her hotel room, but we told her she shouldn't go back there because of Virgil. We said we'd all chip in for a different hotel for her.

But she wasn't interested in our offer. "I'm not afraid

of him," she said. "He better be scared of me. I'm not going to change what I do for the likes of him."

Cloris had stopped in the pub below for another drink and brought it with her to Angela's. "I understand," I said to Cloris, "but why don't you find another room just in case."

She stumbled as she walked to the door. When she regained her balance she turned around. "All right," she said. "I might sleep here tonight. I'm going back to Texas pretty soon, anyway." She finished off her drink in one final gulp and slumped into the sofa.

"Why me, God?" Liz said loudly.

We all turned to her.

"Why did this happen to me?" she continued. "I feel so out of control." She let out a huge sigh. "Don't you care, Lord? Are you there?" She sat on the sofa next to Cloris and dropped her head into her hands.

Tex and I turned toward Jane in unison. Since she'd turned his life around when he was in the hospital, we thought maybe she could help Liz. I didn't know what to say. I'd never heard Liz question God before.

Jane got the message. "Faith is all you need," Jane said calmly as she sat on the sofa on the other side of Liz.

Liz sighed again, louder this time.

Jane continued. "Having faith doesn't mean you won't face difficulties. It can't control what happens to you. What it can do is give you the strength to get past painful situations such as this, and the strength to live through all of life's challenges and each time come out a stronger person."

Liz held her eyes on Jane, but her expression showed

she was still confused.

Jane studied Liz for a few seconds. "I think you know this, but when we are in the midst of a problem, in a place where we need God the most, we often blame God. When that happens, we lose our faith. We don't realize it, but that's just the opposite of what we should do. It's human nature, I think. We can't help it. Remember, faith leads to peace. Faith comforts."

"What a bunch of baloney," Cloris said from her perch on the other side of Liz.

Liz turned to Cloris. "No. Jane's right. All I need is faith. Bad things happen. God doesn't keep us from the evils of others. But faith helps us get past them." She smiled. "I know that. I tell people that all the time. It's just when it hit so close to home, I went off my rocker. Temporarily, that is." She looked around the room as if daring anyone to disagree.

"Amen," Tex said.

"Oh, right," Cloris said, "that's the answer. You just have faith while Virgil steals us blind." She turned to Liz. "How's that working for you?"

Liz smiled. "I don't know what God has in mind yet, but I'm going to find out. I'm not going to sit around feeling sorry for myself. God will show us the way."

"You're such a sap," Cloris said. She stood and walked to the kitchen area and deposited her empty glass in the sink.

No one spoke for the longest time. Finally, I couldn't stand it any longer. "I know things seem pretty hopeless. I have no idea what to do next to find Virgil. Intellectually, I suppose we should go home. But, intuitively, I keep thinking there must be something we can do. Any suggestions?"

"Yeah," Cloris said. "Go home and forget you ever heard of Virgil Golden."

"We don't have a fallback plan?" Jane asked. "Or do we? I guess we could stay a few days. I've got that bodybuilding contest Thursday night. Tomorrow we can see some of England before we go home." She looked at Tex. "Okay, honey."

"Sure," Tex said.

"That's good," I said. "But let's keep thinking of ways to find Virgil. We had him within reach. Maybe we can do it again."

"Until I scared him away," Liz said.

"Don't blame yourself," Cloris said in a rare loving way. "He's a slippery one. We might as well forget about the money he stole. We'll never see it again."

"Well, I'm not ready to quit," Liz said. "I'm going to pray for faith and keep a positive attitude."

Liz jumped as if she'd been jabbed. "Hey! You know what I just thought of?"

"What's that?" I asked.

"Jane said something about a bodybuilding contest. Cloris, I'm betting Virgil calls you tomorrow if nothing else to cuss you out for what happened in Stratford."

"Yeah, so?" Cloris said. "Won't do him any good."

"Well, when he does, tell him you didn't know anything about us being there and that we must have followed you from Texas. Tell him there's a way to get back at us for what we did."

"Okay," Cloris said. "And that is…?"

"Tell him about the bodybuilding contest Jane's in."

"Hmm," Cloris said. "Knowing him, he'll want to go just to gawk at the contestants."

"That's good," I said. "That means we get another chance to follow him, right?"

"Yes," Liz said. "Another chance."

"I'll try. Write down the time and place," Cloris said to Jane. "I've decided to go on back to the hotel after all. Staying here is too much like being in church." Cloris took the note from Jane and left without a good-bye.

"I hope she'll be careful," I said.

"Yeah," Tex said, "I'm worried about her. Should we try to stop her?"

"I don't see how we can," Liz said.

"Let her go," Jane said. "If we're right about Virgil, he's not going to hurt her. I've got something else to talk about. Do you think we could rent a van with wheelchair access? This city is not easy for Tex to get around in."

Liz jumped from the sofa and danced around, more like her usual self. "No, but I know where we can get a bookmobile with a wheelchair ramp."

"Why a bookmobile?" I asked.

"We could use it the same as a van. The library in Norwich has a used one for sale. I got a brochure about it last week."

"We can't buy anything like that," I said. "The bookmobile fund is gone."

"Maybe they'd let us test drive it," Liz said.

"I doubt it," I said.

"Well," Liz said, "why don't we go find out. Who

knows, it might be just what we need for the library. Meanwhile, we could use it to tour the country. Does anyone know where Norwich is?"

Jane pulled up Google maps on Angela's computer. "Norwich is northeast of here," she said. "Google shows it's 116 miles by car. Says it'll take about two hours to get there by train. But, we'll have to take the Underground or a bus to get to the right train station. I'll check on the details later. When should we go?"

"How about tomorrow?" Liz asked.

"Tomorrow's Wednesday," Jane said, "and I've got that competition Thursday. Friday would be better for me."

"Yeah," Tex said. "Jane needs time to prepare. Liz, you and Chris could go sightseeing around London while I help Jane get ready."

"How do you prepare for bodybuilding competition?" Liz asked. "You've already built up your body."

Jane laughed. "Yes, I've done most of the work. But I'd like to run and work out at the gym. Plus, I usually find a place for a fake tan. That helps."

"Haven't you been running every morning since you got here?" I asked.

"I have. But a few more miles tomorrow could make my muscles look bigger."

I was in favor of delaying or canceling the trip to Norwich for any reason. If we could get involved with finding Virgil, Liz might forget about buying that bookmobile in Norwich. I liked the way the possibility made her happy again, but buying something that big without money was a little bizarre, even for Liz.

***

When I saw Virgil running down the street outside the Garrick Inn in Stratford, I thought he'd blame Cloris for the ambush and never speak to her again. But I was wrong.

He fell for the enticement to go to Jane's competition. Cloris didn't say it when she talked to Jane by phone, but I think when Virgil learned we were going to the competition, he may have thought that was the only reason we were in London, and that we hadn't come to find him after all.

The competition was held in a theatre much like the ones where you would go to see a play or a musical. It was cozy in size, small enough for everyone to see the stage. It was also difficult to hide from anyone there.

We had reserved seats so we waited until the last minute to enter in hopes of spotting Cloris and Virgil without them seeing us. We hadn't found them by the time we had to go to our seats. Tex rolled into a wheelchair space in the center of the last row of the first section. Liz and I had seats next to him. I quickly scanned the rows in front of us, but didn't see Cloris or Virgil. There was a balcony, but it was difficult to see the people sitting there since we were so far from the stage. I took my phone and pointed it to the empty stage as if preparing to take a photo. Instead, I switched lenses and aimed it toward the balcony and snapped a picture. I zoomed to see if I could find Virgil or Cloris in the photo, but didn't see either one.

Knowing where Virgil was didn't matter so much now, but when the competition ended and everyone started to leave, I wanted to follow him. Our plan was to assume he'd take Cloris back to her room afterwards and we could follow him from there. Something about that plan bugged me, but I wasn't sure what.

The lights dimmed, the music volume rose and a man in a blue sequined tuxedo stood center stage in front of the curtain. The sequins glistened in the spotlight. In a loud, lyrical voice pumped with emotion, he told us what to expect.

"And, now, ladies and gentlemen, please welcome tonight's contenders..." As his voice rose so did the curtain, the stage lights, and the applause.

I didn't know what to expect when we first talked about going to see Jane compete, but when twelve bikini-clad women appeared on stage, I had an inkling of what was coming. I saw more of Jane than I probably should have. Especially with her being a chaplain. But this is what she enjoyed doing, and she certainly appeared healthier than she did a year ago. Tex cheered and clapped along with the rest of the crowd. Liz got my eye and we both gulped. Her eyes were tall circles which I'm sure mirrored mine.

I looked around at the other women on the stage, but my eyes kept jumping back to Jane. Her muscles were rippled, all of them. She was darker and gleamed as if she'd added baby oil to her body. For some reason I thought an ordained minister would be a little more self-conscious dressed the way she was. But she wasn't.

And I thought how the smile on her face made her more attractive than usual. Her saunter and posture oozed with self-confidence. This was good for her. We all need to succeed at something.

Jane stared directly at me and as soon as our eyes locked she pointed her eyes to the far left side of the balcony. She'd spotted Cloris. I nodded, but I didn't turn around.

On cue, the women moved to another spot on the stage. When they did, I couldn't help noticing the bikinis didn't cover much of their backside. I reached for my program about the time Jane faced the other direction and I noticed Liz looked away, too.

I wasn't sure how the event worked, but this must be an introduction to all competitors. After a swell in the music along with movement on stage, we were left with four women standing side by side near the front of the stage. Jane wasn't in this group. The four went through a routine without being prompted. Each one raised her arms to show her flexed biceps. Naturally, her abdomen and thighs were flexed, as well. Next, each one held her arms in a near akimbo position while she tightened every muscle in her body. All the women's trapezius muscles stood high above their shoulders and their deltoids flared as well. They turned around together as if choreographed and showed their back muscles to the audience. From this view I could also see their triceps and other muscles I didn't have names for.

After showing off their bodies in a variety of positions, the four left the stage and were replaced by another four, and then the last group, the one with Jane in it came on stage. I could tell the crowd loved her and she was clearly the most well-developed of anyone I'd seen. And, I was nearly right.

There was a short intermission to give the judges time to decide the winners. I took the opportunity to go upstairs to see if Cloris and Virgil were there. I spotted them, but they weren't in the balcony. They were walking through a fire exit on the side of the theatre. I could have followed them if they'd gone out the front door with other people, but not since they were alone, probably in a dark alley. I went back to my seat and told Tex and Liz what I'd seen. We agreed I would go to Cloris's hotel to see if we could find Virgil there.

Just as I got to the back of the theatre to leave, the emcee came on and announced the winners. I waited. Jane got the third place trophy in the Bodybuilding Masters 35 and older category. She was presented with a trophy plus a bouquet of red roses.

After that, I made my way to Cloris's hotel and watched the entrance for three hours without seeing either one of them coming or going. That was when I gave up and went back to Angela's flat.

CHAPTER FIFTEEN

The next day Jane called Cloris several times before we left for Norwich, but she never answered.

Liz was so excited about the possibility of getting a bookmobile, I didn't have the heart to remind her she didn't have the money to buy one.

"I bet they'll let us drive it around to test it," she said. "It's been for sale for over a year now, so they're probably anxious to find a buyer. If they say okay to a test drive, we'll have a vehicle to use while we're in England."

I looked at Tex and he raised his eyebrows, and added a grin just for me.

Jane caught on to our silent communication and put an end to it by giving us the evil eye she used on her kids. "While we're in Norwich," she said, "there are some cool things to see. It won't be a wasted trip at all. First, the library itself should be interesting. I did a search after we talked about going there and learned the Norwich Millennium Library was recently named the most popular library in the UK for the sixth year in a row."

"That's right," Tex said. "She showed me a photo of the place. It's huge."

"Plus," Jane continued, "Norwich has a castle, museums, art collections, churches, and many other things to see. We could spend several days visiting there and still not see it all." She spoke a little softer as she added, "with or without a bookmobile."

We found the library with the help of a woman from Norwich we'd met on the train. The four of us approached the checkout desk of the library with the luggage we'd brought in case we stayed overnight. When we asked about the bookmobile that was for sale, we were directed to the administrator's office on the second floor. Jane found an elevator and we all went in.

The administrator had an incredulous look on his face as Liz gave him a Texas hug and pumped his hand for all of us.

"Howdy," she said in her best imitation Texas accent. "I'm the director of library services in Austin, Texas. I've been admiring the used bookmobile you've had for sale for the past year or so."

She was such a trusting person, she opened the conversation with what she thought would give us a vehicle to use for the rest of our stay in the UK.

"Bookmobile?" he asked.

"Oh, I think you call it mobile library," Liz said. "What we'd like to do is take it for a spin for a few days to see if it'll work for us. If it does, we'll buy it and ship it to Texas."

The administrator scratched his bald head and stared at her a few seconds before he scanned us with his eyes taking in the luggage we'd brought.

"A spin?"

Liz could be blunt at times and I couldn't think of a way to help.

He shook his head and crossed his arms. "Oh. No. I'm afraid that won't be possible. And, in fact, if it were allowed, it wouldn't be necessary. The vehicle is for sale as is. You can examine it and you can have a mechanic check it over, but we can't let anyone test drive it. Liability and all that, you understand."

Liz's bottom lip puffed out, but only briefly. "I understand." She looked at me first before turning to Tex and Jane. "I'd still like to see it. As long as we've come this far. Okay?"

We nodded.

"Can we see it?" Liz asked the man.

"Certainly," he said. "It's out back in the parking lot. Right this way."

"Before we do," I said, "we want to make sure it's legal to ship it to the States, and that it won't cost us an arm and leg."

"Yes. Quite." He stared down his nose at Liz then back to me before he took in a big breath and exhaled slowly. I had the feeling he felt sorry for me. "A vehicle such as this can be shipped to the United States only if it is new..."

Liz gasped.

"...or if it is more than twenty-five years old," he added.

"And?" Liz asked. "Is this one old enough?"

"Yes. Just barely. But it is legal according to your laws and ours."

Liz did a little jig.

"And how much does it cost?" I asked.

Liz stopped dancing and turned to the administrator.

"Ninety-nine thousand, nine hundred ninety-nine," he said.

"Is that dollars?" Liz asked.

"No, that's pounds. Hang on a moment, let me check that for you." He pulled out his phone and punched some keys before glancing back to Liz. "That would be approximately 155,000 in US dollars, based on today's exchange rate."

"And the shipping cost?" I asked.

"It is quite expensive," he said. "However, it is irrelevant."

"Irrelevant?" I asked. "What do you mean?"

"The advertisement Ms. Siedo referred to was in an American Library Association's publication. To simplify the transaction, we included the shipping cost in the price."

"Well, show it to us." Liz was all smiles as she locked elbows with the administrator. We all followed, dragging our suitcases behind us.

I was surprised to see the bookmobile was a vintage red double-decker bus that had been refurbished. I wondered if Liz knew that when she'd admired it in that ad. I also wondered if it was legal to drive back home. Would it fit under the phone lines and railroad overpasses?

But it was too late. As soon as we entered the vehicle I saw Liz's mouth and eyes pop open as if connected together. She was in love with this giant red library on wheels. I kind of liked it too, and began to wish there was some way to buy it.

We climbed in. Tex used a state-of-the-art wheelchair lift he operated himself. The windows on the first floor had been filled in and the walls were covered with empty bookshelves. It was spacious and looked more like a room in a library than a vehicle. There were stairs at each end, and the administrator motioned us toward the nearest one.

"Perhaps you'd like to see what we did with the top deck?"

Tex stayed downstairs with the administrator while the rest of us went up.

The covered top floor—or deck—had been converted into a cozy reading room. It was carpeted, with tables firmly attached to the walls so they wouldn't shift around while the vehicle was in motion. Windows provided light and I saw a section for computer desks. Several easy chairs were located around the space.

"It's perfect!" Liz said. She ran up and down the stairs several times, causing the vehicle to shake. Each time she passed Tex she told him about another feature on the top deck. When she stopped running about, she pulled me outside to get away from the others.

"Chris, I've got to have this bookmobile." It was almost a whisper.

"Have you forgotten, the bookmobile fund is gone? I like it too, but you can't buy it without money."

"Our patrons will love this. And think of all the publicity we'll get for the library. This bus will be the talk of the town."

"Yes, but is it legal in the States?"

"Oh, sure. That upstairs will stay busy at every stop. People will come just to see the bookmobile."

She turned to me, smiling, ignoring my question about the legality of it. "We had nearly enough money in the bookmobile account to buy it."

"Aren't you forgetting something? Virgil? The money is all gone."

"That's okay. All we need is a short-term loan. You're going to recover that money from Virgil. I prayed about it and I'm sure you can do it. Also, I saw that drone you built. Now all we have to do is find where Virgil is and you can send that helicopter in and, voila, we get the money and pay back the loan. Nothing to it."

"What?" My heartbeat rose quickly. How could she seriously think about spending that much money? What if we didn't find the stolen money? "How can I recover the money if we can't find him? Don't forget, you scared him away and now he knows we're searching for him. He's going to be extra careful now."

"We'll find him," she said. "Now, where can we get a loan? I know Brian would lend us the money, but I think he's in California. What about Matt? I've got his phone number in France. He could wire us the money, couldn't he?"

I still didn't understand how I could help her repay a short-term loan, but her enthusiasm was so contagious my mind began to search for a way to buy that red double-decker bookmobile for her. "It would be best to get someone local. Sarah's brother, Andrew, works for a large bank in London. I can call him and ask him about a short-term loan."

"Perfect," Liz said. She nodded toward the administrator who was talking to Tex and Jane. "He'd probably prefer working with a bank in England. Can you call him now?"

I took out my phone and checked my contact list. When I found Andrew's name, I pressed call. Liz went inside the bookmobile, leaving me alone to make the deal. I was close enough to hear her telling the administrator she'd buy the bookmobile and Andrew had yet to answer his phone. What was I getting myself into?

"Hello," Andrew said.

"Andrew, it's Chris."

"How are you? Enjoying your visit?"

"Yes. Great. Listen, I'm in somewhat of a bind. I hate to ask you, but I need your help with a financial matter. The director of library services from Austin is here and she has found a used bookmobile she'd like to buy and ship home."

"Like a mobile library?"

"Yes. It's actually a refurbished red double-decker."

"What can I do to help?" he asked.

"We need a short-term loan to make the purchase in

Norwich. It'll take about thirty days to get our funding together at which time we can pay you back."

"How much are we talking about?"

"Ninety-nine thousand, nine-hundred ninety-nine pounds."

"Ouch. You want to borrow that much for thirty days?"

"Yes. Can you do it?"

"It's highly unusual. Are you sure your funding is coming in?"

"Of course." I wasn't sure of anything. "Besides, if it doesn't, you'll still have the bookmobile."

"I think I can do it, but only because of Sarah. Don't let me down. I could lose my job if you don't come up with the money on time. And you know you'll have to leave the bus in the UK until the loan is paid off."

"Of course. Thanks, Andrew. Don't worry. I'll get the money to pay you back." I hoped we could find Virgil. I hoped he hadn't spent all the money, or otherwise squirrelled it away somewhere out of reach. There was always a possibility that Liz's millionaire friends would help, but that was out of my control.

Andrew and I talked longer and made the final arrangements. He said he would fax the papers for Liz's signature to the Norwich Library. As soon as they were signed and returned, he'd authorize payment.

I stepped into the bookmobile. "Okay. The money is approved." I passed the phone to the administrator. "Would you talk to our banker? He wants the particulars and your fax number."

Three hours later the Norwich Library administrator

handed Liz the keys to the bookmobile. Liz sheepishly held the keys out to me. I shook my head and held my hands behind my back at first, but I soon realized I was the best choice to be the driver. I didn't like to think about my obsessive behavior, but I was forced to admit to myself that it often helped me do new tasks better than some people. After all, learning anything new was a matter of concentration, and I had tons of that.

The administrator got his bookmobile driver to move the vehicle to the main street while I sat next to him and watched. The driver talked to me constantly, explaining everything he did. It wasn't as hard as I'd thought it would be.

"Not my business," the driver said after he stopped and motioned for me to take the driver's seat, "but I guess you know you need a special driver's license for this bus."

I hadn't known that. "Sure," I said.

"Yep," he continued as if he didn't believe me, "most of the older Routemasters that aren't used to carry passengers are exempt. This one isn't. It's too new. Just twenty-five years old, it is." He looked at me with a twinkle in his eye. "The engine's newer. You should like that. When the old one gave out, we replaced it with one that we could use on the motorway. Came in handy when we took books to other towns."

"Is that right? How fast will it go?" I wasn't too worried about the driver's license. As a tourist, I could probably feign ignorance.

"Seventy miles an hour and more. Before, it had a top speed of forty-five, maybe fifty."

"Good. I'm glad to hear it can be used on the motorways."

"Yep. And, all that talk about it being haunted, that's hogwash. I'd drive it today, if they'd let me."

"Haunted?" But the driver was walking away in a hurry.

"Before we leave Norwich," I said, as soon as everyone was on board. "I want to remind everyone of all the wonderful sights Jane told us about. Should we stay over a night or not?"

"I think we should go on to London," Jane said. "There's lots there we haven't seen."

"I agree," Tex said.

"We can come back another day," Liz said. "It's been an exhausting trip."

I liked Liz's idea.

We pulled away from the curb slowly and headed for London. All three of my passengers reminded me to drive in the left lane frequently until we got to the A11. By then, I had started doing it automatically. Jane handled the map, directing me to the M11 that led us back toward Angela's flat. By the time we got to the main road, I had begun to enjoy driving this vehicle and was astonished by the help I got from the friendliness of other drivers.

***

When we got to London, I learned how difficult it was to find a place to park a red double-decker bus close to Angela's flat. I dropped the others off and kept searching. I eventually found a lot that took oversized vehicles. For an oversized fee.

When I rejoined the group, we all walked to Cloris's hotel to see if she was okay. She had not returned any of our calls during the trip to Norwich and we were beginning to worry about her. She'd talked about going back to Austin, but I didn't think she'd leave without telling Jane.

We walked cautiously into her hotel, afraid we might see Virgil, or rather, he might see us. The guy at the front desk assured us Cloris hadn't checked out.

"Let's go to her room and see if she's there," Liz said, walking toward the elevator.

"Why don't you two wait for us here," Jane said, joining Liz. "We don't want to overwhelm her."

The lobby was spacious enough for Tex and me to wait without the fear of being spotted by Virgil if he should come in through the front. We drifted over to a corner where we found brown leather chairs, indented from years of use. I took one near a large plate-glass window that provided a view of the sidewalk leading to the hotel's main entrance and Tex rolled in near me.

"Keep an eye on the elevator," I said. "Wouldn't want Virgil to spot us here."

Tex wheeled around for a view of the elevator. "Right," he said. "Don't know how to hide this chair, though, if he does show."

I watched people walk by, all dressed in cold-weather clothing, and thought about how warm it must be back home. Not that I minded the colder weather.

"Speaking of Virgil," Tex said, "there's a possibility he

could be there with Cloris right now. Think we should've insisted on going with Liz and Jane?"

"They should be okay. Besides, I doubt if he's there."

The elevator sounded, indicating its arrival. We both watched the door. Liz and Jane exited and looked around. I waved and they walked toward us, Jane shaking her head in answer to our unspoken question.

"Nobody was there," Liz said. "We knocked pretty hard and waited some. No response. I put my ear against the door to see if I could hear anything."

"Not a sound," Jane said.

"She could be touring the city," Tex said.

"Or making travel arrangements to go home," Liz said.

"Or," I said, "she could be on a plane headed for Texas without the desk clerk knowing she was gone."

No one said the obvious. She could be with Virgil somewhere.

For the next week, we were tourists, enjoying the sights in and around London. We'd bought the bookmobile to make it easier for Tex to get around, but we left it parked most of the time.

All during our sightseeing time, no one mentioned Virgil or the missing money. I couldn't stop thinking about the balloon payment coming due in about three weeks, but I didn't want to take away from everyone's enjoyment by mentioning it. I hoped we wouldn't get Andrew in trouble with his bank for going out on a limb for us, but I was beginning to wonder if we would be able to pay off that loan on time.

That wasn't all I worried about. It was January 18, the

first day for classes at Austin Community College. I used my laptop and Angela's wireless router to meet my students. After that, it would take several hours a night to maintain my classes. I was beginning to tire from touring the city by day and working at night. To make things worse, I hadn't heard from Angela and had no idea when I'd see her again. I started to wonder if my idea to stay until she returned was realistic.

Even though I knew I needed to spend more time with my students, I went with the gang to see more of the city.

That day, we walked to Buckingham Palace and watched the guards. Everyone took pictures, and we headed back.

"Hey," Jane said when we got to Angela's flat. "Did we leave the door open when we left?"

Sure enough, the door was ajar. "Maybe she's home," I said.

"Shh. Or, Virgil," Tex said softly as he rolled to the door in his wheelchair.

I followed him. The hair on the back of my neck sprang into action. I listened for a few seconds before quietly pushing the door the rest of the way open. Tex and I peeked in. No one was in the living area. The bedroom door was closed.

"Tex, do you usually leave the bedroom door closed like that?" I asked.

"I don't know," he said.

"No," said Jane and Liz simultaneously.

"Then someone has been in the apartment," I said.

"Or is still here," Tex said.

I walked to the bedroom door. Tex rolled over to the kitchen area and grabbed a broom before he joined me. I put my ear to the door to listen for movement inside. Nothing. I turned the handle slowly, without making a sound. When the catch was clear I pushed the door into the room and waited for someone to rush out.

But no one did. The room was empty. We checked the closet. No one there either.

"Check to see if anything is missing," I said.

"Nothing's missing," Tex said.

"All my stuff's okay, too," said Liz. "Do you think it was Angela?"

"Maybe," I said. "I guess I could try to call her. If she's back, she'll answer. Otherwise, I haven't been able to reach her by phone."

I called her number and let it go to voice mail. "Hi, Angela. Miss you. Give me a call if you get a chance. Love you."

After I put my phone away, I noticed everyone was smiling, probably because of the "love you" part of the message, but I didn't care. It was time they knew.

"I'll ask Clarence if he saw anyone snooping around," Liz said.

"Who's Clarence?" I asked.

"My friend in the pub," Liz said.

"Good idea," Jane said. "He'll know if Angela is back."

Liz left and we continued to survey the contents of the room. With my crazy memory, I actually knew everything was there and where it should be.

Liz returned.

"Well, it was Virgil."

"How do you know?" Tex asked.

"Clarence described him to a T. Smarmy with slick black hair acting like he owned the place. He came in asking about the guy in a wheelchair. Clarence didn't know better, so he gave him our room number."

"What on earth was he searching for?" Jane asked. "And how did he find us?"

"He may have followed Cloris when she first got to town." Tex said.

"I doubt it." I said. "That was two weeks ago. Why would he have waited so long to break in here?"

"Or," Jane said, "he may have forced her to tell him." She bowed her head. "Dear Lord, please care for Cloris and keep her safe."

"Amen," everyone said.

A sudden feeling of joy came over me. Not because of Jane's prayer, but because Virgil had been here. It meant we still had a chance to catch him. I hadn't told the others, but I'd given up on ever seeing that money he'd stolen and was considering other ways to pay back the loan. But now everything had changed. I knew we'd catch that creep.

"You all know what this means, don't you?" I asked.

"What?" Liz asked.

I gave them my biggest smile. "It means we're back on his trail."

She thought about that a few seconds before it hit her. That was when she danced a jig, causing everyone to laugh.

"What about your room, Chris?" Jane asked. "Shouldn't you see if he was nosing around there, too?"

I hadn't thought of that. He could've taken my laptop, or..., what? The drone? "Yes," I said and moved quickly through Angela's door to mine.

My door was locked, but I went in and checked to see if anyone had been there. It bothered me that I'd allowed Virgil to be in Angela's flat, but it appeared he hadn't taken anything. I searched my space thoroughly and couldn't find anything missing. I went back to tell everyone, told them goodnight and pulled out my laptop.

CHAPTER SIXTEEN

As soon as the laptop booted I knew something was wrong. The hair on the back of my neck told me someone had messed with my computer.

It didn't take long to find it. Virgil may have thought he was a computer expert, and he had managed to steal a lot of money from Liz by computer, but he was an amateur compared to me.

As soon as I fixed my system I went over to Angela's flat.

Liz was on the couch, her hair in curlers, reading a magazine.

"What's up?" she asked.

I stared at her. Curlers? Her hair was always unruly. Why did she bother?

Jane came in from the bedroom, wearing a robe. "Is

something wrong?" she asked.

"I know why Virgil was here. He put a program on my laptop that records all my keystrokes and periodically sends the data to an e-mail address I don't recognize."

"He bugged your computer?" Tex asked as he rolled into the room.

"Yes. I think I better check Angela's system to see if he got to it, too."

"Yeah," Tex said.

"Just a minute," Jane said. "I don't know how things like that are done, but in the movies, they'd leave the bug and send erroneous messages. Should we do that?"

"No," I said. "I don't think it's worth it. We need our computers and we don't want him to know what we're doing. I didn't remove what he'd done on mine. All I did was change it so he doesn't learn anything important. It'll still send him messages, but it'll look like he goofed up when he installed the program."

I turned on Angela's computer and found the same bug there. I fixed it the way I fixed mine and we all said goodnight for the second time.

***

I was awakened the next morning by a knock on the door. The sound caused me to sit up quickly. The cot I called a bed sagged in the middle so much it was like sleeping in a hammock. The bed and the linens had a smell that reminded me of a Boy Scout campout.

"Hey, sleepyhead," Liz said through the wooden

156

door, "breakfast is getting cold."

Breakfast. Yes. My mind was muddled from lack of sleep. I could smell the bacon.

"Okay. Y'all go ahead and eat. I'll be there soon."

I'd worked late. Again. There was always more to do at the beginning of a semester. Once the students got a feel for the course and what was expected, I wouldn't have to spend so much time with them. All my textbooks were the same as last semester, so I had read them. That also meant I could use the same lectures and the same exams. All the assignments were on Blackboard, an online software tool ACC used, and the tests were set to pop up automatically when the students were scheduled to take them. All I had to do was adjust the dates from last semester to match the schedule for this semester. Blackboard also graded the tests and let the students know which questions they'd missed and the part of the textbook where they should study more.

Teaching computers with computers was easy, but sometimes I missed grading printed tests and talking to students face-to-face. Doing it the old-fashioned way gave me a better feel for how each student was doing and allowed me to help them before it was too late. With online classes, I didn't know what they looked like, other than what I saw on the 72-pixel ID photo the school posted. If I had time, I'd try to get to know them better by the end of the semester. I'll encourage them to get to know each other, as well, to make the experience more like what goes on in a classroom.

By the time I got dressed and crossed the hall to

Angela's place, Liz was washing dishes, Jane was clearing the table, and Tex was sipping a cup of coffee while reading a newspaper.

"Well, about time," he said when I entered the room.

"Morning. I had to teach last night," I said, putting air quotes around the word *teach*. "Stayed up past midnight." Thinking about how busy I was reminded me I was also supposed to be working on the new textbook. I poured a cup of coffee and could tell by the viscosity it was no longer fresh. But, it was hot and dark. Just what I needed.

"I don't know how you do it," Liz said. "I simply have to have eight or nine hours of sleep every night just to function. Without sleep, you might as well put me away. Sit down, sweetie, I kept your breakfast warm. Do you want some fresh coffee? That stuff's thicker than motor oil."

She put a plate in front of me heaped high with pancakes and English bacon.

I tipped my cup. "No, this is fine. What's the plan for the day?" I asked as I slathered the pancakes with soft margarine.

"It's time to get serious about finding Virgil," Tex said. "The three of us talked while waiting for you and came up with a strategy."

I topped off the margarine soaked pancakes with syrup. "And?" The smell of maple syrup reminded me of my mother and the way she served pancakes every Saturday while I was growing up. She still does.

"Well," he said, "since we know he's been in this room, he must have walked the streets nearby. If he's watching us now, as you suspect, he's still out there."

"Sounds reasonable." I forked a wedge of pancakes and dipped them into the excess syrup.

Tex continued. "We can't stake out the place. He'd recognize us in an instant. So, Jane and I are going to change the way we look and watch for him to walk by again."

It was hard to respond with a mouthful of pancake, but Tex waited while I chewed. "Don't you think he'll see through that after the incident at Stratford?"

Jane brought me a glass of orange juice. "We thought of that," she said. "In Stratford, I wasn't in costume. This time I will be. He might see a guy in a wheelchair, but he'll never notice us."

"And if you see him?" I asked. "What are you going to do?"

Tex raised his brows at his wife. "Well…uhh…we haven't worked out all the details."

"I could follow him," Jane said.

"And call me?" I asked.

"Yes. That's it," Tex said.

"Or me," Liz said. "Call me. I'd love to get my hands on him again."

"Remember," I said, looking at Liz, "we want to find where he lives. The goal is to get into his bank account and get your money back. We don't want to scare him off again. You haven't forgotten the huge balloon payment coming due soon for that bookmobile, have you?"

"No," she said, but she had a pout on her lips.

My phone rang. I took a quick sip of juice and

grabbed the phone, hoping it was Angela.

"Hello."

"Chris," a man's voice said. "Andrew here. You asked me to watch for any info on a Virgil Golden."

I stood, hoping he had a lead we could use. "Yes. Do you know where he is?" I punched the speaker button so my friends could hear. Liz and Jane came to the table where Tex and I sat and we all listened.

"It's Sarah's brother, Andrew," I said softly.

"I don't know if it is the person you're searching for, but a Mr. Virgil Golden opened an account in one of our branch banks in Scotland. It is an account of a significant size so I wasn't sure if it was the same person or not. The money was actually transferred from a small institution in Italy, one we've often associated with the so-called gypsy population there."

"It's him," Liz said. "I bet he's a gypsy. He looks like a gypsy."

"Andrew, that was Liz. She's the director of libraries in Austin. Virgil stole about $150,000 from the bookmobile fund there. Was the amount of the deposit similar to that?"

"Much more than that," he said.

"That's him," Liz said. "He's stolen from me and Cloris and no telling how many others."

"Do you have his address?" I asked

"Yes, but I don't think it will help you find him. It's one of those commercial post office box numbers people use to hide their home addresses."

"Can you give me the bank name and his account number?"

The silence was deafening.

"I can't do that," Andrew said. "Family or not, I can't give out that information. If something happened to the account, the bank could be liable and I could be out of a job. It's quite a good job, I might add."

"But, if the money was stolen, you shouldn't get in trouble if we happen to recover it, should you?"

"Sorry. No way I can help you do that, if it is even possible."

"It's possible," Liz said.

"I don't want to know about any of that," Andrew said.

"Okay," I said. "Thanks for alerting us about this. Is there anything else you can tell us?"

"No. But, I'll keep digging around and call you back if I learn more. I think we should have more identifying information, but I wanted to call you as soon as I saw the name."

"We appreciate it."

"Pardon for asking, but paying back the loan isn't dependent on finding Virgil, is it?"

"Oh, no," I said and hung up.

"Interesting," I said, "but I'm not sure knowing about Virgil's bank account is useful, yet. We still don't know where he is."

"Can't you just look for all new accounts at that particular bank?" Tex asked.

"No, it's not that easy."

"Let's go to Scotland and look for him," Tex said.

"Scotland is a big place," I said. "Where would we start?" My unusual memory jumped into action and I saw that the population of Scotland was in the millions.

"I always wanted to go to Edinburgh," Liz said.

"We can't go to Scotland to try to find Virgil," I said. "Not without more information about his whereabouts. There are five million people there."

"You're right," Jane said. "Maybe only his money is in Scotland. Let's do what we planned. We know he was in this room yesterday. Let's watch the streets a few days and see what happens."

"Right," Tex said.

"Okay," Liz said. "But as soon as we catch him I want to go to Edinburgh."

***

Later that day Jane and Tex prepared to walk the streets between Angela's place and Cloris's hotel.

Tex appeared to be eighty or ninety years old. Makeup added wrinkles and a gray wig and flat cap took the place of his Stetson. Jane was dressed as a bag lady. When I saw her in her dirty clothes, stockings partially rolled down, carrying two shopping bags stuffed with junk, I thought of the Jane who had just won third place in the bodybuilding competition. The transformation was extreme. Today, she looked like an old woman, down on her luck, hoping for a few handouts for food and a warm place to sleep for the night.

While Tex and Jane were on the streets, Liz and I went to Cloris's hotel to see if she was there. We'd been calling her phone number each day, without success.

When we got to her room, we saw a "Do Not Disturb" door hanger.

"That's new," Liz said.

"Yeah. Maybe she's sleeping."

Liz knocked anyway and we both waited. No response.

"She may have checked out and gone back to Texas," Liz said. "I think I'll go talk to that desk clerk again."

"I don't think it'd say 'Do Not Disturb' if she'd checked out. Bet the guy at the desk was wrong about her still being a guest here, and someone else is occupying the room now."

"Either way, we need to talk to the desk clerk."

"I guess," I said. "If she hasn't checked out, see if you can talk him into giving us a key. Tell him you're her mother or something. People always like to make you happy. I bet he'll do it."

Liz looked at me as if she didn't know that about herself.

When we got to the front desk, Liz got the clerk's attention. "Excuse me. Is Cloris Parker still a guest at this hotel?" She put on her best smile.

He checked his computer screen. "Yes. She's still registered."

"Oh, no," Liz said with a pout. "I hope she's okay. I've been trying to reach her for days. She's never in her room and doesn't answer her phone. Could she have left without checking out?"

"I guess she could leave without saying anything. But it's not likely. She's paid for a few more days. The maid would have let me know if the room was empty."

"Even with that 'Do Not Disturb' sign on the door?" Liz asked.

"Oh," he said. "Maybe not."

"She's my sister," Liz said, glancing quickly toward me as if daring me to think she was old enough to be Cloris's mother. "And I'm worried about her. She may have left or she might be sick or something. Would you be a dear and lend me a key to her room so I can check on her?"

He looked at her suspiciously.

"Or you could go see if there's a dead body in the room yourself," she added.

"She's your sister, you say?"

I'd need to compliment Liz for the way she got a squeamish desk clerk to hand over the room key.

"Yes. My younger sister. And I'm worried about her." She leaned in on the desk with pouting lips and eyelids blinking.

He stuck a plastic access card into a machine, typed a few strokes on the computer's keyboard and handed her the card. "Let me know what you find."

"Thank you, my dear man," Liz said.

We moved quickly to the elevator.

When we got to Cloris's room, I slid the card key through the lock. A green light flashed, indicating the door was unlocked. I pushed the door in for Liz to go in first. She didn't and neither did I. All we could do was stare, at first.

We didn't see a body, and I don't think either one of us expected to. But what we found surprised us nearly as much.

CHAPTER SEVENTEEN

We could see it from the hallway. The suitcase stood ominously not more than six feet from the door, its pull handle extended and pointing away from us. It looked as if someone had rolled it in and left it sitting there.

We entered the room without a word. The bathroom was to the left of the entry way, and its door was wide open. No one was there unless he was behind the shower curtain. I nodded to Liz and turned in to check the tub. I've watched enough TV to know there was not a dead body anywhere. If there was, we would have smelled it. But that didn't mean a live body couldn't jump out of the bathtub when the curtain was pulled back. It didn't.

We continued into the room, walking past the suitcase. No one was there. The bed was made and there were no used towels in the bathroom. There was nothing out of place. Except the suitcase that stood at attention guarding the entrance.

Liz looked at me with question marks on her face, then, without hesitating, she hefted the bag to the bed and checked the name tag hanging from its handle. "It's Cloris's," Liz said as she opened it.

It was full of clothes and other personal items, but what surprised me was the passport she found in one of the outer pockets.

Liz opened it and held it for me to see. "Cloris's. This proves she's still in the UK."

"Maybe," I said. "All we can say for sure is that she hasn't gotten on a plane to go back to the States. Not unless she has another passport."

"That's not likely," Liz said.

"Something's wrong. That's for sure. She's not in her room, she's not answering her phone, and her passport and clothes are here."

"We've got to do something," Liz said.

My phone rang.

"We've spotted him." It was Tex.

"Can you follow him?"

"Don't have to. He parked a rental car and went into the hotel."

"Get the license number, make and model," I said.

"Got it."

"Also the name of the hotel," I said.

"Cloris's hotel."

"Virgil went into Cloris's hotel?" I looked at Liz. Her eyes popped open.

"That's where we are. We're in her room."

"Be careful," Tex said. "We'll sneak in and see what he's doing."

"Okay." I hung up. "He parked a rental car outside and came into the hotel. Either he has a room here or he's coming to this room. We better get out of here now."

"But what about Cloris? We have to call the police."

"We'll do that later. We can't let Virgil see us and blow our chance of getting the money back."

We closed the suitcase and put it back where we had found it. Liz had Cloris's passport in her hand.

"Shouldn't you put that back?" I asked.

She stuffed it in her purse. "No. We may need it."

"For what?"

"I don't know. To show the police or somebody." She moved toward the door.

My phone rang again.

"He just got in the elevator," Jane said.

"Virgil?" I asked.

"Yes."

"Did he see you?"

"He looked right past me."

"Good. We'll take the stairs and meet you and Tex at Angela's."

I ended the call and put my phone away. "We've got to go. Virgil's in the elevator."

We left the room and shut the door. There wasn't time to argue the pros and cons of taking the passport. Right now I was more concerned about our safety. I searched the hallway for an exit sign and found one just as the elevator beeped its arrival. I grabbed Liz's hand

and pulled her toward the stairwell. We opened the door and stepped in. I motioned for her to be quiet and wait. I left the door open just wide enough to peek out to see who exited the elevator.

Sure enough, it was Virgil. And he walked straight to Cloris's room. He looked around before placing a keycard in and opening the door.

"Let's go," I said. "He went into Cloris's room."

When we got to the ground floor, Liz walked toward the desk. I grabbed her arm.

"Let's go. Virgil could come down anytime."

"But," Liz said, "I promised the desk clerk I'd tell him what we found."

"I know, but we can call him or come back later when it's safe."

Still, I had to urge her out of the building.

***

A few minutes later all four of us were in Angela's room, reviewing what had happened.

"Why'd you take her passport?" Jane asked.

"I don't know," Liz said. "I guess I panicked. At the time I thought of her as a missing person and I wanted to have the passport to show authorities. Maybe the United States Embassy."

I said, "It was strange to see her unused room and her suitcase sitting there like it hadn't been touched."

"Yeah," Tex said. "She might have left her bag there while she went for some last-minute shopping or whatever. What if she comes back and can't find her passport?"

"Don't worry," Jane said. "She'd call me if that happened."

"There was a 'Do Not Disturb' sign on the door," Liz added.

"So?" Jane said. "I do that when I don't want a maid to come in while I'm having breakfast. It doesn't mean she should've been in the room."

"Sounds like she didn't need a maid," Tex said. "Maybe she's been staying with Virgil in another room. We don't know that much about her. What little we do know is that she is unpredictable."

"I think we should have left her passport in the suitcase," I said. "But with Virgil on his way, there wasn't time to talk about it." I looked at Liz, who quickly turned away.

"So what do we do now?" Tex asked.

"We've learned two things," I said. "One, Virgil has a rental car we can follow, and two, he has access to Cloris's room. I'm not sure what to do with the second bit of information, but I suggest we move the bookmobile to the street so we'll be ready to follow him when he leaves."

"Good idea," Jane said. "See if you can find a place to park near Virgil's car and make sure the bookmobile is pointed in the same direction. We'll keep a lookout at all times and be ready to follow him when he takes off."

"I can point the vehicle in the right direction," I said, "but I'm not sure if I'll find a parking place big enough. I may have to double park and move around when I'm forced to. I'll take the drone with me in case we have to leave in a hurry. Tex, be sure to pack your disguises, just in case."

"I will," Tex said. He still had his wrinkles, but had removed the wig. "We need to be prepared for a quick trip."

"I'm worried about Cloris," Liz said. "I'm afraid to call her now. If Virgil can walk into her room like that, he has access to her suitcase. He could have her phone, too. Our hands are tied if we can't call her without fear of tipping him off."

"If Angela was home," I said, "we could get her to help, but I don't know anyone else in law enforcement in England."

"Law enforcement. That's it," Liz said. "I'll call Tom."

"Who's Tom?" Jane asked.

"Tom is the chief of police in Austin," Tex said.

"Oh, that Tom," Jane said.

Tex turned to Liz. "How's he going to help with a missing person in London?"

"I don't know," she said, "but I'm calling him anyway. I see it on TV all the time. Police departments talk to other police departments, even those in other countries. We've got to do something. We're her only friends in a foreign land and we can't sit by while she's missing."

Liz had her phone in her hand as I headed for the door. "I'm going to move the bookmobile. I'll take the drone with me. Tex, you or Jane watch for Virgil. We don't know if he is staying at the hotel or just went there to see Cloris. We need to be ready to move at a moment's notice."

I drove around the block several times, keeping an

eye on Virgil's rental car. I didn't see a place big enough for the mobile library so I drove toward the city bus line near Victoria Station. Before I had gone far, I saw Jane in the street, waving. Liz was behind her pushing Tex's wheelchair. I stopped and waited while they got aboard. Tex had his disguise case in his lap and he pulled the lever for the wheelchair lift and rolled on when it was down. Jane assisted a breathless Liz.

"Phew," Liz said, "I'm not used to running so fast."

"Virgil must be leaving." I said.

"Yes," Jane said. "We better hurry."

"There he goes," Liz said. "Oh, no. He's making a U-turn. Hey! That's against the law. You're not supposed to do that."

Luckily, he couldn't hear her.

I drove to the next intersection as fast as the traffic allowed so we could reverse our direction. It was tight, but we managed with the help of the pedestrians who waited calmly while I maneuvered the large red double-decker. Several people on the street helped with hand signals. When we got turned around I gunned the engine, hoping we'd catch up to Virgil. It wasn't long before Tex spotted his car stuck in traffic. After that we managed to stay close behind him all the way to the M1 heading north. I was glad Norwich Library had replaced the engine with a new one.

Three hours later, I wondered if we should've packed some clothes for an overnight stay. I also wished I'd brought my computer so I could stay in contact with my students back home.

When Virgil stopped for gas near Leeds, so did we,

staying as far away from him as possible. While Jane worked the pump, I checked the map.

"Remember what Andrew said about Virgil depositing a bunch of money in Scotland?" I asked everyone.

"Yes," Liz said.

"I think that's where we're going."

"Oh, goody," Liz said. "I always wanted to go to Edinburgh."

"Liz," I asked, "did you talk to your friend back home?"

"Tom?"

"Yes. He hadn't heard anything about Cloris, but he's going to look into it."

"Good."

***

Virgil drove past Edinburgh, so we did too. Liz looked sad as we bypassed the city she was dying to visit. But we didn't go far past it.

Virgil stopped in St. Andrews, known as the home of golf. He parked in front of a B&B there and went in, carrying a suitcase. We were careful not to let him see the bookmobile, but that wasn't easy to do. The vehicle was so large, and apparently a curiosity in this area, it was difficult to be stealthy while following someone.

We found a B&B around the block from where he stopped that had three rooms available. The owner looked puzzled when she saw the bus and again when she asked why we didn't have any luggage.

"It's on the bus," I said, noting to myself how I had started lying more easily as time went by. "We'll get it later."

We had to drive all the way to Dundee to find a store open. There we bought a few necessities such as underwear, shirts, socks, toothbrushes and toothpaste. I also filled the tank with gas so we would be ready to roll should Virgil decide to leave. Since he had a considerable amount of money in a Scotland bank, money I wanted to grab, perhaps he'd stay put for a long time. I hoped so. I was considering ways to fly the drone into his room to search for bank account information. I knew how to hack banks, but I needed some basic information first. What I wanted was the bank identifier and the name on the account. A bank account number would be icing on the cake. A password would make it child's play. I didn't need to stare at the information for long because of my ability to remember what I saw.

The owner of our B&B wasn't there when we got back to our rooms to see us carry our "luggage" in. She'd probably expect us to have suitcases when all we had were plastic shopping bags.

We took turns watching Virgil's car, but it stayed where he'd parked it all night.

We had a typical English breakfast complete with eggs, bacon, sausage, tomatoes, canned beans, and mushrooms. When I finished eating, I relieved Jane, who was on Virgil-watch duty outside.

It a matter of minutes, I spotted Virgil walking toward his car. I alerted the others and we jumped in the bookmobile to follow him. Jane was the last one on board, carrying a napkin full of sausages to munch on since she'd missed breakfast.

If Virgil knew we were in the red double-decker, he didn't care. There was no way to tail him on the small curvy roads without him seeing our vehicle. But he never hesitated. He drove straight to St. Andrew's Old Course. We parked as far away from him as possible, while keeping him in sight. He got out of his car and stood near the clubhouse. After a short time, three men joined him. They all had golf bags. One of the three had an extra bag he handed to Virgil.

The four men looked so much alike they could have been brothers. All had dark hair slicked back with too much oil. They were in their forties or early fifties and acted like it was the first time they'd played golf. This wasn't ideal weather for the sport and the course wasn't too busy, but they wore clothes more suitable for hunting than golfing. That is, plaid shirts instead of polo.

We watched quietly from a distance until the foursome completed teeing off on the first hole.

"What do we do now?" Liz asked. "They're not using golf carts at this course. How can we follow them?"

"Does anyone know how to play golf?" I asked.

Everyone shook their head.

"I guess we wait until they return." Tex said.

"Or we could leave and come back," Jane said. "How long does it take to play golf?"

No one knew. But I had some answers. "A foursome would need about four hours to play eighteen holes, but sometimes golfers elect to play only nine. But I think that time estimate is with golf carts. They don't allow them here except for seniors and those with a disability."

"How do you know that?" Jane asked.

"I don't know. I must have read it somewhere."

"Tex has a disability," Liz said.

"Who says?" Tex asked, clearly miffed.

"Yes, but he's not a golfer," I said. "Besides, he'd need a note from his doctor."

"We'll see," Liz said. She took off toward the club house. "Come on, Tex. You need a golf cart."

She went into the clubhouse and we all followed. She stood in front of the counter and Tex rolled up beside her. Jane and I stood behind.

"I need a golf cart for my friend," she said indicating Tex.

"You mean a buggy?" the man behind the counter said.

Liz looked at me and I nodded. "Yes, a golf buggy. It's for my friend in the wheelchair."

"I'm sorry but we only allow buggies to be used between April and October," he said. "Driving on the course at this time of year would damage the greens."

"So," Liz said, "you're denying access to my friend in this wheelchair who can't play golf without a buggy?"

"No buggies this time of year," the man repeated. "Besides, he'd need to be registered as permanently disabled to use a buggy at the times of year when they are allowed."

We left, but I suspected Liz wasn't ready to give up. I could tell she had a plan by the way she walked. We followed her as she went around to the side of the building. Before long, she found a golf cart parking lot. She looked around until she found a black buggy with a key in the ignition. She climbed in and turned it.

Nothing happened. She looked at me, but all I could do was shrug. My special memory didn't help. I'd never read anything about driving a golf cart.

Liz didn't care. She saw a man walking near us and asked him. "Hey. How do you start this thing?" she asked.

"Just turn the key," he said.

"I did. Nothing happened."

He looked at her over the top of his glasses. "It's electric. You won't hear anything, madam. Put it in gear and step on the pedal."

"Gear?"

"The handle near where you are sitting. See the forward and reverse indicators?"

She pushed her dress out of the way and peered around. "Oh, yeah. Thanks."

She pushed the gear shift handle to reverse and the buggy started beeping. She stepped on the accelerator pedal and the buggy jerked backward, moving it away from the other buggies. Once it was away from the group, she shifted gears and drove away. The beeping stopped. One thing you could say about Liz, once she decided to do something, she found a way to make it happen.

"Climb in, everybody. We're going to catch a crook."

Jane helped Tex into the back seat, leaving his wheelchair sitting with the unused buggies. She sat next to him. I took the front passenger seat with Liz.

"Liz, what do you have in mind?" I asked. "We can't catch him. That'll blow the whole plan. And we can't drive across the golf course looking for him. He'll spot us for sure since we'll be the only buggy here. Remember, our goal is to get into his bank account."

I didn't, but I could have repeated we had less than three weeks before the huge balloon payment for the bookmobile would be due.

"I don't care," Liz said. "I want to nab him and force him to give the money back. Remember, he and I have a history. Once I approach him face-to-face, I think he'll do the right thing." She sped up and drove past three men who appeared to be teeing off. They were surprised to see us. One of them yelled, but we were too far away for me to hear what he said. I could read the waving arms and other gestures. They weren't happy.

"I think you're fooling yourself." I had to shout over the rushing wind. "At the time you thought you two had something special, he was romancing Cloris and stealing her life savings. And we don't know how many other lonely, trusting women were conned by Virgil. Do you truly think he will listen to you?"

"I wasn't lonely," she hollered, clearly irritated with me and disregarding the rest of what I'd said.

Liz drove like a crazed woman from one flag to another, surprising players along the way and causing many of them to yell at us. Others laughed or looked mystified. She didn't care. She stomped on the accelerator, determined to get to Virgil and mess up all the planning we'd done to get the money back.

We had yet to see Virgil and his friends when I saw

a buggy heading toward us. This one had a huge sign on the front that said MARSHAL, and it was approaching rapidly.

CHAPTER EIGHTEEN

Liz saw it, too. She jerked the wheel away from the approaching buggy and pushed the accelerator as far as it would go. This maneuver took us to the edge of a sand trap where she turned sharply to keep from falling in. The marshal's buggy was gaining on us. She drove around the sand trap while the other buggy followed.

"We have to stop," I said. "We're too weighted down. We'll never outrun him with four of us to his one."

"I'm not stopping until I have to," she said. "I want to find Virgil."

I looked over my shoulder and saw Tex and Jane holding on with both hands. The marshal was closing in. I could see his face. That was when I realized who was driving the pursuing buggy. "That's not the marshal. That's Virgil!"

But it was too late. Virgil rammed us. We tumbled into the sand trap. I grabbed the window frame and held on as we fell about three feet below the green into the sand. We hit with a thud and stopped immediately. Our buggy lay tipped on its right side with me in the sand and Liz on top of me. I got out from under her and onto my feet quickly to fend off Virgil, but as soon as I stood, I saw his buggy speeding away.

I helped Liz to her feet. "You okay?" I asked.

She had sand in her hair and her dress was twisted around. She jumped up and down frantically shaking her head and arms. I wondered if she'd been hit on the head. But she soon relaxed.

"Everything's working," she said. "Tex and Jane okay?"

I found Tex sitting a few feet away. Jane stood over him.

"Y'all okay?" I asked.

"I think so," Jane said. "Good thing we landed on a soft spot. It was a rather abrupt stop, thought. Threw us to the ground with a jolt."

Liz looked toward where Virgil had gone. "We almost caught him, this time," she said, with both arms in the air, laughing like a crazy woman.

I couldn't believe what I was hearing. "Are you kidding? Don't you see what's happening? He's chasing us now."

Jane and I were able to get the buggy back on its wheels, but before we had time to check to see if it would run, we were surrounded by golfers and others concerned about our welfare, including the guy from the clubhouse who appeared in a buggy. He was concerned about our condition and helped lift Tex into his vehicle for the trip back. The rest of us walked. Liz was offered a ride along with Tex, but she was too pumped up from the encounter with Virgil and wanted to walk with us.

When we got to the clubhouse, we told them what happened and offered to pay for the damage. However, since the buggy we were in was rammed by the marshal's buggy, the manager said he'd take care of it. I think they were somewhat embarrassed that someone had stolen the marshal's buggy and rammed us into the sand trap.

Still, we had to wait around for the police to get there. They asked dozens of questions about the man in the buggy that ran into us, and we cooperated the best we could. That was when I realized how little we knew about Virgil.

We filled out a few forms for the insurance company and then we were free to go.

**

We retrieved Tex's wheelchair and went back to our B&B, rubbing our bruises. Liz's initial upbeat response to what had happened was waning. She made several half-hearted attempts to pull us out of the doldrums, without success. Virgil's rental car wasn't at his B&B when we got there.

We took turns all night watching for him to return, but he never did.

The next morning we met in the dining room and discussed what to do next.

"I'm sorry, folks," Liz said. "I blew it again. I scared him off once more and I don't think we'll get a third chance to catch him."

I agreed with her, but kept my mouth shut. No one responded.

She continued her rant. "Chris warned me we'd lose our chance to recover the money, but I couldn't help myself. I wanted to hurt him the way he'd hurt me. It became more than money to me. When Virgil first came along, treating me so fine, I put my feelings out there for the first time in years. It hurt to have them stomped on the way he did."

Jane had tears in her eyes, but she didn't say a word. Tex looked away.

"I shoulda listened to Chris. We had a plan. We said we'd determine where he was staying so we could get information on his bank account and hopefully recover the money he took from me and Cloris and no telling who all. I'm sorry."

She paused and let out a big sigh.

"Liz," I said, "don't beat yourself up about this. Like I told you yesterday, things are changing. And, after sleeping on it, I think the change is to our benefit. Virgil made a huge mistake on the golf course. Since he knows we're searching for him, all he had to do was hide. Instead, he came after us. I'm confident he'll do that again. And every time he does, we get another opportunity to find him. I'm a little concerned about how long this is taking and whether we can retrieve the money before the bank payment is due, but we can worry about that when the time comes."

Liz's eyes popped open. "You mean I did good?"

"Well," I stalled. "The original plan wasn't bad. But at least we didn't lose him altogether like I thought we would. What you did may help us in the long run." I had to give her something. She needed it.

She jumped to her feet and danced around the room. Our old Liz was back.

"So, what's next?" Tex asked.

I wanted to get back to London, back to my computer so I could check in with my students. But we didn't have a lead. We didn't know if Virgil was still here or had headed back himself. "I think we should go back to Angela's flat and wait for Virgil to make another mistake."

"Oh, oh," Liz stuttered. "Can we stop in Edinburgh on the way? I always wanted to go there. So many writers either lived in or wrote about Edinburgh. Robert Burns, Robert Louis Stevenson, Sir Walter Scott, and Arthur Conan Doyle. It is a dream place for librarians."

"Don't forget JK Rowling," I said. It wouldn't hurt to take a couple of days off from the search. I had an idea of a way to use the Internet to get help tracking Virgil. Maybe a rest in Edinburgh would help solidify the idea. If only I had my laptop.

"Oh, yeah," Tex said. "She's my favorite. I've seen all the Harry Potter movies."

"But have you read the books?" Jane asked.

"Please, can we go?" Liz asked.

"Sure," I said. "It'd be silly not to see Edinburgh when

we're this close." I thought about the bank loan and the approaching due date for the balloon payment, but only briefly.

We paid our bill at the B&B and climbed into the bookmobile for the fifty-mile trip to Edinburgh. We found a place to stay there and spent two glorious days touring the city. We didn't get to see everything Liz wanted to see, but we were there long enough to make her happy. We had to go shopping again. I had to buy another shirt and more underwear and socks. No one complained about not having their suitcases and Liz was in what she called hog heaven, especially when we found a tour of the city that highlighted places where famous authors had lived or visited. In my spare time, I made notes about a plan I began to call The Thief.

***

When we got back to London, I dropped everyone off at Angela's building before going to park the bookmobile. After pulling into my usual spot, I took my recently purchased clothes and toiletries and the drone suitcase and walked to the pub. As soon as I got to Angela's floor, I was met by Liz, Jane, and Tex.

"Somebody was here again," Liz said.

"What?" I asked. "Was Virgil in Angela's room again?"

"No," Tex said. "Your room."

"And it wasn't Virgil," Jane added.

The thought of anyone in my room uninvited irritated me. "Slow down and tell me what happened."

"When we got to Angela's door," Liz said, "some man came out of your room. I thought he was from the pub downstairs and I was going to give him a hug. That spooked him."

"I recognized him," Tex said. "It was one of Virgil's golfing buddies. He pushed Liz out of the way and ran. I hollered at him to stop, but of course he didn't. He went down the stairs. Jane chased him, but he got away."

"Are you okay?" I asked Liz.

"Sure. I hit the floor with my bottom, so I had plenty of padding." She laughed at her joke.

"What was he doing in my room?"

"We don't know," Liz said. "You better check to see if anything's missing. We checked Angela's room and I think everything's there. Of course, we'll need you to look, too. He may've messed with her computer again."

I went into my room and was followed by the three of them. We'd left town in such a hurry, I'd left everything here except the drone. The first thing I checked for was my laptop. The textbook I was writing was on it, but it was backed up on the cloud every time I made a change to the files. It was there. Right where I left it. Everything else, clothes, suitcase, and all were there.

"I don't see anything missing," I said. "Was he carrying something when he left?"

"There was nothing in his hands," Tex said. "But if you had something small he could have put in his pocket."

"I had my billfold and passport with me. Maybe you

scared him away before he had a chance to do anything, or get anything."

"I hope so," Liz said.

"Looks like we might be dealing with a gang, not just a lone man," Jane said.

"That's possible," I said, "but I don't think we need to do anything differently because of it. We have to find where Virgil put the money and try to get it back."

I headed toward the door, but stopped when an idea hit me. "Wait a minute. Maybe he's the computer expert for Virgil. He could be the one who planted the computer bugs and he came back to fix them."

"Didn't we think it was Virgil based on Clarence's description?" Jane asked.

"Yes, but, based on Clarence's description, it could have been Virgil or any his friends."

I grabbed my laptop and turned it on. Everyone waited silently. "Yep. He fixed the bug."

"And probably the one across the hall, too," Tex said.

I modified the bug again and then we all went to Angela's flat to check the computer there. It had also been tampered with. I fixed it while the others checked to see if anything was missing.

"Anyone want tea?" Liz asked.

"Sounds good," I said, glad to see she was back to normal.

Tex helped Liz while Jane and I sat at the dining table.

"Something's been bothering me," Jane said.

"What's that?" I asked.

"Isn't it against the law for you to break into

someone's bank account and take money out of it?"

Tex rolled over to the table carrying a tray of cups and saucers that clinked as he went. "It's not Virgil's money. It's Liz's and Cloris's," he said as he distributed the dishes.

"So," Jane said, "you're saying it's okay to steal the money because he stole it first? Two wrongs don't make a right, you know." She glanced to Liz. "Surely you see the problem with this plan."

"I certainly do," Liz said. "That's why I've instructed Chris to remove only the money we know was inappropriately taken. That is, we will take only the funds he stole from the bookmobile account and the money he took from Cloris."

Jane threw her hands into the air. "Don't you understand that's illegal?"

Liz gazed at me for the longest time before her eyes narrowed. "Is she right? Would you be breaking the law by getting my money back?"

Before I could answer, the electric water-heating pot signaled it was ready. I waited as the bubbling sound of boiling water diminished.

Liz poured water into the four cups. "Well?" she asked.

I put a tea bag in my cup. "Jane is technically correct. It is illegal for me to transfer money out of Virgil's bank account."

"Well, then we can't do it," Liz said. "I'll not have you break the law. I couldn't live with myself if you went to prison because of me."

I wished Tex would help, but he shrugged before I

asked him.

"Look," I said. "If what you're concerned about is me going to jail, that's not going to happen."

"How can you be so sure?" Liz asked.

"Yes, how?" Jane added.

"Chris knows how to get in and out electronically without leaving a trail," Tex said.

Jane continued to talk to me. "What about the place where you transfer the money," Jane asked. "Can't the authorities find you that way?"

"First of all," I said, "Virgil isn't going to report a theft. What would he tell them? How could he explain the money?"

"His bank may report the missing money to law enforcement without Virgil doing anything," Jane said.

"No they won't," Tex said. "Not unless Virgil complains, and I don't think he will."

"Even if someone reports the missing money, no one will be able to trace it. I've set up a special place for the money to be sent. It's an account controlled by law enforcement and it's untraceable."

"Your dad helped, huh?" Tex said.

"So, it's illegal, but law enforcement will know about it and help you hide the money?" Liz asked.

"Sort of," I said. "A special branch of law enforcement, anyway."

"Okay," Liz said. "I say we do it."

"I guess," Jane said, not sounding convinced. "I still don't like it."

I changed the subject before Jane had time to ask more questions. "Liz, when was the last time you tried to reach Cloris?"

"Oh, I don't know. A couple of days ago, I guess. About the time my cell phone battery was drained. I'm charging it now. I guess we should go over there again and see if she's returned."

"Have you heard back from the police chief in Austin?" I asked.

"No. But he may have called while my phone wasn't working."

"She may have checked out," I added. "Let's go over there as soon as we finish our tea. Take her passport with you."

"Oh, yeah. I forgot I had that."

CHAPTER NINETEEN

"She's still not answering her phone," Liz said. "Of course, she could be on a plane heading home."

I doubted it. Liz had her passport. We agreed to go check on Cloris as soon as we finished our tea, but I didn't remind Liz and soon I was busy on my computer talking to students and doing my job as a teacher. That, plus thinking about Angela. We hadn't had much time together and there was a lingering concern she might be closer friends with Andrew than I had thought. Still, I was glad for the short time we'd had together and I wanted more. Bottom line, I was willing to stay as long as necessary.

Thinking about Angela made me want to hear her voice. I took my phone and went to the hall. She didn't answer so I left her a voice mail message. "It's me. I miss you. Call first chance you get. Love you."

I was getting pretty gutsy saying "I love you," like

that, but it was true. I just hope it didn't scare her off, especially if Andrew was still in the picture. Or, ever had been. To be honest, I didn't know.

When I got back in the room, Jane was talking about how she longed to see the kids.

"I just miss them so much," she said. "This is the first time we've left them. I trust Tex's parents to care for them and I talk to them every day, but I need to hold them in my arms."

"Me too," Tex said. "I guess if we were doing more good, like if we had Virgil in our sights, I'd want to stay longer. But I don't see that happening. Not only has he kept us from following him, he's now stalking us."

Jane leaned over and hugged him. "And don't forget about school. This is your senior year and you've already missed the first week of classes."

"I'd forgotten about that." Tex glanced at me. "Hey, buddy, I'm sorry, but I think we better go home as soon as we can make flight arrangements."

I nodded, but didn't say anything.

"I understand, Percy," Liz said. "You two go on home and hug those babies of yours."

I thought I saw a tear in Liz's eye, but she turned and walked away before I could be sure. She was always so strong on the outside, it was easy to forget she could be hurting.

She twisted back toward us. "I guess we all should go home." She looked me in the eye as if waiting for me to argue with her. I kept quiet.

"We've lost the bookmobile fund, haven't we?" It was more of a statement than a question. "And now we owe

Andrew for the bookmobile I insisted we buy. I'm not an administrator. I'm a librarian. I need to realize I don't know the first thing about managing a library. I'll resign as soon as I get back home and beg them to let me go back to working as a librarian. Maybe on the bookmobile, if we have one."

"Ma'am," Tex said. "Don't put yourself down like that. What happened to you could've happened to anyone. You're an excellent boss and I'd hate to lose you."

She smiled, but it was forced, not her usual full-blown smile. "Thank you, Percy, but you know I don't know anything about being a boss. I didn't get my degree until I was in my sixties and I never worked for anyone until I was hired as the bookmobile librarian in Austin. I still haven't learned to use a computer."

"But you're a natural leader," I said. "I've seen the way you get people to do things and, at the same time, make them feel privileged to do it. You call on experts when you need to. Everyone loves you, and the library has prospered under your direction."

"Thank you, Chris," she said, "but I know my limitations."

"Liz," Jane said, "I often caution against making decisions such as this hastily. I hope you'll wait until you've been home for a while before you do anything official."

"Right," I said. "Besides, I still think we can get the bookmobile money back. I understand if you all want to go home. I'm going to stay until Angela returns, and while I'm here I'm going to keep trying to find Virgil."

"But you don't know where she is or when she'll be back," Jane said.

"I know, but I can stay rent free and I can do my work from here so it doesn't affect my job."

"What about your apartment back home?" Jane asked. "Need us to check on it when we get back to Texas?"

"No. I got my neighbor to keep an eye out. I stopped the mail and I'm paying my bills online."

"I feel bad leaving you here all alone," Liz said, "but I'm going home. I'm going to call Matt and Marie the way they told me to. If they're going home soon, I'll hitch a ride with them. Otherwise, I'm flying commercial."

"Okay," I said, "but promise me you won't resign as director of library services until you give me a little more time to get the money back."

She didn't respond right away. "Okay. But I don't think I should wait long to do this. A week okay?"

"Sure," I said, thinking a month would be more like it, based on our progress so far.

Liz called Matt, but there was no answer. She left a voice mail telling him she was ready to go home.

We never did go to Cloris's hotel to check on her. I thought of it before I said goodnight and went to my room across the hall, but I didn't tell Liz. We could do it just as well tomorrow. Besides, I wanted to get started on my new plan.

***

I stayed up past midnight working on my idea. It was worth it. Before climbing into bed I had a new website on the Internet. It told the story of how the bookmobile money had been stolen and provided an easy way to send donations to help Liz get the bookmobile she wanted. All I needed now was a little publicity.

I knew Liz would never approve the request for help so I decided not to tell her. I sent the URL to Brian and asked him to let everyone know about the webpage and the need for donations without telling Liz. He promised to take care of it, and I knew he would. Knowing him, he'd pay for advertising if he had to. He was that kind of guy and he had a special love for Liz.

I woke to the sound of someone knocking on my door. As soon as she spoke I knew it was Liz. "Hey, sleepyhead, are you in there?"

"I'm here."

"Well, it's time to get up. Breakfast is ready."

"Okay, thanks. Be there in a minute."

The magic aroma of coffee reached me from across the hall. I slipped on pants and a shirt and trudged to Angela's in my bare feet. Coffee first, shower later. I followed my nose in my quest for a cup of java and soon got a whiff of bacon cooking. That put more snap in my stride.

I sat at the table across from Tex who had already cleaned his plate and was sipping his coffee while working on a crossword puzzle.

"Where's Jane?" I asked.

"Running," he said.

"Is that safe?" I asked. "Her being on the streets alone

like that?"

"I don't think she'll hurt anyone," he said. "Unless they deserve it."

Liz laughed.

"You know what I mean," I said. "Since Virgil and his friends are stalking us, we need to look out for each other. That means not going out alone."

"You've seen her muscles," Tex said. "She keeps them that way by what she eats and how she exercises. She runs every day. I can't stop her and can't run with her."

"We need to be more careful," I said. "There's no telling what Virgil might do."

"Jane can take care of herself," Tex said.

The door opened and Jane came in. I knew it was cold outside, but she wore a tee shirt with "I'd flex, but I like this shirt," on the front of it.

"I heard my name mentioned through the door. What'd I do now?"

Tex laughed. "Chris is worried about you running alone."

"Percy said you wouldn't hurt anyone unless they needed it."

Jane didn't respond to Liz. She'd probably heard Tex say the same thing before. She turned to me for an answer. Sweat glistened on her body, but she breathed normally.

"I'm concerned about Virgil and his friends. I think we need to watch each other's backs while you're here. That's all."

"Thanks, Chris," she said, "Want to go with me tomorrow?"

Tex snickered.

I wasn't about to let Tex see me try to get out of it. Besides, I needed the exercise. Before this trip, I had been going to the fitness center regularly and could now walk without pain from the gunshot wound I had gotten when Sarah was killed.

"I'd like that," I said. How hard could it be? They planned to go home soon anyway.

Tex and Liz looked at me with raised eyebrows.

"I may not be able to keep up with her," I said, "but at least I'll be nearby if trouble arises." And hopefully not too exhausted to help.

"Don't worry," Jane said. "We'll be leaving soon. We're waiting for Liz to hear from her friends with the plane. She said it was big enough for all of us. I usually go about seven each morning, and I can take it a little slower if you like."

"Seven, it is," I said, hoping I wouldn't make too big a fool of myself.

***

After breakfast, Liz and I went to check on Cloris while Jane and Tex got into costume to watch for Virgil on the street.

We didn't go to the desk clerk first. Instead, we went directly to Cloris's room. The "Do Not Disturb" door hanger was no longer there. I wondered if Virgil had removed it when he was there the other day, or whether it was an indication that Cloris had been there.

Liz knocked.

No answer.

Liz tried the keycard the desk clerk had given her the last time we were here, but it didn't work. It was probably only good for that day.

We took the elevator to the ground floor and found the same desk clerk on duty.

"Hi," Liz said holding out the keycard. "Remember me?"

He glanced at her and quickly changed his initial frown to a forced smile when he saw who it was. He took the keycard and put it on the counter.

"Yes," he said. "You were here last week to see your sister."

"That's right," Liz said. "My younger sister Cloris."

"I hope you found her," he said.

"Nope. Still looking. Did she ever check out?"

"No, but her paid time expired so we assumed she left without checking out. It happens all the time."

"When we were here last, her suitcase was in the room. You didn't happen to find it, did you?" Liz asked.

"Let me check."

The clerk entered a room next to the main desk. When he came back, he said, "It's not where we keep unclaimed property so I guess she took it with her."

Liz looked at me and I shrugged.

"You don't happened to have a guest by the name of Virgil Golden?" I asked.

He pulled the computer monitor closer to him and punched some keys. After a few seconds, he responded. "No one registered by that name."

"Thank you," I said.

Liz and I sat in a sofa in the lobby near the hotel entrance, far enough away so that we could talk without the clerk hearing our conversation.

"You know what's odd about this," Liz said, "is that I still have her passport."

"I was thinking the same."

"Without a passport, the airline wouldn't let her get on a plane back to the States."

"I guess she could've gone to the US Embassy and got her passport replaced. But that would take time, and, like Jane said, she'd call."

"It's been five days since I took it."

"I don't know how long it takes to get a new passport, but I suspect it could be done in that time. I wonder if the Embassy will tell us whether or not she was there."

"Maybe. Do you know where it is?"

"No, but we can find it."

We stood to leave, but an idea hit me before we moved. "Liz, I know you've been calling Cloris frequently, but have you tried her home phone?"

"No. I've been assuming she was still in London. Do you think she could be back in Austin?"

"Well, she could be if she got another passport."

"I guess," Liz said, "but that doesn't explain why she hasn't answered her cell phone."

"Perhaps she lost it."

"Could happen." Liz said. "But I don't know her home number."

"I can find it on my phone, unless it's unlisted." I clicked on the White Pages app and typed in her name, city and state. A listing popped up. I showed it to Liz.

"You want me to call her? All I have to do is touch here to call her home phone number."

"Do it."

I pressed the number and waited. My phone was set to automatically add the country codes so the phone began to ring. I pressed the speaker button so Liz could listen in.

"Hello," said a man's voice.

"Hello," I said. "Is Cloris there?"

"Who's calling?"

"Uhh, this is a friend calling for Cloris Parker. Is she there? This is an urgent call."

Liz nodded.

"What's your name?" the man on the phone asked.

Liz moved the phone nearer to her mouth. "Listen, this is Liz Siedo in London, England. That's in the United Kingdom. We're calling to see if Cloris got home okay. Who are you?"

"You say you're in London?"

"Yes we are. Now, who are you? I'm going to call my friend Tom, who happens to be the chief of police there in Austin, if you don't tell me why you're answering Cloris's phone."

"Liz Siedo? Are you the library director? What are you doing in London?"

"Until I know who you are," Liz said, "that's none of your business."

"Ma'am, this is the Austin Police and we're at Ms. Parker's home investigating a crime."

CHAPTER TWENTY

"A crime?" Liz asked. "What kind of crime?"

There was a long pause.

"Ma'am, I'm sorry to tell you your friend is deceased."

"Deceased?" Liz said. "Oh, my. That's terrible." She looked at me with eyes opened wide and mouthed the word "deceased" as if I hadn't heard it already.

"How did she die?" Liz asked.

"We don't have all the details, but the investigators suspect foul play."

"Was her body found in her home?"

"No, ma'am. Her body was found floating in the Thames near the Tower of London."

"Oh, my goodness," Liz said. "She died in London?"

"Yes, ma'am. The police there are going to want to talk to you. Can you tell me where you're staying and how they can reach you?"

"Of course," Liz said.

We gave them Angela's address and Liz's phone number before we said good-bye. We stayed in the hotel lobby staring at each other without speaking.

Finally, Liz pulled out Cloris's passport and thumbed through it. "She didn't need this after all. Makes me wonder how they identified the body," she said.

"She could have had her purse with a driver's license in it."

"I guess," Liz said.

"The police will probably want this passport and want to know when we saw her last and all that."

"I'm sure."

Liz held her head in her hands. She was quiet for so long I wondered if she was praying. We sat there a few minutes more before Liz stood and kicked the sofa we'd been sitting on. She kicked it hard enough for the desk clerk's head to turn toward us. I stood, too, thinking we should leave before Liz alerted the desk clerk more.

"Virgil did this," she said, with her hands on her hips. She locked her eyes on mine. "Did you think he'd do this? I didn't think he was a killer. A con man, yes, but I didn't think he'd actually hurt someone. I can't believe I cared for that creep the way I did. And I can't believe I didn't warn Cloris to stay away from him. I didn't know. I should've helped her."

I wanted to put an arm around Liz and calm her, but I couldn't. She was so agitated she kept moving around. "He fooled us all," I said. "But I felt he could be dangerous. Remember how close he came to killing

Karen several times before he disappeared. And, if you remember, Jane warned Cloris about him."

"I know about Karen. I guess I wanted to believe he was just trying to scare her."

"He did that and more," I said.

"I'd planned to go home and forget about this, but not now. I'm staying until we catch him."

Liz headed toward the door and I followed.

When we got to Angela's flat and told Jane and Tex about Cloris's death, they both were shocked. Jane prayed to help us all regain our balance. Tex and Jane talked alone for a few minutes and said they had decided to stay and help find Virgil, too. Jane called Tex's parents and asked them if they could keep the kids longer and they were delighted.

An investigator from Scotland Yard showed up and took statements from all of us.

Liz called Matt and Marie and told them she'd decided to stay in England longer. When I told Jane I'd run with her, I had thought it would only be that one time and then they'd be gone. But now that they'd decided to stay, I had to keep at it. That's why, when my phone rang early the next morning, I was awake and in the process of getting my running clothes on. I looked at the phone and the caller ID was a number I didn't recognize.

"Hello," I said.

"Thank God!"

"Angela?"

"Don't scare me like that. What's going on?"

I'd never heard her sound so concerned about me. It

was sort of nice. Except I didn't like being the cause of her emotional outburst.

She didn't wait for an answer. "My office contacted me and said my address had come up as the site of a murder investigation. All I could think of was something had happened to you. Who was it?"

I thought about how she was probably behind enemy lines, or what special agents considered lines, and how the nature of her job frightened me daily. And here she was worrying about me. I understood why. She had received a report that something was seriously wrong and she didn't know who was involved.

"I'm sorry," I said. "It was Cloris. Her body washed up on the Thames near the Tower of London. We don't know what happened yet, but we think Virgil may have killed her. We gave your address to the police in case they wanted to talk to us."

"Who is 'we'," she asked.

"Oh, I guess I haven't talked to you in a while. First, Tex and Jane came with Cloris so Jane could follow Cloris to find Virgil. He would've recognized me and Tex. Just as we had him where we wanted him, Liz appeared unexpectedly and scared him off."

"They're all there?"

"Yes. I hope you don't mind. They're staying at your place."

There was a long pause. "No. That's okay. I don't know when I'll be back. But I'm concerned about all of you. If Virgil murdered Cloris, that means he's more than just a thief. He may decide to come after the rest of you. I think you should all go home and let law enforcement handle it."

"Law enforcement isn't going to get back the money he stole."

"Don't risk your life and the lives of your friends for money. It's not worth it."

"We'll be careful."

"Who found the body?" Angela asked.

"I don't know. We hadn't been able to reach her so Liz and I called her home phone to see if she had left without telling us. The Austin police answered. I guess they'd been investigating there after Scotland Yard contacted them. Since Liz works for the city and knows the police chief in Austin, they gave us more information than they would give just anyone calling on the phone." I felt strangely happy to know that Angela called. "So how did you hear about it?"

"I haven't heard any details," Angela said. "All I know is that my London address is included in a murder investigation database. My office watches for things like that. They cross-reference employee addresses with criminal investigations, just in case."

"Actually, Liz, Jane, and Tex were planning to leave soon. Now, after hearing about Cloris, they want to stay and help find Virgil."

"What about you? Were you planning to leave?"

"No. I'm going to stay until I see you again."

"That's nice. I..." Her voiced changed from concern about my wellbeing to something I thought could be love. "I don't know when that will be. What about your job?"

"It's okay. All my classes are online and the college

told me I don't have to attend faculty meetings again until I feel like it."

"Must be nice."

"It is. I love the freedom to travel, especially if it means I can see you."

"So, what are you going to do about finding Virgil, or the money?"

"You said Virgil may come after us. Well, I think he already has. Not to harm us, but to scare us off. We have reason to believe he and some friends are stalking us now, but we're being careful and trying to use it to our advantage. Jane has been running every morning to stay in shape so I go with her to watch for possible danger. We're all being careful and watching each other, and especially since we heard about Cloris."

"You're running? That's great."

I wasn't sure if she was saying I needed to lose a few pounds, but I decided to take her words as a compliment. "Jane takes exercising seriously. Since you saw her last, she has become a physical fitness prize winner. She's lean and muscular and full of energy. Sort of like you."

"Prize winner? You mean for bodybuilding?"

"Yes. She's got trophies all over the house. Got one in London. We used the event to lure Virgil out, but we lost him again."

"Well, that's wonderful. Not losing Virgil, but Jane's competition. It's not my thing."

"Yes, but you are lean and muscular."

"I stay in shape, but for different reasons."

"I know, you need lots of stamina for your job."

"Right. Well, I'd better get off this phone. It's for business only. I was so worried about you, I had to call. If I can't talk you into going home, I will get my office to send you what they learn about Cloris's death. Someone will deliver it to my flat soon."

"Thanks. I'm sorry I scared you." My mind told me to shut up and get off the phone, but my mouth kept talking. "Angela, is there anything between you and Andrew?"

"Are you crazy?" she asked.

"That answered my question. Remember, I'll be here until you get home. Love you."

The phone call ended without her loving me back. After she disconnected, I began to wonder if she asked me if I was crazy for thinking there was something between her and Andrew or because I asked during an emergency call.

***

Two days after I talked to Angela, Jane and I returned from our morning run to find a young man in a black suit and crew cut in the hallway outside Angela's flat. He was just about to knock when we got there. When he saw that I had a key to the room, he handed me a package.

"This is for Angela," he said without a greeting or as much as a smile, and thrust the object toward me.

I knew he must be the courier from Angela's London office. That didn't stop my body from going on full alert. I had become suspicious of everyone. The manila envelope was approximately nine by twelve inches in size and had a white label with Angela's name written by hand with a thick black marker. He must have known she wouldn't be home. He didn't ask for her and gave the envelope to me.

"I'll make sure she gets it," I said, assuming we were playing a game of making the transfer of information to me an acceptable transaction.

That was all it took. The young man turned and left without another word. I wondered what he would have done if I'd told him the truth and said she wasn't here and I didn't know when I'd see her again.

I shut the door and held the envelope for all to see. "I think this is the report on Cloris's death from Angela's office. But what if it's something for Angela?"

"Open it," Tex said. "She told you she'd have her office send us case reports."

"Yeah, but is this it or something for Angela alone? It doesn't say what's inside." I flipped the envelope over and showed him the name label.

"Don't worry," he said, "if it was for her only, the messenger would have said so. If it's not what we think it is, we'll apologize later."

It still bothered me to open it, and I wasn't sure why. I could feel my stress level rising and I obsessed on the envelope for a few seconds wondering why the label was crooked. It's not that hard to use a ruler and put labels where they should be. If Angela was here she'd stop me about now and tell me to relax. My need for an orderly world sometime got in the way of living.

I opened the envelope with the crooked label and

placed the contents on the table. Tex and Jane leaned in.

Liz moved away. "Oh, please," she said, "don't let there be any photos of the body. We don't have to see the body, do we?" She turned around with her back to the table. "Tell me when I can open my eyes."

I checked through the papers and didn't find any photos. "There are no photos, Liz. You can turn around now. However, there may be a description of what they found."

"That's okay," Liz said. "I can read about it, but I can't stand seeing it."

We pored over the documents for the next hour. None of us were trained in law enforcement, but Tex and I had seen similar reports during our criminal investigations. We learned Cloris died from blunt force trauma and was dead before being placed in the river. The marks on her face were consistent with being struck with fists.

"Who found the body?" Jane asked.

I scanned the report. "Seems an off-duty Yeoman Warder, whatever that is, spotted something unusual in the water at the Tower of London. After determining it was a body, he called Scotland Yard."

"Do they know time of death?" Tex asked.

I looked through the documents. "Yes. It's estimated to be January 22. That was the day after we saw Virgil at the golf course."

Liz pushed away from the table. "That poor woman. What's going to happen to her son Heath? His life was getting better with Virgil out of the picture. Now this. We need to pray for that boy."

"I will," Jane said.

Liz continued. "He's been staying with his stepmother, Karen, and Brian while Cloris was here. I suspect they'll take care of him."

"Why is living with his mother?" Jane asked. "Does he have mental problems or anything?"

"No," Liz said. "Nothing like that. It's just that Cloris sheltered him in a cocoon of hate and atheism for so long it will take time for him to become a man on his own."

"That's sad," Jane said. "I'll add him to my daily prayer list."

"Let's see what else we can learn about Cloris's death," I said, shuffling the papers on the table looking for ones we hadn't studied. "Here's a summary. It says her injuries couldn't have been caused by falling and that they had to have been caused by another person."

"I'm thinking Virgil did it," Liz said. "I'm just thankful it didn't happen to me."

"We all are," Jane said.

"But," I said, "there's nothing in the file indicating Virgil is responsible."

"He did it," Tex said.

"I agree he's the most likely, but it could have been one of those guys we saw with him at the golf course."

"Yeah," Liz said, "but he'd be involved. They would have done it for him."

"What else do we know?" Tex asked.

I held out a piece of paper. "Here is a list of Cloris's credit card charges for the past week."

Everyone leaned in to see the list.

"When did we see her last?" Liz asked.

"Jane talked to her on the phone January 10 and I saw her that night at Jane's competition."

Everyone stared at me.

"What?" I asked.

"How do you do that?" Jane asked. "That was two weeks ago. You said that as if you know it's true without looking at a calendar."

Tex snickered. "He remembers things."

I shrugged. "I don't know how I do it. Until I started school, I thought everyone remembered things like that. Cloris went to Stratford with us on the eighth. We all came back here. That night she left saying she was going back to her hotel. Jane talked to her by phone reminding her to get Virgil to go to the competition two days later. I saw them leave through a side door. We never talked to her or saw her again after that."

Tex held the credit card charges report. "Either they're wrong about the time of death or someone used her credit card after she died. Look at this."

Tex pointed at the sheet, placing his finger on the activities after the estimated time of death. "It's mostly hotel charges, but there are several purchases made at petrol stations."

"It's possible she had given the hotel her card number and they charged to it daily for as long as she stayed there or some date she'd given them. Virgil could have easily used her card for gasoline without anyone questioning him. I guess law enforcement will check security cameras at the fuel stations to see who used the credit card after the time of death."

"Probably," Liz said. "But what good would that do?

We know what they'd find."

"Not necessarily," I said. "Don't forget he had three friends with him at the golf course."

"Anything else in those papers?" Jane asked.

"No," I said, "that's about it. Not much to go by is there? Nothing that will move us closer to finding Virgil or the money, anyway."

"Still," Liz said, "we've got to locate him. Not just because of the money. We need to make sure he's taken into custody and stands trial for what he did to poor Cloris."

Liz's phone rang.

"Excuse me," she said as she grabbed it and pressed the answer button.

"Hello," she said with her happy voice as if we hadn't been going over murder investigation records all morning. "Thanks for calling me back. How is Heath doing?"

She was silent for a while.

"I'm so glad he is with you and Karen. That boy needs help to get through this. I'm thinking God picked you two and put you into Heath's life just in the nick of time."

She listened again.

"He did?" She looked at me with piercing eyes.

"Well, thank you for letting me know. Yes, I'll tell Chris. Give my love to Karen and Heath. Good-bye."

"So, they know about Cloris." Jane said.

Liz didn't take her eyes off me. I knew the last part of the call wasn't about Heath.

"It seems Chris has been working his Internet magic

again. Evidently, he has created some type of webbie something or other for people to donate money to replace the stolen bookmobile money."

"Hey! What a great idea," Tex said. "I wish I'd thought of that."

"Yeah," Jane said. "Why does that upset you, Liz?"

"I don't want to ask people to donate more money just because I was stupid enough to let Virgil steal what they already gave us. It's a little embarrassing, don't you think?"

"It shouldn't be," Jane said. "It wasn't your fault. He's a con man. That's what he does."

"Yeah, but I should have been smarter about it. I can usually read people better than that. Ask anybody who knows me."

"Sure, "Tex said, "you're great at understanding honest people, even those who hide their true feelings. You're good at getting them to talk, too. Virgil is a sociopath. He is a good actor and he lied by telling you what you wanted to hear. You trusted him because you thought he was sincere." Tex rubbed his hands together. "So, how much money did the webpage bring in?"

"Were you in on this, too?" Liz asked turning her glare to him.

Tex showed his palms. "No. All Chris's idea." He laughed. "How much?"

A grin popped onto Liz's face as if she could no longer hold it back. "Brian said the money is still coming in so there's no telling how much more there'll be. Right now we already got twice what Virgil stole."

"Twice?" I asked. I was surprised. Since activating the

site and asking Brian to publicize it, I hadn't checked to see how it was doing. I didn't expect anything like that. I wouldn't be surprised to learn Brian and his friends had made some hefty donations. But, Liz didn't need to know that.

"Yes," Liz said. "He said money is coming in from all around the world, not just from the library patrons in Austin. He said something about twittering and viral stuff. Not sure what all that means. It seems there are many people in this world who love libraries and bookmobiles and hate crooks."

"Thank God," Jane said. "That takes away the pressure of trying to get the money back from Virgil in time to pay off the bank loan. We can go home now."

"Not so fast," Liz said. "I'm glad we don't have that loan deadline to worry about, but I'm not going home until Virgil is in custody. Chris, I want you to empty his bank account if you can."

I smiled. "I can, if we can find him."

Jane didn't say more about going home, but I could tell she was disappointed.

CHAPTER TWENTY-ONE

No matter how hard we worked for the next week, Virgil couldn't be found. Tex and Jane continued to get into costume each day and go on the streets to watch for him. Liz and I wore sunglasses and hats to disguise ourselves and periodically checked Victoria Station and the Underground.

The courier in the black suit brought daily updates on Cloris's murder investigation, but nothing in the subsequent reports helped us find Virgil. He wasn't included in the reports as a suspect.

I continued to connect online with students, but it was routine. My heart wasn't in it. I wasn't making much progress on the textbook and the contract I'd signed with the publisher had some key completion dates looming. I didn't care. Mostly, I thought about

Angela and how much I missed her. She hadn't called again, so I didn't think I'd see her anytime soon.

No one mentioned sightseeing. There were several landmarks on our list of places to see, but I didn't want to do anything that would take time away from the search and I think the rest of the group felt the same. We spent most of each day walking around the neighborhood or thinking and talking about Virgil and making plans to find him.

Nothing seemed to work, though, and I could sense the growing discouragement in our group and suspected they'd be talking about going home again soon.

Jane prayed for guidance every morning after breakfast and I believe the prayer on this eighth day was the reason for the nudge I got. The idea was so beautiful it had to be a God-thing.

Ever since Brian called and told Liz about how the website I'd created had brought in so many donations for the bookmobile fund, I'd been checking it several times a day. Donations continued to come in, although at a slower rate. Still we had twice what was needed to repay the loan. But, beyond the donations, I noticed people were asking if we'd found the thief yet, and they asked if there was anything they could do to help. I was particularly interested when I saw a large number of librarians and bookmobile drivers from the United Kingdom leaving comments and tweeting. That was when the idea began to take shape. But it wasn't until Jane's prayer today that I knew what to do.

"Listen, everyone," I said. "I have an idea. Come join

me at the table so I can describe what I have in mind and get your reaction. I want to know if you think it will work."

Liz and Jane, shoulders drooping and faces sagging, silently left the comfort of the sofa and sat around the table. Tex rolled over to his spot beside Jane.

"Okay. Here it is." I took a deep breath. "Just after Jane's prayer, a fully-developed, detailed plan for catching Virgil came to me."

Liz yawned. Tex sneaked a peek at his crossword puzzle. Only Jane smiled.

I continued. "With the success we've had raising money for the bookmobile fund, I propose we use the same webpage to get people to watch for Virgil."

Tex frowned. "The donations are coming in from around the world, aren't they?"

"Yes, but a substantial number are from the United Kingdom."

"How substantial?" Liz asked.

"Dozens," I said.

"That's not many," Jane said.

"It's more people than we have sitting here. And, if this works the way I think it will, more people will join in the search. These are people Virgil won't recognize. Not just here in London. There are people all over England, Scotland, Wales, and Ireland who are asking how they can help find the thief."

I looked at my three friends. They weren't sold yet. "All we have to do is ask them to watch for him and let us know if they see him. We will also ask them to tweet about it and ask all their friends to watch, too."

"How will they know what he looks like?" Tex asked.

"We'll post photos. I checked and I have several pictures of him on my phone from when we did that investigation for Brian and found him with Cloris when he was supposed to be dating Liz."

"Don't remind me of that," Liz said. "So how are you going to show people his photo?"

"I'll create a public Google map and add pins showing the dates and places where we've seen Virgil. Of course he can see the map, if he happens onto it. However, I don't believe he'll find it. Just in case he does a vanity search, we won't post his name. We'll just call him the thief. That's the name that's gotten started on the web anyway."

Liz looked around the table. "I don't know what Chris is talking about. Does any of what he's saying make sense to y'all?"

Tex smiled and pushed his ten-gallon hat back on his head. "It's brilliant."

"I understand the map part. What about the photos?" Jane asked, looking at me.

"I'll post the photos on the webpage along with his description. If we get feedback, the map will show where he is, or where he was. All we'll have to do is follow the map. People who spot him will add to the map, either a note or a photo at the scene."

I grabbed my pen. "Tex, could I have a piece of paper?" Tex removed the small spiral notebook that was in his left breast shirt pocket and pushed it across the table to me. "Thanks. Now, let's make a list of places where we've seen Virgil and when." Because of my crazy memory I could do this alone. However, I thought it might help everyone's spirit to work on it together. By lunch we completed the list and, after I made a few corrections, I posted the information on the Internet.

Brian must have seen what we were doing and joined in by posting a snapshot from his wedding album. It was a beautiful picture showing Liz and Virgil together at a happier time. Seeing it reminded Tex he had a photo of Virgil on his phone, too. He found it and we added it to the webpage.

Soon, UK librarians and bookmobile drivers added their location pins to the map to let everyone know where they were watching for the thief. Each time someone joined the search, we sent a message and asked if they would invite their friends to help. The number of pins on the map increased rapidly. By the end of the day, there were hundreds of pins all over England, Wales and Scotland, and a half dozen or so in Ireland.

We were no longer alone in our search for Virgil. We had an army of people helping.

***

The next morning, while Jane was lacing her running shoes and I was taking a last sip of coffee, Tex hollered. "There he is!"

He was at the kitchen table in his unusual combination of pajamas and cowboy hat. Instead of his crossword puzzle, he was checking his laptop. "Looky here, everyone. It's Virgil." He pointed to the screen while grinning from ear to ear.

Liz came running from the bedroom, wearing a bathrobe and had her hair wrapped in a towel. "You found Virgil?" she asked.

"Yes," Tex said. "Someone just posted a photo of him on the webpage."

I moved in closer to the screen. "Where is he?"

"I don't know if it says," Jane said, "but you can see he's at an Underground station."

"Which one?" I asked.

"Look," Tex said, "here it is. The guy who posted the photo says it's Tower Hill. Is that an Underground station? I don't recognize it."

"Liz, do you still have that Tube map we got at Victoria Station?" I asked. That was something I hadn't memorized yet.

Liz grabbed a colorful brochure from the table near the sofa. "Yes. Here it is." She placed it on the table next to the computer for us to see.

"Tower Hill," I said, pointing my finger at the map. "There it is. It's east of here, but I can't tell how far away."

"Look," Tex said. "Here it is on Google maps. I think it's about five miles away."

"Should we go now?" Liz asked. "It's not too late, is it?"

"The idea was to watch for a pattern. See which direction he goes," I said. "A single sighting doesn't tell us where he'll be next. Tower Hill is on both the Circle Line and the District Line. He could go either way."

"But," Jane said, "we don't know if anyone will spot him again."

"I think they will," I said. "See how fast this came in.

And see all the map pins along the route. Several of these people, if not all, will go out of their way to find him and at least one of them will see him."

"Some may be busy at work, Chris," Jane said.

"I want to do something," Tex said. "I can't just sit here hoping someone happens to be in the right place to see him. I'm going to Tower Hill." He rolled away from the table.

"Me too," Liz said, pulling the towel off her head, revealing her gray, stringy hair, still wet from her shower. "Just give me a minute to get dressed. If I can find the person who posted that photo, I'm going to give him or her the biggest hug ever."

I searched the faces of my friends and saw smiles that hadn't been there for weeks. "Well, count me in," I said.

After Liz was dressed, we hurried to the Tube Station at Westminster and took the elevator to the next car headed for Tower Hill. I had the laptop with me, but since it only worked with Wi-Fi, we had more success watching the website on my phone.

By the time we got to Tower Hill, no one had posted another word about the thief, so we split up there. Tex and Jane took the Central Line while Liz and I took the District Line.

Tex called when they got back to Westminster and said they were going to Angela's flat. Liz and I took a long, uneventful trip to the end of the line in Upminster. We headed back, still without another thief sighting posted on the webpage. The morning delight brought on by the possibility of finding Virgil quickly turned to disappointment and frustration. I actually wished Jane and I had gone running as we'd planned instead of chasing Virgil.

***

We retreated to the flat to strategize. The new interactive website didn't go viral the way we'd hoped it would. With all the people who had signed up to help, I would have thought there would be a number of Virgil sightings after that first one. But, no. There were none. Jane was right. We couldn't expect people to watch for Virgil around the clock. And to make things worse, there were no additional entries for the next two days. It was discouraging, but we kept watching the screen and asking for help. I used an automatic tweet program and scheduled tweets about the thief for the next few days. There was nothing else we could do since we'd given up sightseeing. I spent some of our down time modifying the website by adding a feature to have it e-mail me when a new comment was posted. I also played with the drone some. Practicing, I called it. While experimenting with the drone I added a new feature. It now had the capability to take a still photo and e-mail it to me.

And, after our experience with the laptop not working without Wi-Fi, we bought a portable satellite dish and router so we could use the laptop pretty much anywhere we wanted. It was expensive, but Liz said we could pay for it out of the bookmobile donations.

Mid-morning on the second day after we'd made the fruitless run to Tower Hill, Jane suggested a prayer meeting. I agreed. We needed some encouragement. But, then something strange happened. As Jane prayed, she described our concerns in a way that seemed too specific, too centered on what we wanted. It wasn't the way I'd been taught to pray.

Still, it worked.

I guess one could argue that what happened next was not related to her prayer at all. If anything, it could be called coincidental.

Immediately after Jane said "amen," the laptop beeped, announcing an incoming message. We all jumped and ran to the table. Before we got there, it had beeped five more times. My phone was beeping, too, because of the e-mail notification feature I'd added to the website. Little pins with photos appeared on the map showing the pattern I'd been hoping for.

Virgil was on the move and was being tracked by a host of helpers, most of whom identified themselves as librarians. The path showed Virgil taking the Underground south to where it ended. From there he was reported to be on a train, continuing south. The last entry was from a librarian in Brighton named Juliet who, after she saw he was heading toward her town, left work early and got to the train station in time to see the thief getting off the train. She posted his photo and followed him to a car rental desk where he rented a beige car and was driving east. She also posted a photo of the rental car and another that zoomed in on the car's license number. She followed him and continued to post comments. When Virgil left Brighton on the A259, she asked for help since she had to get home to fix dinner for her family.

"Let's go," I said. "Now we have a pattern. We have a place and we know what kind of vehicle he's driving."

"Okay," Jane said. "Let's take our suitcases this time. I don't want a repeat of what happened in Scotland."

Liz opened her suitcase and added her toiletries. "I'm ready."

"I'll go pack," I said, heading toward the door to go to my room.

"Don't forget the drone," Tex said.

"Right."

We were in the bookmobile driving toward Brighton when we learned Juliet had been relieved by Thomas, a retired librarian from Newhaven in East Sussex. Thomas's first report was that the thief was heading toward Seaford.

We continued to monitor the webpage as we drove south on the A23 then the M23. It took us about two hours to get to Brighton. From there we took the A27, bypassing the city traffic and getting to Newhaven faster. By the time we got there, Thomas left a post saying the thief had stopped at a grocery store in Seaford, come out with three bags and driven to a residential neighborhood nearby where he parked his car in a garage next to a home and entered the front door with a key, taking his groceries in with him. Thomas posted the address and a photo of the house.

"Tell Thomas we're on our way," I said from the driver's seat.

"Right," Tex said. "I will. Anyone know how long it will take us to get to Seaford?"

"Let me see," Jane said, unfolding her map. "I'd say we should be there in less than thirty minutes."

"Great," I said. "Tell Thomas that and ask him to wait there until we arrive."

"Will do," Tex said.

I was encouraged about how Virgil acted like he was going into his own house, with groceries no less. That could be the place where we get his bank information.

"Thomas said he'd wait for us at the end of the block," Tex said. "He said he can keep an eye on the house from there without being seen by the thief."

Seaford was a small town so we found the street where Thomas waited for us without delay. This neighborhood resembled the suburbs back home, not like the residential areas we'd seen in the larger cities in England. There was little traffic and, unlike the larger cities, few vehicles parked on the street. The yards were smaller than those in the States, with the front of the home a few feet from the street.

"This red double-decker is going to be as conspicuous as a fire truck," I said. "Virgil will spot it for sure."

"Yeah," Jane said. "What can we do?"

There was an intersection ahead. "First, I'm going to get off this street. After we check in with Thomas, I suggest we rent a van."

"Good idea," Liz said.

"There's Thomas's car," Jane said.

A man in a brown corduroy coat and a matching cap stood next to the car. I stopped close to him and opened the bookmobile's front door. "Thomas?"

He nodded with a tip of his hat and climbed on

board.

Liz had him in a bear hug before he was all the way in. "Thank you. Thank you," she said so loudly I was afraid Virgil would hear and recognize her.

Thomas pulled away with a wry grin on his face, perhaps a little alarmed by Liz's outburst.

"You're welcome. You must be Liz the librarian. We were all sorry to hear about the library fund being stolen." He walked to the front window of the bus and pointed. "See that house with the brown stone and green shutters? That's where the thief is. I'd say he plans to stay a while."

"Thomas, this is Percy and his wife, Jane," Liz said. Percy works at the library and Jane's here to help us find Vir...ah, the thief.

Thomas nodded to them. "Nice to meet you."

"You, too. Call me Tex. Is the garage attached to the house?"

Thomas shook his head. "There's no door to the house from inside the garage, if that's what you're thinking."

"Good to know," I said. "So if he leaves, he'll have to leave by the front door to get to the car."

"Right," Thomas said.

Thomas stared at the bookmobile. "Say, isn't this the old Norwich mobile library?"

"Yes," Liz said. "It's a beauty, isn't it?"

"It is," Thomas said, "but some say it's haunted."

"Haunted?" Liz asked, her eyes popping open. "What do you mean?"

"Oh, it's just a rumor. Seems the driver and the

SIDNEY W. FROST

librarian disappeared one day and were never found. Some think they ran off together, but others suspect foul play. The library couldn't get anyone to staff it after that. I guess that's why they put it up for sale."

"And," Jane said, "that's why it is in such great shape. We thought they'd decided to sell it because it was worn out."

"No," Thomas said, "it's not too old. I bet you got a good deal...long as you don't believe in ghosts. By the way, this thing's going to be hard to hide around here. What's the plan?"

"We were just thinking the same thing as soon as we saw the neighborhood," I said. "We're thinking about parking it in town and renting a van to stake out the house."

"Good idea," Thomas said. "If you like I could stay here while you nip into town and sort out that rental. I'd lend you my car, but I see you need a bigger vehicle than I've got."

"Thanks," I said. "Liz, why don't you and Jane stay with Thomas while Tex and I go into town?"

"Okay with you, Thomas?" Liz asked.

"Absolutely. Come on." He climbed out of the bookmobile and held open the door of his car. Jane climbed into the back and Liz took the passenger seat in front.

"Call us if the thief leaves the house," I said. I shut the door and drove away, following the route that would lead back into the main part of town.

"Tex, while I'm driving, can you update the website? We need to let everyone know where we are and what's

226

going on."

"Sure will."

It was mid-afternoon and I wanted to rent a van and find a place to store the bus and get back before Virgil was on the run again.

CHAPTER TWENTY-TWO

Tex and I had been on enough stakeouts in the past two years to know how boring they can be. Liz was snoring in the back seat. Jane was reading her Kindle. Tex was playing Solitaire on his phone. I was staring at the house where Virgil was and trying to think of a way to make something happen. If he would leave, perhaps go out for dinner, I could break into his house, find his bank account information and retrieve the stolen bookmobile money plus what he took from Cloris. But Thomas had said Virgil looked as if he was settled in for the night. With those groceries he'd bought on his way there, he was probably enjoying a home-cooked meal while we ate chocolate bars and potato chips Liz had brought with her from London.

I was anxious to try the drone, but if all went as

planned, it'd be faster and easier to go in by foot. Of course, that increased the chance of being seen and getting caught.

I opened another candy bar and the sound or smell woke Liz. Now, instead of snoring, I heard her stomach growling. I tossed her a chocolate candy bar.

"Listen," I said, "we need a plan. As you can tell by my snacking and Liz's stomach, we can't sit here all day and night hoping Virgil will go somewhere. We'll need real food, drinks and restrooms before long. Also, we should change where we park from time to time. There aren't many vehicles on this street, so sooner or later one of the residents is going to get suspicious and call the police."

Liz's stomach growled again, louder this time, causing everyone to laugh.

"I'm okay," she said. "Don't change plans because of me. I can go for hours without eating." She bit off half the candy bar I'd given her.

"Chris is right," Tex said. "Virgil could be hunkered down for a long time waiting for the police to lose interest in him."

"I agree," Jane said, "he may not leave for days. We need to prod him out of there so Chris can get in with the drone and find where the stolen money is stashed. Is that what you're thinking, Chris?"

"Yes. Rather than wait for him, why not let him know we're here and see what happens."

"Good idea," said Tex. "And if this is his own house, the way it appears, or if he has stayed here for any length of time, there's a better chance we'll find the bank information we need."

"Sounds logical," Jane said.

"I got an idea," Liz said. "When we let him know we're here, he'll either chase us or run. Either way, you wait with the drone and investigate the place while he's gone."

"How are you going to lure him away?" I asked. "It could be dangerous. We don't want him to catch you."

"We could take the van," Jane said. "You don't need it to fly the drone. All you need to do is hide around the corner there until he takes off after us."

"But," Tex said, "Chris may need transportation. How about this? What if we take the bookmobile instead? He'll probably recognize it. There's a good chance he saw us in St. Andrews since he was following us on the golf course. That way, Chris could stay in the van. He can monitor the drone easier and he'll have a way to take off in a hurry if necessary. "

"That makes sense," I said. "But who will drive the bookmobile?"

"I will," Liz said, waving her hand in the air. "I drove Brian's several times back when I worked on the bookmobile." She smiled. "Oh, those were fun days. All I did was talk to people, interesting people, and check out books. I didn't care one wit about an annual budget or hiring and firing people. It was just plain fun. Maybe I should demote myself when I get home. It'd be my last official act as director of library services."

I shook my head. "This bookmobile is not as easy to drive as Brian's is. It's twice the size and slow when you take off. Plus, it has a stick shift. Have you driven a vehicle with a stick shift?"

She laughed, her trademark guffaw. Even though we were a block away, I was afraid Virgil recognize her laugh it was so unique.

"You are so sweet. Haven't you noticed I'm older than automatic transmissions? If not, thank you. When I learned to drive, and for years after that, all we had was stick shift. Some of the richer folks had automatics, but it was years before we common folk did." She laughed again just to make her point.

I was still concerned about whether she could drive the double-decker bus. "Liz, you know the steering wheel is on the right side and gears are shifted with your left hand?"

"Well, sure," she said. "I can do it."

"While driving on the left side of the road?"

"Sure."

"And while someone is chasing you?"

"Huh? Oh, yeah. Sure."

"Jane," I said, "what do you think? It's dangerous, but I can't think of a better plan."

Jane paused, as if thinking it over. "How about this. We'll call a taxi to drive us to the bookmobile so we don't have to abandon the watch. While we're gone, you can get the drone ready to fly. Before we return, Liz will practice driving. Tex and I will make sure she's qualified before we attempt anything more. Is that okay with you, Liz?"

"Yes. That's an excellent plan."

"And," Jane added, "you agree to abide by our decision?"

"Huh? Oh, of course."

"Okay, Jane," I said. "I think this will work. And once y'all lure Virgil away, I'll stay on the phone with you the entire time. Not a phone call from time to time, but an open line. Agreed?"

"I can handle the phone," Tex said.

"Okay," I said. "And when you get back, turn the bookmobile around before you let Virgil know you're here."

"Good idea," Tex said. "But instead of turning around, we'll just drive around the block so we'll be heading away from here." Tex pointed to the street he was talking about. "That'll make it easier for Liz."

"That's better," I said. "How are you going to let him know you're here?"

Everyone was quiet.

"I know," Tex said. "I'll toss a rock at his window to get his attention."

"Should work," I said, looking at Virgil's house. "Toss it at the window just left of the door. And make sure it breaks the glass."

"Be glad to," Tex said, smiling.

"Why break the glass?" Jane asked.

"To give Chis a place to get in," Tex said.

"Yes," I said. "The window opens left and right and it's a perfect place to fly the model helicopter into the house. If it's locked, the broken pane will give me a way to reach in and unlock the window."

"You be careful, Chris," Liz said.

"You, too. Now where are you going to lead Virgil?" I asked.

"What about those tourist signs we saw on the way in?" Jane asked. "They mentioned the name of a park nearby."

"The signs said SEVEN SISTERS COUNTRY PARK," I said.

"That sounds good," Jane said. "Perhaps we won't get caught in traffic in a park."

"It should be easier to drive there than on the highway," Liz said.

"Sounds good," I said. "But don't get close to the top. I read somewhere that Seven Sisters refers to cliffs similar to the cliffs of Dover." I wondered where that bit of information came from.

"We'll be careful," Jane said.

"One last question," I said. "What will you do if Virgil catches you now that we know how dangerous he is?"

"He wasn't dangerous in Stratford when I knocked him to the floor with my suitcase," Liz said.

"Where's your suitcase?" Tex said with a chuckle.

"Don't worry. It's in the bookmobile."

"Seriously," I said. "We know what he is capable of now. You must avoid confrontation with him. All you have to do is entice him to chase you and keep him away from the house long enough for me to check the inside. If I find the bank information, I can memorize it and leave. When I do, I'll tell you and you can call the police and drive toward town so there will be less chance for him to harm you."

"Okay," Liz said.

"Sounds like a good plan," Tex said.

"I'll pray for you, Chris," Jane said. "I'll pray for all of us."

***

We found a listing for local taxi service on my phone, called one, and told the dispatcher what we needed and waited.

The taxi approached the van slowly, probably wondering why we needed a ride. I had the feeling he was going to zoom away after seeing the van with all of us in it. We sent Liz to charm him so he wouldn't be afraid of us.

That worked. The driver jumped out of his vehicle, smiling. That's when Liz gave him a hug. He helped Tex from the van to the taxi. I'm not sure what Liz told him about my staying behind, but when they got ready to leave he shook my hand and wished me luck. He said he'd be praying for me.

My suggestion to position the bookmobile for a quick getaway made me think to turn the van around as well. It was parked so I could easily see Virgil's house and garage from the driver's seat. However, I didn't need to be on the same street to fly a drone into his house. I would be directing the helicopter by what I saw on the monitors. I chuckled every time I called my toy a drone. It was merely a remote-controlled helicopter with webcams and transmitter added. Still, it should do the job. I just hoped there was something in that house to see. I didn't want to scare the others, but what I was doing was burglary. That was why I wanted the others away from here. I had justified it in my mind, but I'm not sure I could explain it to the police in a way they would understand. And being in a foreign country made me more vulnerable. If I got arrested, the FBI couldn't help this time and Angela couldn't, either since she was gone.

I cranked up the engine and moved the van to a side street just around the corner from Virgil's house. With the vehicle pointing away from the house I was ready for a fast departure. I saw a face in a window of another house. Someone was checking me out and I knew it wouldn't be long before the police arrived to see why I was here. Hopefully, I'd be gone by the time they got here. I opened the rear door and placed the monitors in the luggage space to allow me to stand behind the van while flying. This also allowed me to easily peek around the corner with less chance of being spotted by Virgil. The monitors were working and everything was ready to go. Now all I had to do was wait for the group to return and get Virgil out of the way.

I called Tex.

"Hello," he said softly. "Everything okay?"

"Yes," I said. "Virgil hasn't moved. But I have."

"What do you mean?" Tex asked.

"Didn't want you to be alarmed when you get back. I turned the van around and moved it off Virgil's street. I can still see his house and I'll be able to see the bookmobile when you arrive."

"Okay. We're on the way. Liz practiced driving and proved she could do it. We'll be there in a few minutes."

"Good. You got something to toss at Virgil's window?"

"Yes," he said. "I found a brick in that vacant lot next

to the car rental office where we'd left the bookmobile. Should work just fine."

"Good. Like I said, I may have to go in that window after you draw him out of the house."

"Oh, we're closer than I thought. We're about a block from you. I better get ready."

"Okay, don't forget to keep this connection open so we can talk when needed."

"Roger. Bye for now."

Tex was right. They were close. I saw the lights of the bookmobile as it slowly moved toward Virgil's house. The distance from the street to the house was only ten to fifteen feet. I expected to hear the sound of broken glass but the street was quiet.

"What's happening, Tex?" I asked on the phone.

"Change in plans," he whispered.

"What? Why?"

"I can't throw the brick from my sitting position in the vehicle. Jane is going to take it to the top deck. It'll be easy from there. Gravity will help. I hate to say it, but it would take me too long to climb those stairs."

Crash!

Jane succeeded. Liz hit the throttle and started moving away from the house.

"Wait," I said to Tex. "Let Virgil see you before you get away."

"Stop, Liz," Tex hollered.

The bookmobile quivered as it squealed to a stop and the horn sounded. I don't know if Liz did it on purpose or by accident, but it was a nice touch either way.

Virgil's window opened just the way I hoped it

would. He leaned out and pumped his right arm in the air. I couldn't hear what he said, but it must have been clear enough to Liz. She stepped on the gas again and headed off.

"That's good, Tex," I said. "He knows who it is. Now don't get too far ahead of him."

"Okay. We won't. Liz, slow down. Let him get to his car. Chris, you be careful."

In a matter of seconds Virgil came running out the front door, pulling a coat on as he ran toward the garage. He opened its door, started the car and backed out, burning rubber in his haste to follow the bookmobile.

"He's on his way," I said. "Let me know when you see him."

"Okay, we'll give him a chance to get closer to us, but not close enough to catch us."

"Good. Interesting situation here. He left in such a hurry, the front door and window are both open."

"Well, that'll make it easier for you to fly in. Keep us posted."

"I will, and don't forget to keep this line open and let me know what's happening with you."

"Roger," Tex said.

I stared at that door for a long time, thinking. The fastest way to get the information I needed was to walk in and search the place in person. The door was open. It was inviting me in. I wouldn't need the drone. I walked toward the house, checking to see if all the racket had alerted the neighbors. Someone had probably called the police already. If they hadn't, they would soon.

However, since that one person peeked out and then quickly shut the curtain, no one had acted interested in what was going on. That didn't mean no one had called the police.

I was more than halfway there when a woman came to the door from inside Virgil's house. I froze. She stepped out, looked left and right, before going back in and shutting the door. If she saw me, she wasn't concerned about it.

I ran to the van and started the helicopter's engine. It was time to go to work and I didn't care if that woman saw the intrusion or not.

CHAPTER TWENTY-THREE

I revved up the helicopter's engine with the remote control then realized I didn't have a plan for entering the house. When the woman closed the door, I rushed back to the van so fast I forgot to check the window. I knew Jane had broken it and Virgil had opened it. But was it open wide enough for the drone? Was the curtain out of the way?

I had to go back.

I turned off the motor and grabbed my phone in case Tex said anything. I ran back to the house and stood outside the window listening for a few seconds. Since I didn't hear anything, I opened each side of the window covering as far as possible. I reached in and slid the curtain to the side. The helicopter could probably make its way through the flimsy drapery, but as long as I was here, I might as well make it easier to fly in. I just hoped the woman wasn't in the room where the window was. Knowing Virgil, I didn't think the woman would call the police, but she may have a weapon.

"Look out!"

I jumped while searching for danger around me before I realized it was Tex on the phone in my jacket pocket.

I retrieved the phone. "What happened?" My heart pumped harder now, even though I knew the danger was there, not here. I checked my surroundings again before I moved quickly back to the van with the phone held tightly against my ear.

"We're okay now," he said. "Liz sort of ran off the road."

"What? What do you mean? Are you still moving? How close is Virgil?"

"Whoa. We're okay. We're in the park. The road is narrow and there are no obstructions along the sides. Liz took a shortcut by going straight where the road curved. That's all. Scared me, but we're okay. Sorry you heard me."

"What about Virgil?" I asked.

"He's gaining on us. I hope you can finish your job at the house so we can call the police to help us with Virgil or at least scare him off. How's it going there?"

"Okay. I have the windows open and I'm ready to fly the drone into the house." I didn't want to worry the others with the fact that there was a woman in the house. He had all he could handle there. I could tell him later, after I got the bank information.

"Good," Tex said. "We're counting on you, Doc. Liz, you're on the grass again. Do you see those cows?"

"What is she doing now?" I asked.

"I'm not sure. She's completely off the road and we're heading toward the edge of the cliff. Right where you told us not to go." His voice rose. "Watch the edge, Liz. There are no barriers there. What?"

"What'd she say?" I asked.

"She saw some people there and thought Virgil might act differently with a few witnesses around."

"Okay. That's a good idea. Be careful. I better get this helicopter going. Keep this line open."

"You're too close, Liz. Turn, turn, turn. No, not that way!" Tex was yelling. "Hit the brakes! Stop!"

I couldn't quit listening to their venture long enough to do my job. But, I had to. I needed to get to work finding the bank information. After all, that was the reason my friends had put themselves in danger. I started the helicopter engine, wondering if the fuel tank was full.

"Are you okay?" I asked.

He didn't answer.

"Tex! Are you there?"

There was a long pause.

"We're okay. For now. The front two wheels are hanging over the cliff. Liz has it in reverse but I think we're stuck here. Virgil has parked and is walking toward us."

"What about the people Liz saw there?" I asked.

"They're still a hundred yards away. They're walking toward us now. Some are running."

SIDNEY W. FROST

"Any chance the bookmobile will fall over the cliff?"

"I don't think so, but we moved to the back to weight it down."

"What's Virgil doing now?"

"He's pushing on the back of the bookmobile."

"With his body?"

"Yes."

"Is it moving?" I asked.

"No. Not at all. With two wheels off the ground, it'll take more power than that to move this monster."

"Good. Ask Jane to use her phone to call the police so you can keep this line open. I've got to get this helicopter into the house before it runs out of fuel."

"Uh-oh," Tex said.

"What's happening?"

"Virgil is in his car and he's trying to use it to push us off the cliff. He'd actually kill all of us if he could. Don't worry, it's not working."

"Chris, Jane here. How do I call the police?"

"The emergency number in the United Kingdom is 999," I said, wondering how I knew. Having an over-achieving memory was sometimes fun and sometimes a benefit, but often unnerving.

I heard Liz hollering in the background, but couldn't make out what she said.

"What's Liz saying?" I asked.

"She says there are three of us and we should go grab him and arrest him until the police get here." It was Tex back on the phone.

"Tell her to wait," I said.

"Liz," Tex said. "Take your suitcase. Knock him down

242

like you did in Stratford."

I heard the sound of a gunshot through the phone.

"Everybody get down!" Tex said.

"What's happening?" I asked.

"Just a minute," Tex said.

I waited, but he was silent. The helicopter was ready. I couldn't wait any longer. "Tex! Is everyone okay?"

"No one's hurt. We're just hiding. Liz had just stepped out when Virgil pulled a gun and fired at her. The bullet hit her suitcase. Probably went through it. She dropped it and fell back into the bookmobile. She's okay. Looks scared, but that's all."

"What about the people who were heading toward you?" I asked.

"I'm not sure where Virgil is now and I'm already up pretty high because of this chair. Jane, can you see where the people are now?"

There was another pause and I could hear Jane's voice faintly.

"They've turned away," Tex said. Probably heard the gunshot. I suspect they'll call for help. There's not much on the hill in the way of cover."

I heard the sirens from where I stood, not sounds over the phone. "Someone called for help or Jane's call got through. I hear sirens."

"Good," Tex said. "I hope they get here soon. To scare Virgil off."

More gunshots.

"What happened?" I asked.

"Several gunshots came through our back window." It was a stage whisper.

"Is everyone okay?" I asked.

There was no response. I stared at the phone to see if I still had a connection, but there was none. Tex may have dropped his phone in the excitement of being shot at. Or perhaps, it was worse. I wanted to call back, but I had to finish my mission. Every fiber of my body said I should jump in the van and go to them. Help them. But I couldn't. They were counting on me. They were in harm's way so I could do my part of the job.

I heard sirens, hoping it was help for my friends. I stared at the phone one more time and looked in the direction of where I thought they were. I had no other choice. I grabbed the remote controls, guided the homemade drone into the air and turned it toward the open window at Virgil's house.

***

As the helicopter flew toward its target, I stood outside the back of the van and stared at the two display screens in the luggage area. I used them to guide me to the window. I was amazed how easy it was. The sun had started to go down so there was no glare on the screens. At the same time, it was light enough to see everything I wanted to see.

When the helicopter got to Virgil's house, I slowed the forward motion of the helicopter to make sure the window was still open and the curtains were out of the way. When I saw the opening, I flew into the house slowly. The helicopter made noise as it flew, so I knew Virgil's house guest would hear it. I counted on her being too surprised to do anything about it.

I was right. The helicopter hadn't been in the house more than a few seconds before I saw her on the front camera's monitor looking straight at me. I let the helicopter hover there for a few seconds as the woman stared into the lens. She was frozen in place so I zoomed the drone toward her, and stopped just before it would've hit her in the face. She screamed and retreated. Soon after that I saw her without the need of a webcam and monitor running and screaming as she ran toward me. She ran past the van and kept going.

With her out of the way, I went to work. I searched the house with the drone and quickly found an opened laptop computer on a small table. The bottom webcam helped more than I thought it would. It meant I could look down with one camera and forward with the other to watch for intruders while searching for information. However, with my eyes on two monitors, Virgil could drive by and I wouldn't know it. That was a disadvantage of working alone. If Tex was here, he could watch my back.

It didn't take long to find what I wanted. It was so easy I laughed. Everything I needed was written in large letters on a legal-sized yellow pad sitting on the desk next to the computer. Mostly numbers, but I knew it was a bank account number along with a URL and password for online access to the bank. Because of my special memory capability, my job was finished. I'd probably never forget what I was looking at. Just in case, I took a photo and e-mailed it to myself.

A maniac-like laughter ripped through the sound of

the helicopter's engine. I turned the camera toward the interior door to see if the woman had returned, but saw it was Virgil. He must have arrived while I was busy flying and gotten into the house without me knowing it. I'd been so busy, I didn't realize how much time had passed.

But I didn't care. I had done what I set out to do. The only way he could stop me now would be to change the bank password. If he did, there was a pretty good chance I could still break in to his account. He'd have to actually move the money to another bank to stop me now.

He walked toward the helicopter and I buzzed it toward him the way I'd scared his lady friend away earlier. It didn't faze him. He swatted at the helicopter, but I moved it up and away before he could reach it. He laughed and turned away. In seconds he was back with an umbrella. Before I could get the helicopter away he swung the closed umbrella like a baseball bat causing an awkward, static view of the room. I tried the controls, but the view didn't change.

I peeked around the corner toward his house and saw him leaning through the window, laughing.

My brain told me to grab the money quickly and don't take a chance on what Virgil might do. I couldn't wait any longer. I had to check on my friends. The last message from Tex was that Virgil was shooting into the back of the bookmobile and I didn't know if anyone had been hit or not.

I shut the back of the van, praying my friends were safe. I didn't know where they were, but I knew the

general location and I was positive it'd be hard to hide a
red double-decker bookmobile.

CHAPTER TWENTY-FOUR

I raced to the driver's seat and jumped in, only momentarily thinking about the monitors loose in the back. They'd probably roll around and break, but it didn't matter. Not now. The helicopter was gone, probably smashed to pieces by Virgil. The drone had served its purpose. Now it was time to find my friends.

Tex had described their route, but I couldn't visualize it. I turned east onto the A259 and watched for the Seven Sisters Country Park sign to follow the same route my friends had. I was forced to pull over when a fire truck approached me from behind with its siren blasting and lights flashing. I suspected they were going where I wanted to go, so, as soon as the truck passed by, I moved in behind it.

I doubted my decision to go behind the truck when

it drove past the entry for Seven Sisters Country Park. Perhaps it was a short-cut. My friends had been on a cliff and the scene to my right was a green pasture on an incline that could lead to a cliff. I was relieved when the emergency vehicle eventually turned right. I stayed close behind the truck. But we were in a residential area, not a park. This couldn't be right.

I was about to turn around and go back to the Seven Sisters Country Park road, when the surroundings changed again. No more houses, just short grass on each side of the road. We turned a couple of times and ended up on Beachy Head Road.

Without slowing, the fire truck swerved off the road and into the pasture. I did too, and saw the bookmobile ahead at the end of the gradually-sloped hill covered with short grass. What a relief.

The fire truck stopped with its front bumper ten yards behind the bookmobile. I parked on the right of the truck. Two firefighters ran toward a crowd on the grass off to the right of the bookmobile. Two others connected a heavy twisted metal cable between the fire truck and the bookmobile.

I walked to the front of the bookmobile and looked down. There was a steep cliff with the ocean about a hundred feet down. The water slammed repeatedly against huge rocks.

I went to where the crowd was, searching for Tex. Or Liz. Or Jane. The money hadn't been transferred yet. But I didn't care. I had to find my friends.

Liz sat on a large boulder while Jane fanned her with Tex's hat. It wasn't hot.

"Is she okay?" I asked when I got to them.

Jane smiled. "She'll be all right. Just had the wind knocked out of her."

Liz jumped up and pulled me into a bear hug. "Chris, thank God you're okay," she said.

"Don't hurt yourself," Jane said.

"Ouch!" Liz said. "Too late."

She sat back on her rock and took several large breaths.

"Where's Tex?" I asked.

"I'm here," Tex said.

He was on the ground behind the boulder Liz was on. I hardly recognized him without his wheelchair and cowboy hat.

"Where's your chair?" I asked.

"It's in the bookmobile. When Virgil started shooting we had to dive down to keep from getting hit. Liz and Jane did okay, but I couldn't get to the floor fast enough. They both grabbed the arm of my chair and pulled it and me over. They got me down, but the chair and I landed on top of Liz. She's still a little stunned, but the EMS gal said she'd be okay. Maybe have some bruises is all."

"So, why'd you leave your chair in the bookmobile?"

"People here got us out after Virgil left. Now, everyone's afraid the bookmobile is going to go over the cliff so no one wants to go in there and get my wheelchair. Jane would do it, but the EMS people won't let her. Too dangerous, they say."

"I just saw the fire department hook a cable onto the bookmobile, so it'll be secure enough to go in now. Want me to get it?"

"Sure," he said, "but first tell us how the bank transfer went."

"Oh my gosh." I turned and ran to the van trying to remember the bank information. My brain was going through the sequence of steps to follow if I didn't. Get on Internet, check mail, open photo, hope the image of the yellow pad was clear enough to read. Another problem popped into my head. What if Virgil had moved the money? He could have. Why had I waited to finish the job? The way he'd laughed when he smacked the helicopter made me think he thought he'd stopped the invasion in time.

At the van, I turned on the laptop and the portable satellite dish. Then it all came back. I saw everything I'd seen on the yellow pad. I logged in and entered the information as it was called for, moving methodically until it was time to transfer the money. I froze with my fingers hovering above the keyboard. Liz had said to take only what he'd stolen from the bookmobile fund plus what he took from Cloris.

It wasn't that simple. There was £249,000 in the account and no time to compute how much to take so I transferred it all. Once the transfer had taken place, I relaxed, and without the stress of having to work so fast, easily computed Virgil's balance was about $372,000, much more than Liz wanted me to take. We'd have to sort that out later. I'd told Liz the money would go to a law enforcement account. That was a stretch. I transferred it all to my dad's business account. Being a computer consultant for the FBI put him into the law enforcement field. I made a mental note to call and tell

SIDNEY W. FROST

Dad what to expect. We'd figure that out later, too.

***

When I looked away from the screen, the trio of friends were staring at me. I hadn't noticed they were there. Tex had his wheelchair back and his ten-gallon cowboy hat, only slightly dented in the wrong places, sat perched at its usual position. Jane stood behind Tex holding the wheelchair handles. Liz stood beside Jane with her arms crossed in front of her chest. She appeared to have recovered.

"Well?" Liz asked, "did you do it?"

"I was so worried about you three," I said. "I heard gunshots on the phone just before I lost contact."

"We were a bit busy about that time," Jane said. "I think that's when Tex's phone hit the deck and splintered into several pieces."

"I knew you were in danger when I heard the shots. I was so worried I was afraid I couldn't do my part. But I didn't want to let you down. I saw a woman in the house after Virgil left—"

"A woman?" asked Jane.

"She didn't keep you from finding the money, did she?" Tex asked.

"I thought she might. When I flew the helicopter in, it scared her so much she ran out the front door and down the street. The last I saw she was running and screaming around the corner."

"So, you got the money?" Liz asked.

"Before I could get the helicopter out of the house,

Virgil appeared and swatted it with an umbrella."

"You got what you needed first, right?" Tex said.

"Yes, but I lost the helicopter and the webcams."

"We'll buy you more toys if you got the money," Liz said.

"You got the money, right?" Tex asked.

"Yes, but—" I said.

"Wonderful." Liz was all smiles now. She leaned toward me. "You got the whole amount and Cloris's money, too?"

"Well, sort of."

"What do you mean?" she asked.

Tex smiled. I think he had figured out that I'd taken it all, but he enjoyed watching me squirm as Liz quizzed me. He whispered something to Jane and she smiled, too.

"I got so rattled I couldn't convert pounds to dollars and I was afraid to take more time. I kept thinking Virgil was logged in to the bank at the same time moving the money before I could."

"So you took it all," Tex said.

I nodded.

"You took it all?" Liz said. "How much?"

"Three hundred seventy-two thousand dollars," I said.

She dropped her arms. "Good. After ducking his bullets, and having Tex fall on top of me, Virgil deserves to lose it all. It's probably all stolen anyway."

That was a relief. "I figured we could decide where the money should go later."

"So," Tex said with a grin as wide as that time we met

the president of the United States, "we did it." He took off his hat. "See, honey, this is what I've tried to tell you before. Doesn't if feel good to right a wrong?"

Jane nodded with a smile. "It'd feel better if we could put Virgil in jail."

"Yeah," Liz said. "The goal was to get the money back. But, he should pay for what he did to poor Cloris." She looked around at each us. "What can we do about that?"

"Did you call the police?" I asked.

"Yes," Liz said. "They got here soon after Virgil left and we told them everything we knew. They called back a few minutes ago and said they'd searched the house, but there was no one there. Virgil's car was in the garage and the garage door was open, but he wasn't there. The officer I talked to said they'd watch for him but they didn't think he'd return. They said the Chunnel is only seventy-seven miles away and Virgil could be in France by now."

"There's not much we can do," Tex said.

"Isn't there?" I asked. "We still have the webpage for tracking the thief. It helped us find him once. Maybe it'll work again. Let's find out." I opened the webpage to check for new thief sightings.

"Anything?" Jane asked.

"They got him!" Liz said.

She must have been reading over my shoulder. "Wait, there's more. 'Thief in custody. If you want to see him before I turn him over to the police, let me know where you are.'"

"Who's it from?" Tex asked.

"There's no name," I said.

"It could be a trick," Tex said. "Maybe Virgil found the webpage and is using it to find us."

"That doesn't make sense," Jane said. "He knows where we are."

"Yeah, but he doesn't know where Chris is. Maybe he learned the money was gone and wants to force Chris to give it back."

"He's not that smart," Liz said. "He'd probably run while he had the chance." She looked at me. "Why don't you just ask for a name and see what happens?"

"Okay." I typed it in and we all waited for the reply.

The reply came quickly and I read it aloud. "The brown-haired beauty."

I quickly typed in our location and added, "Hurry."

"Who is that?" Liz asked.

Tex smiled.

CHAPTER TWENTY-FIVE

Liz stared at me, waiting for an answer, but I turned to Tex.

"You're grinning. You remember, don't you?" I asked him.

He beamed. "Yes. That's what you called Angela before we knew her name." He pushed his hat back and looked at me in disbelief. "How on earth did she nab Virgil?"

"And how did she know our nickname for her?" I asked. "I didn't tell her, did you? That's probably her coming now."

The sun was low, but it was still light enough to spot a car coming in the distance. As it got closer, I could tell it was a police vehicle, not Angela. I wanted it to be her. I wanted to see her again and spend time together the way we planned to when I first got to England. I gazed beyond the police car, but there were no other vehicles in sight.

"It's the police," Tex said.

"Yeah," I said. "Probably coming to check on us. I suppose they're going to want us to get our bookmobile out of the park as soon as possible."

"We called a wrecker," Liz said. "The firefighters said to ask for a big one. I did, but they said it'll take them a while to get to us. They're having to bring it from Dover."

"I'm just glad the fire truck can stay until the wrecker gets here," Jane said.

"Me too," Liz said. "They said they'd have to cut the bookmobile loose if they got an emergency call. I don't think there's a chance it'd fall off that cliff, though. They're just being cautious."

The police car stopped next to the van. A policeman got out on the driver's side and a woman got out of the front passenger seat.

It was her.

"Angela," I said. "You surprised me. I didn't expect you to come in a police car."

I walked toward her and she moved rapidly in my direction. We met halfway and fell into each other's arms. Not a Liz hug, but an "I missed you more than I thought I would" hug.

The policeman opened the back door.

"Time to get out," he said into the vehicle.

The man moved slowly out of the car. When his face was visible, I saw a Virgil who was no longer laughing.

Just the opposite. He was frowning, looking like a trapped animal with his hands cuffed behind him. When he saw me, the frown turned into a snarl. A look I took as an expression of defeat.

"Which one of you is Liz?" the policeman asked.

"I'm Liz, Officer," she said, facing Virgil.

I hoped she wasn't going to hit him again. This wonderful, loving, hugger of people everywhere who lived her life helping others made an impression on me when she knocked Virgil to the floor with her suitcase in Stratford. Before that, I never would have dreamed she had it in her. Of course, she regretted hitting him later and prayed for forgiveness, but it proved she could take care of herself if she ever had to. She didn't have a weapon this time, so maybe he'd be safe.

"Madam," the policeman said, "I understand you may have something to say to this man. If you do, go ahead. I have to take him into custody when you've finished with him."

Angela must have arranged it. I took Angela's left hand in my right and we watched Liz. I was ready to grab Liz if I needed to. Jane and Tex looked at each other and then toward me.

Liz turned to Angela and mouthed a silent thank you before her gaze turned to Virgil. "I'm praying for you, mister." She paused. "Without a doubt you're the meanest and the most difficult person I've ever prayed for, but I want you to know I forgive you. My prayer is that you will repent and beg forgiveness for your sins."

Tears came to my eyes. I wished my faith was strong enough to say those words to someone like Virgil.

"I don't want your prayers or your forgiveness," Virgil blurted. He turned to the policeman. "She just stole my life savings. She cleaned out my bank account and now she's forgiving me. Can you believe that? Arrest her, not me. Get my money back. This woman is a thief, I tell you. If that's not enough, she almost killed me in Stratford. Lock her up."

The policeman looked at Angela as if he wanted her to help. Angela shook her head and the policeman acted satisfied with her response and he motioned for Virgil to get into the backseat. As the policeman held Virgil's head to keep from bumping it on the top of the car, Virgil pushed back, refusing to get in.

"Hey, what about my money?" he asked.

"Get in," the policeman said, pushing a little harder. "You can file a complaint about your money when you get to London."

"When you take him in, you may want to see what he has to say about the murder of Cloris Parker in London," Angela said to the policeman.

He nodded, made a note, and said good-bye.

Angela gazed at me. "I guess we need to talk about Virgil's claim."

I shrugged.

"How did you find him?" Tex asked.

"Yeah," Jane said. "We were all surprised."

"Not me," I said.

"Huh?" Liz said.

"We left a trail of bread crumbs so wide anyone could have followed us. We did that on purpose, remember, so all the librarians and bookmobile drivers around in the area could help us find Virgil."

"Oh, that's right," Liz said. She turned to Angela. "Is that how you found Virgil?"

Angela smiled. "You think you're pretty smart, don't you. Yes, that's what I did. When I got home and didn't find anyone there, I checked my computer for clues. It didn't take much to find that someone had been following a website called 'the thief.' After that it was easy."

"You used the website to let us know you were here."

"Yes. I didn't call. I wanted to surprise you."

"How'd you get Virgil into custody?" I asked.

"It was easier than I thought it would be," she said. "Based on the information you provided, the police searched his house. But they didn't find him. Thinking he might return, they left an unmarked car to watch. I spotted the surveillance vehicle when I got there. I was talking to the policeman through his car window when Virgil walked out of his house with a suitcase and went toward the garage. The police didn't know he was there, and we still don't know where he came from. The police are going to investigate the house more carefully tomorrow, and while they're there they said they'd check for a hide-away. Anyway, I quickly grabbed and cuffed him. He saw the policeman behind me, so he didn't try to run."

"They didn't happen to find a helicopter with two webcams on it, did they?" I asked Angela.

"If they did, they didn't mention it."

"Quit worrying about your toy helicopter, will you?" Liz said. "I told you we'll buy you a new one."

"It's not that," I said. "My fingerprints were all over it." Not that I thought it would matter, but I didn't like leaving evidence like that.

"That reminds me," I said. "We better post the capture of the thief on the website."

"Right," Tex said. "So people can quit looking."

"And also to let them know they helped capture him," Jane said.

"Good idea," I said. "Jane, will you write a thank you to everyone for the website? Be sure to mention Juliet and Thomas specifically."

"Be glad to."

I loved seeing Angela again, and I hoped she'd be home for a while. I was thinking of all the things we could do. I wanted to go back to Bath and finish my tour of that area.

I was glad we had to wait on the wrecker to get there. As it turned out we were at Beachy Head at the perfect time to see the most gorgeous sunset I had ever seen. Once the wrecker arrived, we got our luggage from the bookmobile and said good-bye to the firefighters. Liz gave all of them one more hug. She grabbed the wrecker driver next and, before he had a chance to squirm out of it, she had him locked into her trademark hug. When he managed to break away, he was smiling as if he'd enjoyed it. She told him where to take the bookmobile. We all piled into the van and drove toward Seaford.

We stopped at the car rental office to let them know we needed to keep the van longer than expected and signed new paperwork giving us the right to take it to London and drop it off there.

SIDNEY W. FROST

Everyone was tired, prompting a discussion of whether to spend the night in Seaford or Brighton. But, after talking about it, we all said we were ready to get home. By "home" we meant Angela's flat in London.

I didn't care where we went as long as it meant more time with Angela. I wanted that vacation together we'd planned and never got. I turned to see she was looking back at me with a warm smile. I had this strange feeling she could read my mind.

***

We hadn't gone more than a few dozen miles when an enormous gurgling sound filled the back seat and caused us all to laugh.

"Sorry," Liz said. "I don't remember when I ate last."

"Me neither," Tex said. "I'm hungry."

"But I don't want to stop," Jane said. "Can't we wait until we get back to Angela's place to eat?"

"We could eat in the pub there," I said, thinking about how we'd already shattered Angela's food supply plus what we'd bought to add to it.

"I can't wait that long," Liz said.

"How about getting a takeaway or some fast food?" Angela asked. "The fast food places all have toilets."

"That's good," Jane said. "I could use a quick restroom stop."

With Angela's help locating a roadside stop where we could get in and out easily, I pulled over and everyone headed for the restrooms. Afterwards, we met in the dining area where there were several choices of fast food. We all picked our favorites and were back on the road in a matter of minutes.

CHAPTER TWENTY-SIX

It was half past ten when we got to Angela's building, but the pub was still open. We pushed two tables together and ordered dessert and tea. After we'd been served, Frank, the night manager, came over to our table.

"I didn't know you guys knew Angela," he said. "You should've said so, and you'd have got the VIP treatment."

Liz was on her feet before anyone had a chance to respond. "Frank, I don't know how you could have given us any better service than you have." She pulled him to her in a special hug that included a kiss on his cheek. "But now we have to say good-bye. We're going back to the States. Well, most of us. Chris is sticking around for a while longer. I'm gonna miss you, Frank."

His face turned red and he stuttered. "Ah…well, yes…quite so. It was nice meeting you. All of you. Have a safe trip home."

I hadn't thought about it until now, but it was clear that Liz's attitude had changed drastically since Virgil had been apprehended. She was more like her old self than I'd seen since we first learned the bookmobile fund had been stolen.

"Well, silly me," Liz said after Frank said good-bye and returned to the bar. "I told him good-bye as if I'll never see him again and I don't know when or how I'm getting home. I've got to call Matt and Marie and see if they plan to leave France anytime soon."

Angela looked at me with raised eyebrows.

"Matt and Marie are friends from Austin with a plane. They're in France right now," I said.

"Nice," Angela said.

Liz called them as soon as we got upstairs. She was on and off the line coordinating with Jane and Tex, and by the time she disconnected we knew Matt and Marie were flying to London and would pick up all three of them at an Underground station to help them get to the airport tomorrow morning for the trip back to Texas.

After the travel arrangements were taken care of, it got quiet in the room. I sensed a letdown. But we should be celebrating. Our job was done. We'd been successful. Was everyone too tired?

Liz answered my question as she began to dance around the room, moving easily at first, and then with a gradual crescendo, she moved with a rhythm from a song she hummed. Because of her weight I was concerned about the strength of the building. But I remembered it had been here for hundreds of years.

"What are you thinking?" I asked after she came to a stop.

"It just hit me," she said. "We should celebrate our success. And what better way than the annual Vengeance Squad Christmas dinner?"

"Christmas dinner?" Angela asked. "It's February."

"Doesn't matter," Liz said. "We were late for Christmas the year before last, remember? Mainly 'cause Chris and Percy were in the Galveston County Jail."

Angela smiled.

"I remember," I said.

"Don't remind me," Tex said. "They almost kept me there on a weapons charge. If it hadn't been for that fancy lawyer Liz found, I might still be there. I never did get my gun back, not even after the full pardon the president gave me."

Liz raised her eyebrows at Tex. "You don't need a gun, Percy. And, if I remember right, being in jail wasn't all bad. It seems to me Chris found God again while he was there. And Percy, if we hadn't gotten you out, you might not have saved the president like you did. Anyway, it doesn't matter what day we celebrate Christ's birth."

She looked around the room before settling on Angela. "Everybody else knows this, darling, 'cept you. Truth is, after I found the bookmobile money missing, I didn't feel much like rejoicing. I tried to hide it, but this bunch," she nodded, "they knew. They did everything they could to cheer me up." I thought she might cry, but she didn't.

"So," she continued, "I skipped Christmas altogether last December. Now, I'm ready to party. I want a good home-cooked Christmas dinner with turkey and all the trimmings. Can you come?"

Everyone in the room focused on Angela.

"Of course," Angela said. "I love your Christmas dinners. Just say when and I'll do my best to be there."

I hoped Liz wouldn't schedule it too soon. I wanted to spend more time in England with Angela. We hadn't had much time together and I still wasn't sure what kind of relationship we had. In addition, we hadn't finished our visit to Hemington. A sudden feeling of guilt washed over me. Did I want to see more of Hemington because of Sarah?

"Well," Liz said, "how about two weeks from today." She paused. "Is that okay with everyone?"

"A fortnight. Perfect," said Angela. "That'll give Chris and me time to finish that vacation that was aborted because of my job."

That was good to hear.

"Chris, you may want to check on a flight for Thursday. That'll give me four days to show you around and let you get back to school. And, get ready for me to visit you in Georgetown."

"Uhh…okay." I didn't want to leave, but it made sense. It fit into the plans for our belated Christmas party.

"Speaking of food," Angela said. "You know what I miss from my time in Texas?"

"What's that?" Liz asked.

"Mexican food."

Liz's eyes popped open. "We didn't try any, but I saw some Mexican food restaurants here someplace."

"Yes, but it tastes different," Angela said.

"It's not Tex-Mex," Jane said. "Mexican food varies from place to place even in the states."

"Yes," Angela said. "I had some in Georgia and California and it's not the same as in Texas."

"You need to come visit. I'll cook you some Tex-Mex," Jane said.

"Thanks," Angela said.

"Well, Liz, we can be there for the special Christmas dinner," Jane said.

"Okay," Liz said. "Let's meet at my house two weeks from today. Jane, will you plan on something special to lead us in prayer when we get together in Austin? We should thank God for the success we had in England and for guiding me through a rough time in my life. I learned more about faith from this experience. And would you pray for Heath as well? He's going to be grieving the loss of his mother for a long while. Thank goodness he has Brian and Karen in his life now. "

"I would be honored," Jane said. "Is there anything I can bring? Dinner rolls? Dessert? Sides?"

Liz cleared her throat. "I don't like to brag, but lots of people say my turkey and dressing is the best in Texas, even though I grew up in Holly Springs, North Carolina. Still, I never could make a decent batch of dinner rolls. If you want to bring some to dip into my tasty gravy, I'd be obliged."

"What can I bring?" Angela asked.

"What do you like to make?" Liz asked.

"My mother grew up in Georgia and taught me to make pecan pie. I know it's probably not the same as Texas pecan pie, but I think you'll all enjoy it."

"Sounds wonderful," Liz said. "Tell you what. I'll make a Texas one and you bring your Georgia one. We'll need two for this bunch anyway."

"We'll be there," Jane said, "with homemade dinner rolls and anything else you can think of, but right now I need to call and check on the kids. And let them know when we're coming home. I think I'm suffering from some serious mom's separation anxiety." She turned to Angela. "What time is it back home?"

Angela looked at her watch, but before she had a chance to reply, I answered. "It's 5:36 in the evening."

Angela smiled.

"Good," Jane said. "Thanks." She picked up her phone and held it to her ear. Tex rolled over next to her.

"I'm going to get my shower," Liz said, "and get ready for bed." She went into Angela's room and shut the door.

"Mom," Jane said with a smile. "How are things?"

She paused. "Yes, I mean the kids. But we're concerned about you, too. We'll be home tomorrow."

"Ask her if they smoked around the children," Tex said.

Jane shook her head and crossed her lips with her index finger.

Angela and I laughed as Jane continued her conversation with her mother-in-law. When it sounded like the conversation was about to end, Jane said, "Hold on, Mom. Percy wants to talk to you." She handed the phone to Tex.

He didn't look as tough as he had when he'd suggested Jane ask his mother about smoking, but he took the phone anyway.

"Hi, Mom. We sure appreciate what you two have done for us. When we get home we'll tell you how important this trip has been. Not just for us, but in other ways.

"I love you too, Mom. Oh, how did Dad do without his cigarettes? He didn't smoke around the kids, did he?" Tex shrugged.

"Is that right?" Tex said with widening eyes. "He didn't smoke the entire time we've been gone? He didn't go outside and smoke? Not at all?"

He paused, listening. I thought I could see tears in his eyes.

"He doesn't want to ever smoke again. Oh, Mom, I'm so happy for you two. I know how hard it is to quit, but it is worth it. Oh? You haven't stopped yet?"

He listened again, shaking his head slowly. "Well, that's okay, Mom. It takes time. You can do it. Now that I've found you two, I want you to take care of your health so you'll be around a long time, for me and your grandchildren."

Tex said good-bye and hung up just as Liz walked in wearing a bathrobe with her hair wrapped in a towel.

With Liz's entrance, I was probably the only one who noticed the tears in Tex's eyes.

She laughed. "Well, pardon me, Angela. I just assumed I'd be sleeping on your sofa tonight. Now that you're back, we're gonna need to do something different."

"If it's okay with you Angela," Tex said, wiping his cheeks. "Liz could stay on the sofa. Jane and I would like to try that fancy hotel where Cloris stayed. Part of the reason for our trip was to spend more time together without the children and, so far, we haven't had any time alone."

Jane smiled. "Are you sure we can afford it?"

"Not to worry," Liz said. "I think Virgil should pay for a nice room for Tex and Jane. After all the trouble he caused them. Don't you agree, Chris?"

"I'll take care of it," I said.

Jane turned to Tex and they both smiled.

"In that case," Tex said, "I think we could stay another week."

"No, we can't," Jane said. "I miss my babies too much."

"And," Liz said, ignoring Tex's comment, "would you pay off that short-term loan Andrew got us for the bookmobile and ask him to get it out of the repair shop and ship it to Austin?"

Liz was back to her old self. Self-assured, confident, and delegating.

"I'll take care of all that first thing in the morning."

Angela stood and moved closer to me.

"So," she said, "Virgil was right. You emptied his bank account."

"Sort of," I said. "Actually, we could pay for the new bookmobile we bought and buy another with all the donations that have come in. But, as for Virgil's bank account, we retrieved stolen money and are keeping control of it in a special place until we determine who it goes to. We know he took the bookmobile fund, so that's why we're paying the bookmobile loan with the money from his account. We also know he took Cloris's life savings. We'll give that to her son, Heath."

"And the rest?" Angela asked.

"Oh, we'll return that to Virgil," Liz said. She stared at me. "I'm serious. Unless we can prove he stole it elsewhere, we will give it back. He might need it to pay for a defense attorney."

I could see Angela's law enforcement mind working overtime and knew I'd hear from her about absconding with evidence and all that, but in the long run she'd probably agree with us. After all, she didn't work for Scotland Yard.

Tex and Jane left soon after with their suitcases. I said goodnight to Liz and Angela and went to my room. When I got there I called Brian and asked him to ship the ingredients for enchiladas, beans and rice to Angela's place in Hemington.

CHAPTER TWENTY-SEVEN

The next morning, we met at Angela's place for breakfast. All five of us were quieter than usual. We packed our suitcases, cleaned the room and left. No one mentioned a word about parting until we got to Victoria Station.

Liz, Tex, and Jane were taking the Underground to Hounslow West where Matt and Marie would meet them and help them go the rest of the way to Heathrow for their trip to Austin. Angela and I were taking the train to Bath to pick up where we left off before she was unexpectedly called back to work.

Liz hugged us as we said good-bye. I'd see them in two weeks, but I felt dampness in my eyes. My three friends were leaving. We'd spent so much time together during the past month, we'd become like family. At the same time I longed to be alone with Angela. I had no idea where our relationship might lead and I still hadn't gotten a straight answer from her about Andrew. Well, that's not entirely true. She asked if I was crazy when I mentioned it, but that could have been because of when I asked. Still, she was taking me back to her place in Hemington. That was a clear indication of something. I just wasn't sure what.

After Liz, Tex and Jane said their good-byes and were safely on their way, Angela grabbed my arm. "Chris, do you mind if we don't go to Hemington yet?"

"Uhh…no," I said, disappointed and wondering what was going on. "Why?"

"I want to visit my parents. I haven't had much contact with them lately. I don't want them to worry about me. Besides, I'd like them to meet you. Okay? We can spend the night at their place and go to Bath tomorrow."

Her smile and the way she continued to hold my arm as she talked warmed my heart. She wanted to introduce me to her parents. "That sounds good," I said. And to think I was worried she didn't want me to go back to Hemington with her. "Where do they live?"

"York. It's a couple of hours from here by train and not on the way to Bath, but it'll be fun."

The time on the train flew by.

"Tell me about your parents," I said, realizing how little I knew about her.

She smiled. "Mum is a first generation American. Her parents migrated to the United States from Italy as children. Separately, of course, but around the same time as each other. They didn't meet until college."

"What was her name?"

"Gina Romano."

"Where did she grow up?"

"In the Atlanta area," Angela said. "Mum says we still have some relatives there, but I've never met them."

"So," I said, "it must be nice to trace your ancestry back to Italy. I have no idea where my ancestors came from."

She looked at me as if waiting for me to continue.

"My grandparents on both sides died young. I know my mother's family lived in Oregon and my Dad's lived in Oklahoma. But, before that, it's all a mystery."

"Aren't you curious? I love to go to Italy to search for relatives."

"Sure. Now that you've mentioned it." I should ask Mom and Dad and start making notes. With the Internet it was easier to find ancestors. "What about your father?"

"Harold Helmsley was born and raised in York, and has never lived anywhere else."

"Tell me about him."

"He's a teacher. He's a wonderful father. I can't wait for you to meet him."

"You must love him. I can see it in your face when you talk about him."

"I do. I love them both."

How did your American mom meet your English father?

"They met while she was in England doing graduate work. They were in college together. She said she hardly noticed him, but he claims to have fallen in love with her at first sight."

"How did he get her to marry him?"

"After she graduated and went back to America, he followed her and proposed. Mum told me it took her some time to decide, because it meant moving to England. But, of course, she eventually said yes."

"Do you have any brothers or sisters?"

The rapid change in her appearance scared me. As an only child I've heard stories about how lucky I am. You can pick you friends, some say, but you can't pick your family. You have to take them as they are and some are not the type of people you want to be around. I waited for her to regain her composure.

"One brother," she said, swallowing. "Robert was killed in Afghanistan early in the war." She turned toward the window. "I miss him dearly."

"I'm so sorry. That has to be difficult for you."

Our train got to York on time and we took a bus to her childhood home. She continued to tell me stories about growing up in North Yorkshire, including a few about her brother that brought a smile to her face. I loved learning about her life. It made me feel closer to her. I shared a few stories, too, but they weren't nearly as exciting as hers.

When we got to where her parents lived, she paused with one hand of the front-door handle. "Before we go in, I need to tell you they don't know about my job. Don't say anything."

She opened the door. "Mum. Dad. Guess who's home."

So many questions popped into my head. Why don't

they know? What do they think she does? What do I say if they ask where we met? I needed time to prepare answers to every possible question and more time to rehearse.

It was too late. Before I could say anything, Angela's parents stood there bubbling over her and staring at me.

"Oh, sweetie," her mother said, "I was praying for you this morning and hoping I'd get to see you soon. And here you are. Thank God." She squeezed Angela's cheeks. "You could call every now and again, you know."

"Yes," her father said, "I was considering sending a search party." He gave Angela a hug.

Angela's mother had the same dark brown hair and eyes as her daughter. Or was it the other way around? They were both striking. I could see why Angela's father fell in love with her at first sight.

He took my hand and asked, "Angela, who is this young man?"

"Mum, Dad, I want you to meet Chris McCowan. He's from Texas. We're staying with you tonight and I'm taking him to Hemington tomorrow to show him around."

Angela's mother peered at me a little closer than she had before. "Welcome to our home, young man. Where did you two meet?"

And there it was. Just like I knew it would happen. I could feel my face burning. Now what do I say. I looked at Angela for help. Why didn't she tell me about this while we were on the train? If she had, we would have had time to make up answers for such questions. She knew me well enough to know I'd get flustered not knowing what to say. I opened my mouth, but nothing came out. "Ah…ah…"

"Chris was engaged to Sarah." Angela said.

"Oh," her dad said. "I'm so sorry, son."

Mrs. Helmsley hugged me and patted me on the back. "Such a tragedy. We were all sorry to hear about your loss."

"Thank you," I said. Did they know Sarah or had Angela told them about her? I didn't ask. I was afraid I would get mixed up in truths and untruths. Angela hadn't lied, but she hadn't answered her mother's question. We had met while searching for the killers, and for a long time after that, I thought Angela was an FBI agent. It wasn't until much later that I learned Angela had known Sarah.

"And how is Andrew holding up?" Mr. Helmsley asked me.

That question made me wonder again if Angela and Andrew had dated, or were still dating, for that matter. Maybe that was how her parents knew Sarah.

I could answer this question without lying. "I talked to Andrew yesterday," I said. "He's managing, but I know he was devastated by his sister's death."

Angela smiled directly at me.

"We all were, son," Mr. Helmsley said, putting an arm around my back. "We all were."

The rest of the evening was less stressful as time went by. I never did have to lie, but I was ever alert to the possibility. By the time we'd eaten and talked for several hours, I relaxed and enjoyed getting to know Mr. and

Mrs. Helmsley. We talked mainly about what all I'd seen during my visit to England. Since I had not spent all my time searching for Virgil and had seen some of the major sights in and around London, I was able to tell them about my visit without getting into the other reason I was here. Of course a major purpose for my trip was to see Angela and I didn't know how much they knew about our relationship. Actually, I knew little about it myself. When they learned I was teaching school remotely, they were fascinated by that and had many questions regarding how it worked. Angela sat quietly and smiled as if she was enjoying my interaction with her parents.

When it came time to turn in, Mr. Helmsley showed me to a bedroom upstairs. "This was Robert's room," he said.

"Angela told me what happened. I was sorry to hear about your loss. It must be difficult."

Shortly after they left me alone I heard a soft knock on my door. I opened it to see Angela.

"May I come in?" she asked.

"Of course," I said, opening the door wider.

Her eyes shone. "I wanted to tell you how much I enjoyed getting to know you on the train today."

Before I could respond, she kissed me and left. There was much I wanted to say and ask her, but I realized there was no hurry. There was something special about the way she'd kissed me that made me know we would be together for a long time and, in light of that recognition, the thought of being separated the rest of the night didn't matter.

***

The next morning, I woke to the smell of fresh coffee and a pleasant assortment of other enticing aromas. I slipped on my clothes, brushed my hair with my hands and headed toward the smells.

When I got to the kitchen, I found Angela and her mom busily preparing breakfast. Angela poured a cup of coffee and handed it to me with a smile and a kiss.

"Thank you," I said, meaning the kiss as much as the coffee. I'd learned to like the coffee made with what I called a plunger. It tasted fresher than what I made at home in a machine.

"I hope you're hungry," Angela said. "Mum has made the typical English breakfast. Not typical for us, mind, but the type of breakfast Americans must think we have quite often."

"Mmm, smells good. We ate in a B&B in Scotland while I was here and I think they had something similar." I peeked over Mrs. Helmsley's shoulder. "Let's see, eggs, beans, tomatoes, mushrooms, sausage, fried bread, English bacon…"

"English bacon?" Angela acted shocked.

"Well," I said, "that's what it looks like to me."

"Well, it's not. It's bacon. Not that skinny, crispy, little piece of pork you call bacon."

"I kind of miss that skinny, crispy piece of pork."

"You can find it in the UK. Just not here this morning. Besides, Mum made a special effort for you by preparing this meal."

Angela's words made her sound as if she was fussing at me, but we both knew she wasn't.

I played along. "I know and I appreciate it." I went over to Mrs. Helmsley and gave her a hug. "Thank you, ma'am."

"You're welcome. I actually enjoy cooking."

"Breakfast ready?" Mr. Helmsley asked as he entered the kitchen with a newspaper folded under his arm. He had on a dress shirt with tie, but no jacket.

"Just about, dear," Mrs. Helmsley said. "Angela, have you set the table?"

"All ready."

It was a marvelous meal. I decided the typical English breakfast could vary from place to place as much as Mexican food varied in the States. Thinking about Mexican food reminded me of the surprise in store for Angela if Brian shipped the ingredients in time.

The Helmsleys didn't say grace before breakfast nor had there been a prayer at dinner last night. Sarah and I had met at church, and our parents were lifetime church members. My parents were Episcopalian and therefore I was, also. It wasn't until I moved to Georgetown that I visited and soon joined the Anglican church Sarah and her parents attended. It wasn't all that different from the church I'd been brought up in.

With Sarah, there was no need to talk about our beliefs and where we would go to church. But, now, I realized I didn't know anything about Angela's religious beliefs. Her mother had mentioned praying, and she thanked God that Angela came to see them. That was something.

We left soon after eating breakfast. Angela's mother made her promise to come home more often. Her dad said she should call every day, but she laughed about that. They both told me to come back anytime, with or without their daughter.

As soon as we were outside, I asked, "Why didn't you warn me ahead of time that they didn't know what you did for a living?"

She laughed. "I didn't want you to get nervous about it any sooner than you had to. You should have seen your face when Mum asked where we met. It was as red as that double-decker bus you call a bookmobile."

"But—"

"It worked, didn't it?" she asked.

"I could have had more time to think of an answer if you'd told me before we got to their house."

"I don't think it would've helped. You are incapable of telling a lie without blushing."

"Can, too. There have been many times I obscured the truth when I was talking to my parents about investigations I've worked on, especially if it was something that might make them worry about me."

"See, you keep secrets about what you do from your parents, too. And, for your information, you do better on the phone when you know the other person can't see your face. You light up like a Christmas tree when you lie face-to-face."

"What do your parents think you do?" I wanted to change the subject.

"I told them I work for the government in a position that requires me to travel from time to time."

"Doing what?"

"Encouraging companies to move their facilities to the UK."

"You should tell them the truth," I said.

"Why? Your dad didn't tell you he worked for the FBI until he felt you should know. Your mother was upset with him about it for months afterwards."

"I know, but things are better between me and my parents now that I know the truth and they don't have to think about what I know or don't know."

She thought about it. "I guess I should tell them, and I will, eventually. In fact, I'd planned to before Robert was killed. Ever since, I've been afraid to say anything for fear they would worry about losing me, too."

"I can understand that. Still, when the time is right, I hope you'll talk to them. They may be anxious about it, but they'll be proud of you, too. Let them have that. Tell them how you saved the life of the president of the United States. Twice."

"You amaze me sometimes, Dr. McCowan."

That made me smile, but I had a question for her that I couldn't put off. "How do your parents know Sarah?"

She took a deep breath and let it out. "They never met Sarah, but they know of her. Andrew and I were friends at the time she was killed, and he asked me to investigate the case. I went to Texas on holiday to see what I could learn…just to satisfy him. Soon, my superiors decided I should stay and work more closely on the case. And, you know how that turned out."

"Yes, you helped catch a terrorists cell in the US and saved the president's life."

She smiled. "With your help, of course."

Her explanation of how her parents knew Sarah only made me wonder once again about the relationship between Angela and Andrew. Did I want to know?

We went through London to get to Bath and my mind replayed the stop in York, meeting her parents and what was going on between me and Angela. When Sarah died I didn't think I'd ever experience romantic love again. Now I worried that something romantic was happening between me and Angela, something that was getting out of control. Part of me wanted nothing more than to marry her, but another part of me asked if we were compatible for a lifetime together.

At some point along the four-hour trip from York to Bath, my mind began to obsess on Sarah. I wondered if it was because of the Helmsley's questions. For some reason, I wanted to be home, back in my Georgetown apartment. I remembered how I hid there after Sarah's death, and sometimes didn't leave for days at a time. I've done better in the last year or so, but it wasn't always easy. I realized I had taught, wrote, and participated in the occasional criminal investigation with Tex and Liz during the worst of the sad times. I had grieved and I had made it through the darkness. So why did I feel the way I did now?

I was sitting next to a beautiful woman I was clearly attracted to and enjoyed being with. I was pretty sure she liked me in that special way, too. We were talking and getting to know each other. We could have a future together. I should have been happy. Instead, I wanted to run and hide.

CHAPTER TWENTY-EIGHT

We made it to Bath without discussing anything more serious than the weather and, after retrieving the Mini Cooper, made our way toward her house in Hemington. We stopped for a takeaway at a pub in the woods halfway to her house, had a simple dinner and went to bed early, each to our own rooms. I didn't know if she was waiting on me to start a conversation about our future or if she, too, was having second thoughts, or whatever it was that was happening to me.

The next day, Angela showed me the tourist spots in and around Bath. We took a tour of the Roman Baths, visited Bath Abbey, saw the Jane Austen Centre, and had tea and buns at Sally Lunn's House. She explained it all from the viewpoint of a local and I began to relax and feel comfortable.

We had a picnic lunch in the National Trust gardens at Stourhead, and then drove to Stonehenge. Most tourists walked along a path away from the stones, but Angela showed someone her ID and we were allowed to go with a guide into the inner circle and see the famous structure up close.

All in all, it was a delightful day and it wasn't until we got back to her house that I remembered my fear of falling in love again and realized what was wrong.

Once in the house, Angela dug around in the chest freezer. "Let's see what I can find for dinner. I didn't plan anything special for your last night here, but I should have something in this freezer we can cook."

"We could eat out," I said, wishing the Tex-Mex supplies had arrived in time. I'd hoped to surprise Angela by cooking for her, but it didn't look like that was going to happen.

Before she could respond to my offer to go out, someone knocked on the side door. Angela shut the freezer and went to see who was there.

"Hello, Mrs. Simmons," she said. "How are you today?"

"Just fine," she said peering over Angela's shoulder directly at me. "Oh, I see you have company. I took a delivery for you today while you were gone."

"Thank you. This is my friend Chris. He's from the United States."

She nodded toward me and I moved next to Angela.

"Nice to meet you," Mrs. Simmons said. "The package came from America."

I was glad to hear that.

"The box said to store it in a cool place, so I put it in my cellar. Just wanted to make sure you were home before bringing it over."

"Thank you," Angela said.

"I'll help you," I said.

Angela looked at me with raised eyebrows.

"Lovely." Mrs. Simmons smiled and led the way to her cellar.

It was the box from Brian. When I got back to Angela's house I opened it, and breathed in the strong smell of cumin. "Do you have any hamburger meat in that freezer?" I asked. "I've got everything else I need for Tex-Mex."

"You mean minced meat? Let me check," she said, smiling. "Texas-style Mexican food. Just what I've been wanting. It's amazing you were able to get all the ingredients so quickly. Uh…you're cooking, right?"

"I am. Wait until you taste my enchiladas."

"Umm. Sounds wonderful. I thought I was going to have to travel to Texas for a good meal."

She went back to the freezer and pulled out a package. "Yep. We've got minced meat. But, what about the spices? I don't think I have the right ones."

"No problem." I smiled and motioned toward the box contents now lined up straight on the kitchen counter next to the stove. "Everything we need is right here."

"It'll take a while, so try the chips and salsa Brian sent while I start cooking."

I started the pinto beans first since they would take the longest. I preferred to soak them overnight, but there wasn't time. It'd take a couple of hours, but it would be worth it. Brian had sent everything I'd asked for and had carefully packed it for safe shipping. I added onion, jalapeno, garlic, salsa, cumin, and pepper to the pinto beans and turned the burner up until the mixture boiled. After reducing the heat to a simmer, I made sure everything was ready for the enchiladas and rice.

While the beans cooked, all I had to do was check on them occasionally to make sure there was enough water. Meanwhile I went to the living room where Angela sat on the sofa and was reading an old John le Carre thriller. She stopped long enough for a kiss and then went back to the book. I checked the shelves to see what else she liked to read. But what caught my attention was a photograph album. I pulled it off the shelf.

"May I?"

She smiled, closed her book with a dog ear, and patted the spot beside her. "Of course."

I took the seat and opened the album. The first page was a dozen or so photos of her as a baby. Before the timer beeped me away, I had watched Angela grow from newborn to college student.

When the beans were close to done, I got busy and finished cooking the rest of the meal. She watched and took notes.

"You're going to leave these spices with me when you go home tomorrow, right?" she asked.

"Sure." I loved seeing her happy.

The meal was perfect, and Angela thought so, too. She not only said so, but I could tell by the way she ate. Afterwards she started a pot of coffee and thawed a frozen pudding while we waited for the coffee.

"We need to talk," she said, returning to the kitchen table without looking at me.

"I know," I said, but I didn't want to. And to prove it, I started washing dishes. But as soon as the coffee and desserts were ready, I had no excuse not to talk. Still, I let her go first.

"Here's the thing," she said.

I could guess what was coming with a lead-in like that. She was going to say she liked me, but she'd been dating Andrew and it wouldn't be fair to date us both, and blah, blah, blah. Then she'd say it would be best if we didn't see each other again. We lived so far apart she'd add. And when she finished all that, there wasn't a good response. I'd be forced to say good-bye, go home and forget I'd ever met her. In time I wouldn't remember how much I loved her.

"I'm falling for you," she said.

Huh? Did I hear her right?

She continued. "And I don't know what to do about it. I sense you have feelings for me, too. But, is it possible for us to be in a serious relationship? With you in the US and me here? Me doing the type of work where I may have to be gone for weeks, or longer, at a time. That wouldn't be fair to you. It'd be crazy, wouldn't it?" She gazed into my eyes, waiting.

"Not crazy," I said. "It'd be a challenge, but we shouldn't give up on a chance for happiness because it would be difficult."

"So, you feel there's something going on between us?"

"Yes. I felt it when I first met you, too soon after

289

Sarah's death. I can tell you now the guilt was strong. So strong, I tried not to think about you in that way again until much later."

"I didn't know," Angela said with her dark-brown eyes staring at me. "I remember that time you picked me up at the airport for the second Christmas dinner at Liz's. What was that, a year or so after we first met? I remember the kiss."

"Yes. I remember that, too. I was less guilty at that time."

"Oh, how is your guilt now?"

Ouch. She sounded hurt. I was comparing my feelings for her by announcing that my guilt was less.

"I'm sorry," I said. "That didn't come out right."

"No," she said. "You were being honest about your feelings. That shouldn't bother me."

"I shouldn't have mentioned guilt. But now that I have, let me say there is no more guilt."

She stared at me with head raised slightly as if studying me. "Are you sure?"

"Yes. I'll never forget Sarah and what she meant to me, but I know she loved me enough to want me to be happy."

"I believe that," Angela said. "And I wouldn't want you to forget her. Still, we have all these other obstacles. What about the distance between us?"

"Angela, you have an exciting job that you enjoy and I would never suggest you leave it. I enjoy teaching, but I don't have to stay where I am to do it."

"Could you teach here?"

"Probably, or I could continue to teach online the way

I've done for the last two years. I also like to write and that can be done anywhere. So far all I've done is write textbooks, but I've been thinking about writing a novel based on the investigative work I've done with Liz and Tex. I think I could add some interesting computer forensics to a novel."

"That would be something you could do in Hemington," she said, smiling. "Are you sure you'd be okay with me doing what I do and being gone the way I am from time to time?"

"Yes. I'd want you to be happy and I think your work is something you enjoy doing."

"I do."

"I'd be lying if I said I wouldn't worry about you when you're on assignment, but I know you're good at what you do."

"Thanks. I know you'd worry," she said, "mainly because of the secrecy of my work. It's not all dangerous you know. Some of it is routine, boring stuff."

"I need to ask you something," I said, knowing the answer didn't matter any longer, but wanting to get it out there and settled once and for all. "What about you and Andrew?"

She expressed surprise, but smiled after she checked my face. "Andrew?" There was a long pause before she continued. "That's simple. Once upon a time I thought he might be Mr. Right. He wasn't. We agreed to be friends."

I felt relieved. "I thought so. I think he would have liked it to be different. That's why I asked. But I do have another concern."

"What is it?"

"I was brought up in a Christian church and my trust in God has grown stronger over the years. I don't know for sure, but I sense you don't feel the same. Am I right?"

She stood and picked up the plates and walked to the sink. "My parents had me baptized and took me to church on special occasions, but I was not taught much along the way. We didn't pray together or read the Bible at home the way you and your friends do. When I was old enough to make my own decision about going to church, I didn't go. I still don't, except for an occasional wedding or funeral, but I would love to go with you."

She rinsed the plates and put them in the dishwasher and slammed the door. "This is crazy. You haven't proposed, but I feel like we're discussing the pros and cons of marriage. We haven't talked finances yet. Is that next?"

"I'm sorry," I said. "I didn't mean to make you feel uncomfortable. Still, I think talking about religion is something more couples should do before proposing."

"I guess," she said, in a calmer voice.

"And, for the record, I don't see a problem. We're both of the same faith. I'm more active about it, but that's okay. Now, about finances..." I smiled, hoping she'd laugh.

"Are you serious?" She acted stern at first, but it wasn't long before she laughed.

"Well, you said it was part of the premarital discussion. The fact is I don't have much money and my income is miserable. On the plus side, I don't have any debts and I don't have a need to live lavishly."

"A young man with a doctorate and no debts. What about student loans?" she asked.

"All paid up."

"That's admirable."

"Well, I can't take credit for it. Liz arranged it somehow after we rescued the president in Houston."

"But, still, it's something to be proud of. In my case, I make more money than I can spend so the savings have been building up for the past five years. The government pays all my bills except for this house, so I'm in a good place financially."

"Okay," I said. "One more question. How do you feel about children?"

I thought I saw her shiver. Could this be a problem? I'd always thought I'd be a father someday. Could it be she isn't interested in being a parent? How important is it? I think I could marry her if she didn't want children. Just a short time ago, after Sarah's death, I thought I'd never marry.

"I'm sorry," I said, not sure why.

"No. It's an appropriate question." She rubbed her eyes. "I love kids. But, I'm afraid I wouldn't be a good parent. I don't cook much and I'm away from home a lot. That's not good for bringing up a family. The fact that you could put up with my travel is enough of a strain on a family."

"If we can find a way for me to be here with you, and if you can find the time to have a baby, I can take care of the rest."

She smiled. "You'd do that?"

"Of course."

"But a child needs a mother and a father."

"You could be a mother much of the time. You need to be able to leave in a hurry for unknown lengths of time. When that happens, I'll be mother and father."

"I don't know," she said.

"Could you get special duty to have the baby?"

"Course I could. Other agents have got pregnant. That's not a problem."

"So what are you worrying about?"

"It's just that I'm not sure it would be good for the child for me to leave it alone so much."

"It wouldn't be alone. I'd be there."

"I know, but—"

"The only concern I would have," I said, "is that becoming a mother could soften you and make you more vulnerable when you get caught up in a conflict requiring your full attention."

"I don't think that would happen. You've done enough in the field to know response is drilled into you over a long period of time. It becomes automatic. I wouldn't be considering my child while facing danger."

"You're right. The few times where I had to fire my pistol at someone, I was like a robot."

"Are you sure you want to be the stay-at-home parent?" she asked.

"Yes. I will still be able to teach online and write, if I want to, but I could be a fulltime parent if that is what it takes."

"What if Liz and Tex need you for a job?"

I always enjoyed those special times with the Vengeance Squad. I'd miss that. But, if it was a choice between being with Angela or being with them, I'd pick Angela. I wasn't sure how to say that.

"I think the Vengeance Squad is about finished."

"Why?"

"Tex is a fulltime student at the University of Texas now and about to finish his degree and go to work as a drug and alcohol counselor, a job I think he'll be good at. His kids are getting to the age where Jane wants him to spend more time with them, and with her. Liz will probably retire soon. She's already eligible for social security and Medicare."

"Has she said she's retiring?"

"No, I'm just guessing."

"She's quite active. Don't let her age fool you."

"Anyway, I'd be happy here. If they did need me and it didn't affect you or our family, I could go. If I had to say no, I wouldn't regret it."

"We're compatible," she said with a warm smile.

"Good. Now that that's settled…" I knelt on one knee on the stone floor of her kitchen as she leaned against the sink.

"Get up, Chris. When you propose, it'd better be more romantic than that. And you'd better have a ring in your hand."

I stood and hugged her pretending it was a joke. We had a great laugh, but I wished she'd let me propose. I was ready and knew I wanted to spend the rest of my life with her. But I understood.

By the time we said goodnight and went to bed, her to the master bedroom up the narrow stairs and me to the guest room in what used to be part of the chicken house, I knew we'd be married soon.

The next day she took me to the train station in Bath where I began my journey home. She walked with me to the train and waited until boarding time. She promised to see me in Austin for Liz's Christmas dinner and gave me the most passionate kiss yet. My whole body quivered.

She must have noticed the effect the kiss had on me. "That's to remind you to think about me every day," she said.

I made my way to a window seat and looked out. She was still there and she waved. She was so beautiful standing there smiling and waving. I didn't want to leave. I didn't want to return to my lonely apartment. I didn't want to ever be away from her again.

CHAPTER TWENTY-NINE

As strange as it sounds, the whole gang gathered at Liz's house on February 24 for Christmas dinner. She wore a festive Christmas apron and was as happy as ever. She had put up a tree and decorated the house and yard as if it was Christmas. Her neighbors probably thought she'd lost her mind.

There were seven of us there for the big feast. Five adults and two children. Tex and Jane's kids, Anna and Owen, were little angels. They helped Liz in the kitchen and watched the proceedings with interest. The turkey was big enough to feed three times as many people, but Liz said the best part of a meal like this was the leftovers.

She placed a humongous browned main course in the center of the dining room table and surrounded it with cornbread dressing, giblet gravy, mashed potatoes, yams, and green beans, along with vegetables of every type and color. Jane's homemade rolls were steaming and topped with a thin layer of melted butter. Only my enchiladas were out of place.

They weren't on the menu, but Angela insisted and I couldn't resist preparing them for her. I'd offered to make some for us to eat later, but she said she'd been dreaming about them ever since I'd left her house.

Tex, who often wore his cowboy hat inside, took it off and tossed it toward a spare chair in a corner. It took off like a Frisbee and landed gently in the center of the seat. I gave him a thumbs up.

We joined hands without being prompted, and I felt a circle of love around the table. Liz nodded to Jane for the prayer. I silently thanked God for my friends before Jane prayed aloud.

"Dear Lord," she said, "every day is Christmas day for those who love you and you know all those present here are in that group. We not only love you, we worship you. As you know, Lord, we've been on a special journey. Thank you for bringing us home safely. We mourn the loss of Cloris, but we trust you, Lord, and know there are things we don't understand and never will. Watch over her son, Heath. He is hurting now and trying to comprehend why his mother was taken from him just a short time after he joined the church. Lead us, Lord, and show us how to help him during his time of grieving and confusion. Lead us in other ways that you would have us go. And, Lord, bless this meal and bless the cooks. We ask this in Christ's name. Amen."

"Amen," Anna and Owen said together.

"Amen," Liz said. "Thank you, Jane. I knew you'd know exactly what to say. Now, ever'body dig in."

And that's what we did. Utensils clicked on plates, bowls moved counterclockwise around the table and the conversation dwindled right along with the food.

Since returning home, I'd been trying to think of a special way to ask Angela to marry me. Nothing had come to me, but I had the ring in my pocket, waiting for the right time and place.

"Liz," I asked, "what have you heard from London?"

"Yes," Jane said. "We've all been so busy since we got home, we haven't kept up with what's going on."

Liz chewed for a few seconds before setting down her fork. "That's right. Let me give you a quick update. First of all, we got Cloris's body shipped home. Her brother helped. He's a lawyer in town. Brian tells me he's supposed to be well off, and could take care of Heath financially. But Brian doesn't think Heath's uncle would be a good role model for the young man."

"What about Virgil?" Tex asked.

"He's still in custody in London. He claimed Cloris's death was an accident. He said he tried to keep her from running away from him and she fell and bumped her head. Instead of calling for help, he got scared and dumped her body in the Thames." Liz shook her head and stabbed her fork into a large pile of cornbread dressing smothered in giblet gravy. "I guess it could've happened that way."

"Do you think the authorities in London might let him go?" Tex asked Angela.

Angela shook her head. "I've been keeping an eye on

the proceedings. You may be interested to learn Scotland Yard arrested three more men in connection with the case. They were all petty criminals, never been suspected of anything serious. Now, they're all blaming Virgil for everything that happened and are giving the police what they need to prosecute him."

"Probably his golfing buddies," Jane said.

"How did the police find them?" Tex asked.

"The Seaford house was owned by all four of them," Angela said.

"The cops didn't happen to find Chris's helicopter, did they?" Tex asked.

Angela smiled. "As a matter of fact, they did."

"Yes," I said. "She brought it to me wrapped as a Christmas gift. It's beat up, but I think I can fix it. It'll make a nice souvenir either way."

"Wonderful," Tex said.

"Nice touch," Jane said to Angela.

"Guess I won't have to buy you a new one after all," Liz said.

"Well I'm glad Virgil will be charged there," Liz said, "but Tom told me that if he happens to be freed, the DA in Austin has filed several charges against him."

"What has happened to the money we recovered from Virgil?" Jane asked.

Liz shook her head. "We returned more than half of it. I'm sure it was all stolen, but we didn't have proof. Maybe Scotland Yard will look into it when they learn how much money he has."

"What about the bookmobile?" Jane asked.

"Bookmobile?" Anna said and turned to her brother.

"We like the bookmobile."

Liz smiled. "You mean the new red double-decker one?" she asked.

"Yes."

"It's here. We can't use it yet, but it won't be long. At first I thought we might have to park it somewhere permanently and use it like a small branch library."

"Why?" I asked.

"Because I didn't think we'd ever get the proper licenses and inspections and all that. But our lawyers have found one like it in San Antonio and another in Phoenix. Not bookmobiles, but buses. They're used for tours. If they can do it, so can we. Brian and his friends are helping to get ours on the road. "

Tex shook his head. "Don't forget what Thomas said about it being haunted. If word gets out about that, or if anything happens, you're not going to find anyone to go out on it."

"In that case I'll drive it myself," Liz said. "I don't believe in ghosts."

"What about the bookmobile fund?" I asked, knowing it was growing still.

"You won't believe how much money has come in. Since we're getting donations from around the world, there's more money than we need. We'll get a new smaller bookmobile to replace the one provided by Brian and Karen. Still, we'll need to find other ways to use the money. We'll ask them first, but I don't think the donors will object to our using the money for other library-related purposes."

"How about using some of the donations for libraries

in poorer countries?" Angela asked.

"Good idea," Jane said. "Or to purchase bookmobiles to go from town to town in smaller locations around the world."

Liz's eyes popped open. "That's it. What wonderful ideas. Let's get together and do some research about where to start."

"Tex and I can check when we go on our next trip abroad," Jane said.

"Oh?" I asked. "Where are you going?"

Tex smiled. "Can you believe it? We're making another trip. The kids are going with us this time."

"We are?" Anna asked.

Jane nodded at her children.

"Where?" I asked again.

"On the flight home, Matt and Marie offered us their chateau in France for spring break," Tex said.

"Wow." I felt happy for them. Tex, especially. He was a good man who'd lived a rough life and came out on the other side thanks to the grace of God. "That's wonderful."

"Yes," Jane said. "We have to pay our way over and back, but we'll be able to stay free there for a week. Could have stayed longer, but that's all the time we can take off."

"France is not a poor country," Angela said. "They have plenty of libraries."

"Oh, right," Tex said. "I guess we'll need to do that research after all, Liz. Perhaps some places in South America would be good."

"Let's meet tomorrow at the usual time and place,"

Liz said, "so we can research the possibilities. We've got enough money, so it doesn't all have to go to one place. I'll bring some turkey sandwiches."

I didn't want to go to a meeting with the Vengeance Squad while Angela was visiting. I'd promised to show her around. Liz would understand if I didn't attend. Besides, the engagement ring I had bought for Angela was burning a hole in my pocket. If I did any research it would be to find the perfect spot to propose.

After the main meal, Liz took dessert orders and Angela helped. I loved Liz's peach cobbler and I knew she had made a bucket of homemade peach ice cream to go on top. I also wanted to try Angela's pecan pie made from her mother's Georgia recipe. When asked what I wanted, I ordered both.

"Me, too," Tex said. "But give me a small slice of each pecan pie so I can compare them."

"Great idea," Jane said. "I'll take the same." She was on her feet. "Let me help."

"Liz," Angela asked, "I am so glad to see you happy again. I wasn't here, but I know Chris and Tex were worried about you when you first learned what Virgil had done."

Liz had been showing signs of her old self, but I hoped Angela wasn't opening wounds that were not yet healed.

"Thank you," Liz said. "I'm doing good. Yes, it was a rough time in my life to learn Virgil was a con man and had no interest in me as a woman. That hurt. But just because I had one bad experience, two if you count my alcoholic husband near the end of his life, it doesn't mean I have to give up on finding a loving, supportive male friend."

"I'm glad you feel that way," Angela said. "I have a widower uncle who's just moved to Austin. He's in town on the same farm program Sarah's parents are in. I would love it if you'd show him around the area and make him feel comfortable."

"Well, sure," Liz said smiling. "I'd be happy to."

"Good. His name is Samuel Helmsley," she looked at her watch, "and he should be here in a few minutes. I took the liberty of inviting him for dessert. I hope you don't mind."

The doorbell rang.

"Wow," Liz said. "He's a prompt fella, isn't he?"

Everyone laughed.

"I'll let him in," Angela said as she walked toward the front door.

Without discussing it, we formed an impromptu reception line by the time Angela returned to the dining room with her uncle. I could tell she was pleased. For one thing, it made it easier to introduce us.

She stopped in front of Liz first. "Uncle Samuel, I'd like you to meet our hostess, Liz Siedo."

Uncle Samuel locked his eyes on hers and appeared to block out the rest of the world. His gray hair was full and his face had the deep tan of someone who spends day after day on a tractor. A line of lighter skin at the top of his forehead showed he wore a hat when he worked.

"Madam," he said with the slightest bow toward Liz, "thank you for your hospitality. You have a lovely home. Quite in keeping with such a delightful lady."

Liz's face turned red. If I hadn't been standing there looking at her, I never would have believed she was capable of blushing. She wasn't the type. Or so I'd always thought.

"Thank you, sir," she said. "You are too kind."

She recovered quickly, and did what she always did. She pulled Uncle Samuel into a bear hug he'd never forget. And, unlike most of the people who experienced one of Liz's hugs the first time, he wasn't alarmed. Instead, he stepped closer and embraced her right back. The grin on his face showed how much he enjoyed it.

Angela introduced him to the rest of us, and soon after that we all settled down for coffee and desserts. Samuel became the center of attention, telling stories about farming along with a few about Angela as a child. When we finished eating all we could hold, we helped clean up.

When that was done, I put an arm around Angela. "Liz, everything was delicious, but we must leave. I'm showing Angela around while she's in town."

"Oh? I thought you lived in Austin for a while, Angela."

"Yes, but I was working so much I didn't have time to be a tourist."

"Where are you taking her?" Tex asked. "If you need any suggestions, let me know."

"Being from California," I said, "I haven't seen many of the places people talk about around here, so it'll be fun for both of us. We're going to the State Capitol, Bullock Museum, LBJ Library, and, depending on the weather, I want to show her the lakes and other outdoor spots."

"Oh," Liz said, "I know. Show her Mount Bonnell." Liz grinned more than usual and winked at me.

"Mount Bonnell?" I asked.

"Yes." She grabbed Angela's arm and held her close. "But you be careful. There's a legend that says a couple who climbs to the top together will fall in love."

We were already in love, but it sounded like it had that touch of romance that would qualify it for the place I had been searching for. "Where is Mount Bonnell?"

"Are you sure you want to take her there? I went to a wedding there once. They'd planned to wed on top, but it was raining so hard they took their vows in the bookmobile. That was a day I'll never forget."

"Where is it?" I asked again, ignoring her question.

"I'll show you," Tex said. He pulled out the laptop he carried in the backpack hooked to his wheelchair and opened Google Maps. "It's right here." He zoomed to show the route from Liz's house and, after giving me time to view the turn-by-turn details, he zoomed in to show an image of the steps that led to the top of the mountain.

"Thanks, Tex. Want to go see it, now?" I asked Angela.

"Sure." She turned to her uncle. "Will you be okay?"

"I'll be fine," he said. "I'm staying with Paul and Ann until I can get me own place."

The ring in my pocket caused my leg to tingle as we said good-bye to our friends.

CHAPTER THIRTY

I drove to Mount Bonnell without a map. Other than the one Tex had showed me that was still in my head, of course. The lot was empty. That was okay with me. I wanted us to be alone for what I had in mind. We got out and walked hand in hand to the rock stairway. A sign warned against leaving valuables in the car. The stairway was wide with a handrail in the center. We looked at each other briefly before we started climbing. All I could see was a deep forest of cedar trees on each side of the stairs, but we continued up knowing there was a better view from the top.

And there was.

At the peak we could see Lake Austin. In the distance was the arched Highway 360 bridge. Huge, expensive-looking homes rose toward us on the side away from the lake. For a few minutes all we did was take in the beauty of the place, enjoying it as we turned one direction and then the other for a panoramic view.

I patted the ring in my pocket and scanned the area for a place to ask for Angela's hand in marriage. I found a trail leading toward the water. There was more growth there than where we stood, indicating not as many people ventured that way. But it still had a magnificent view. I took Angela's hand and directed her to the trail. We walked a short distance, hand in hand. I turned so that I could see the mountain top, leaving the best view for her. I pulled the ring from my pocket without letting her see it and knelt.

She smiled, clearly not surprised. She didn't tell me to get up, this time.

I open my hand to reveal the ring.

Her smile grew larger. "Yes," she said.

ACKNOWLEDGEMENTS

With each new book I write, I find there are more people to acknowledge. Some by name and some only by how they helped. For example, I learn from every review someone posts about my books. Most are from strangers, people I will never know. I appreciate the time they took to say what they think about a book. Many others write me e-mail messages and I am always amazed at what some find in the stories. God works in mysterious ways.

I also learn from people I talk to at book signings and when I talk to groups about writing. The enthusiasm they have for my books makes me want to write more, say more, be more.

Special thanks go to the many people on Facebook who respond when I need a character name or help with some part of the book. And the ones who consistently encourage me with their words and help me publicize my books.

For this book I learned about bodybuilding from Sue Sieloff, aka Mighty Mouse.

I would like to thank Paul Francis for letting me visit his Hemington farm in the Mendip district of Somerset, England so many times I could write about it from memory.

Special thanks go to Julie Maria Peace, author of *A Song in the Night*. She wrote to me to ask if I would review her book. When I learned she lived in Barnsley, South Yorkshire, England, I asked if she'd read this book. She agreed, and ended up as an unpaid editor of the English part of this book. Thank you, Julie.

Once again, my advance readers are an important part of the success of the book. They make the final pass, checking for errors. They tell me what works and what doesn't work. This time I want to thank Celeste Frost, Peg Case, Joyce Joiner, Malia Barth, and Rollo Newsom.

Finally, only one person knows how many changes had to be made to get to this point and that's Lisa Lickel, my editor. She helped in so many ways from correcting errors to gently suggesting rearrangements and deletions. Thank you, Lisa.

ABOUT THE AUTHOR

Sidney W. Frost is a former Stephen Minister, and a member of his church choir at First United Methodist Church in Georgetown, Texas.

While singing with the Austin Lyric Opera Chorus, he was in 42 productions. He and his wife, Celeste, sing with the San Gabriel Chorale and have been in several Berkshire Festivals.

Until May, 2010, he was an Adjunct Professor at Austin Community College where he taught computer courses. He received the adjunct teaching excellence award in 2005.

After completing service in the US Marines, he attended the University of Texas. He worked part-time at the Austin Public Library driving a bookmobile where he got his first idea for a novel. That book was never completed, but he has included the librarian and the bookmobile in all his books.

He has a Master of Science degree from the University of Houston and a Bachelor of Arts from the University of California at Long Beach.

Awards for his first novel, *Where Love Once Lived*, include First Place in the 2007 SouthWest Writers Contest, First Place in the 2007 Writers' League of Texas Novel Manuscript Contest, Third Place in the Fourteenth Annual Lone Star Writing Competition, Northwest Houston Chapter of the Romance Writers of America, and Finalist in the 2006 Yosemite Writers Contest.

The Vengeance Squad (Kindle edition) has been a bestseller on Amazon.com in the Religious Mystery category.

Love Lives On, the sequel to *Where Love Once Lived*, was published in 2013 and is growing in popularity in the Christian Romantic Suspense category.

AFTERWORD

Thank you for reading *The Vengeance Squad Goes to England*. If you haven't already, I hope you will read *Where Love Once Lived, Love Lives On* and *The Vengeance Squad*. See my website, http://sidneywfrost.com, for the latest information about all my books.

If you would like to see images for this book, go to: http://www.pinterest.com/sidneywfrost/images-for-book-4-the-vengeance-squad-goes-to-engl/.

You may also want to visit the Christian Bookmobile: http://christianbookmobile.blogspot.com/

This is where I talk about writing, review books, interview other Christian authors and occasionally talk about growing up in Austin, Texas.

I also respond to e-mail queries and would love to hear from you: sidfrost@suddenlink.net.